The
Goldhanger
Dog

Wanda Whiteley

The
Goldhanger
Dog

WANDA WHITELEY

Lp
Lammas Publishing

For John

First published in Great Britain by Lammas Publishing 2022

Copyright © Wanda Carter 2022

Wanda Carter asserts the moral right to be
identified as the author of this work.

A catalogue record for this book is
available from the British Library

ISBN: 978-1-9160644-6-1

Printed and bound in Great Britain by
Biddles Books Ltd

CHARACTERS

Real

Lady Mary Tudor, princess
Lucretia the tumbler, fool
Jane Foole, fool
Sir Robert Rochester,
    comptroller
Mistress Susan Clarencieux,
    lady-in-waiting
Mistress Jane Dormer,
    lady of the bedchamber
Sir Henry Radclyffe,
    Earl of Sussex
Lady Anne Radclyffe,
    Countess of Sussex
Dr Scurloch, physician
Lady Eleanore Browne,
    gentlewoman
Cecily, Lady Arundell,
    gentlewoman
Richard Rich, Baron Rich
    of Leez
John de Vere, Earl of Oxford
Sir William Cecil, secretary
    of state
Sir Nicholas Throckmorton,
    politician and courtier
Sir Henry Bedingfeld,
    Norfolk landowner

Invented

Dela Wisbey
Marian Wisbey
Ned, a farrier
Turnspit, a dog
Master Fitzjohn – 'Fitz' –
    Mary's groom
Saltpan Sal, a widow
Rob, her fisherman son
Sir John Tallon, local
    landowner
Fowler, Sir John Tallon's
    gamekeeper
Rosie, a kitchen maid
Alfredo Pisanelli, Lucretia's
    glover uncle
Colin, glover's apprentice
Dumont, Emperor Charles's
    envoy
Sir Godfrey Knowles,
    Mary's hunt master
A chaplain of Mary's
    household

· BLACKWATER ·
ESSEX
~ 1553 ~

New Hall

Goldhanger

R. Chelmer

Little Baddow

Heybridge

Goldhanger Creek

Osea

Woodham Walter

Maldon

Northey

Southey Creek

LONDON

Illustration by Janette Ames

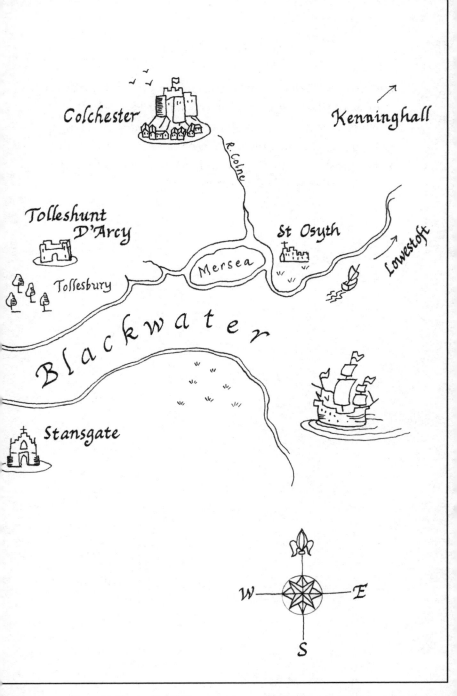

AUTHOR NOTE

The story is set in the few weeks before and after the death of Edward VI, the fifteen-year-old son of Henry VIII.

Mary, the thirty-eight-year-old daughter of Henry's first wife, Catherine of Aragon, is next in line to the throne. Although she is a princess, she is most often addressed as 'Lady Mary' – as was the custom of the time.

PROLOGUE

Barrow Farm, Goldhanger, August 1551

'Dela, it's cold up here. I'm coming down.'

My mother climbed down the ladder from the hay-loft into the stable below. She stood at Bessie's stall and watched me, her eyes following my hand as I brushed Bessie's mane. She hugged her body, arms crossed over her chest.

'Are you feeling all right, Ma?'

'I can't seem to get warm.' Her voice tailed away, uncertain, as if she'd lost the thread of what she was saying.

This was unlike my mother. Marian Wisbey was a definite sort of person. Robust. When she spoke, she knew where she was going with a thought.

'Why don't you go inside?' I suggested. 'I'll do the rest.'

She shook her head wonderingly. 'Thirteen, and you sound like *my* mother.'

She didn't move, just carried on staring at me. Outside, I could hear the comforting cluck of hens as they went about the yard pecking grit. Inside the stable, my unease was catching: the muscles and nerves of Bessie's side rippled and twitched. I wondered, how can my mother be cold?

It was August. A hot day. Scarcely a breath of wind.

It had been like that all morning with her. Something not quite right, as if a picture hanging on the wall had a slight tilt to it.

Earlier, at breakfast, instead of cutting the loaf, she had stared at the knife the longest time and seemed to forget what it was for. My mother had eyes that could pin a person to the spot. Folk used to confess things to her that even our priest couldn't get out of them. But as she sat there, looking at that knife, her eyes were foggy. Apprehensive.

Then she had mentioned Sir John Tallon. That was certainly strange. We had not breathed his name for two years, not since Father's death − as if saying it would put a hex on us. Sir John Tallon … there, I've said it. He's just a man, not a ghoul, but it doesn't stop folk jumping out of their skins at the sight of him. We weren't the only ones to fear him.

'I worry he'll take the farm, Dela.'

'Don't say that. We can manage.' The truth is that Tallon had already taken our land, stripped it off us after he'd hanged my father for treason. All we had left was the house and barn.

'Listen to me. If anything happens, Ned will look after you. You'll have a home with him.'

'Why are you saying this? My home is here with you. Nothing's going to happen.'

I grabbed the knife out of her hand and sawed a slice of bread, then stabbed at the butter roughly. I'd already lost a father. Why threaten me with the loss of a mother as well? It's not as if she needs to put her affairs in order, I thought to myself. It's not as if she is sick. Surely not.

That afternoon, after finishing my chores, I went inside for my supper. I expected to find Mother dishing out the food, bustling about the hearth, but she wasn't in the main chamber. She was in our bedchamber next door, lying on the mattress, face a purplish red. She had the rug and sheepskin over her, but her teeth wouldn't stop chattering. I put a hand to her forehead.

'So cold, so cold ...' she said, between the clackings of her teeth.

Then the sweats came. She threw off the rug and sheepskin and tossed on her mattress, trying to find a cool spot for her burning head. Her clothes were soaked through. She cried out for water. I ran to the pump in the yard, filled the jug. She drank cup after cup. I dashed out to refill the jug and came back to her bedside.

'Mother, tell me what to do.'

She had so many recipes in her head for brews and ointments. If I'd been sick, she would have prepared a poultice. But I hadn't been a diligent daughter. I'd wasted my time picking my way over the mudflats, staring dreamily into pools when I should have been watching her at work. Inside, I raged at myself. *This is your fault, Dela.*

'Mother, tell me what to do.'

But all she whispered was, '*Water.*'

I knew what this was. Sweating sickness had been on our minds for the past month, ever since we'd heard about the two young brothers who fell sick in Cambridge and died within half an hour of each other. Young dukes, which was why every village along the Blackwater had been talking about it.

I didn't dare leave her to go and fetch Ned or her friend Sal. Ned would have been in his forge, Sal out at the saltpan. It was too far; it would have taken too long. I couldn't leave Mother. I needed to shut up the hens or the fox would get them – but even that was impossible.

As night drew in, a mad delirium took hold of her and she began thrashing about. I wrestled with her, panicked. I didn't think I could do it on my own. It took all my strength to keep her on the mattress. Why hadn't I got help earlier? I felt a fool ... that it was all my fault.

Moonlight crept through the unshuttered windows. The fever seemed to have quieted. Mother was calm, said she felt sleepy.

But I knew not to let her sleep.

'Stay awake, Ma. Don't close your eyes. Please ... stay with me.'

Her lids lowered, then lifted a little, then lowered again. It seemed to cost her an immense effort, as if she were trying to lift two great sandbags with her eyelids.

'My little Dela,' she whispered. 'Though not so little now.' The corners of her mouth barely moved, but I knew she smiled.

'Stay awake, Ma. Keep talking.'

'My precious one ... Ned will guard you well.'

'I don't want Ned. I want you! Stay awake!'

'You have the gift. Use it for good things ... My little Dela. Don't be sad.'

'Keep awake!' I rubbed her cheeks, pinched them.

A long, slow breath eased out. I waited for the next. It seemed to take an age to come, then a light rattle as the air quietly leaked out of her. Each time this was repeated through the long evening hours I thought it was the end for my mother, but just when I thought she had finally given up there would be a stuttering wheeze of a breath. Sometime after midnight she stirred, moaned a little, and gave another slow breath, barely noticeable, like a sigh.

I waited for another. It didn't come.

After my mother took that last breath, I took one great big one. Filled my lungs, ready to burst. I howled and I raged. I stamped my feet until the packed earth of the chamber stirred into eddies of dust. My mouth felt as large as the heavens, a wide screaming black hole that would spew forth locusts and frogs if it could – every plague I could summon. Out in the stable, Bessie screamed and stamped the door of her stall with her hooves. In the yard, the hens, not yet caught by the fox, ran into a huddle, while the cockerel flew onto the roof of the barn and crowed through the night, telling the good folk of Goldhanger of Marian Wisbey's passing.

Then matters grew very odd, and I fear to think of it now. Sal told me the whole of it later, as I'd fallen down senseless and didn't witness the half of it. Folk in the village put the strange happenings down to the storm, which arrived at dawn, bursting forth in a great flood of rain, gushing down the thatched roofs of our cottages. Sal said it was like the storm of tears that comes after an infant's fury when things don't go their way.

'Birds and animals, hundreds of them, came up the street, heading for your house in a stream, filling the lane. Geese flapping and jostling into the farmyard, clamouring at your door. Rats swarming out of the barns. And the cats – always a heartless lot – ignoring your summons so they could pounce on 'em. The fishwives said that out in the creek a great shoal of herring came rushing in, though there was hardly any water. Out on the mudflats, it was like boiling silver. The shoal jumped right up onto the quay. Would have thrashed and gulped their way up Fish Street if their gills had let 'em. Such a howling and a honking. Ye must've heard that. And the dogs … every one of 'em busting their chains to get to ye.

'It were your hurt that summoned them,' she told me. 'That's what I think.'

I knew better. It was my rage.

Was this the gift my mother spoke of? How could she have talked of gifts when she knew that the one person I loved with my whole heart was about to be taken from me?

If it is a gift, it must have been dealt to me by the devil himself. I want none of it.

1

A SPY COMES TO THE BLACKWATER

Chapter 1

Goldhanger, May 1553
Two years later

'Dela, come play merels. Keep an old blacksmith happy, will you?'

Ned has set the games board next to the hearth and draws up a stool for me. I make him wait, thumping our wooden supper bowls onto their shelf with a clatter, knowing that his narrow, lined face will be fixed on me patiently, his brown eyes like quiet fingers feeling around the shape of my mood.

Outside in the lane, I can hear folk setting out to Maldon, raucous with excitement, the men jangling the coins in their pockets. It's not that I feel left out – not a bit of it – but what they do on a Sunday evening makes me feel at odds with the world, a stranger to our village.

I dawdle a bit longer, then join Ned, pulling back my stool with an angry scrape. The late afternoon sun is warm for May, the coarse linen of my clothes scratchy against my skin. Our cosy hearth is usually a comfort after the day's work is done, its smoke-blackened beam hung with bunches of fragrant bay, the fire irons Ned made in his forge propped against the wall. But not tonight.

'Here, I'll let you go first,' he says.

Going first puts a person at some advantage in merels, and it is not something Ned normally offers as I'm better at the game than him. He always says that he knows when it's Sunday from the frown that sets itself up between my eyes. I can sense him watching my flushed face as I try to fix my mind on the lines and spots carved into the wooden games board. I thump my first white piece down, heedless of which square I go for.

'You mustn't mind it.'

'Mind what?' I ask, though of course I know.

He places his black pebble on the board. 'The bull-baiting.'

There. He's said it. My mind flicks straight to Maldon and its market place at the top of the hill where they drag the bull to his stake. They'll be chaining the frightened animal to it soon.

Sometimes it feels as if I'm all alone in hating the bull-baiting. So yes, I *do* mind, and I wish Ned didn't sound so easy-going about it.

He raises his eyes to my face. 'That's what's unsettled you, is it?'

'What do you think?' I place my second pebble on the board.

'Reckon it must be hard, you being so keen on animals, but what goes on in Maldon is not something you can change.'

I barely notice him put his next piece down. 'So we just go on putting up with it? Is that what you want?' I thump my piece down on the board and realise too late that I've laid myself open.

He pretends he hasn't noticed he can make a mill – three in a row – and puts his black pebble down on another spot instead.

Which only annoys me the more. 'I'm not a child! You don't have to let me win.'

I want to kick the board so that the pebbles scatter across the beaten earth of the floor, but I know that if I did, he would only fix those wise old eyes on me as if to say, 'See what I mean?'

He leans back against the polished oak of his settle, pride of our cottage, its square panels carved into rough linenfold ridges by his father. 'No need to stick your lip out at me. You look just like your mother when you do that. You'd best tell me what's up. It can't just be the bull-baiting.'

I reckon Ned knows exactly what the mention of my mother will do. I glower into my hair, which always tumbles over my face in unruly black curls when there's no cap to keep it back.

'*If* my mother were here,' I say, 'she wouldn't be resting on the settle if there was something she could do. She wouldn't sit by and let bad things happen.'

But bad things happened anyway. The unspoken words hang in the air between us. I thump another piece on the board without looking where, with the sour satisfaction that I'm ruining the game.

'She didn't want bad things to happen to *you* – that was always her first and last thought,' Ned says quietly. He shuffles his thin haunches in his seat to sit up a little straighter. 'I loved your ma like a daughter. Her father was a good friend to me after I lost Ann.'

I always think of us Wisbeys as the only family Ned's ever had and find myself forgetting he once had a wife of his own. It was such a long time ago that she died, years before I was born.

'Anyway,' Ned goes on. 'I'm not called guardian for nothing, and I *will* guard you, Dela. But there's some things you cannot change, and bull-baiting's one of them. I never want to see another fury rushing on you …' He lets out his breath in a sigh. 'I'm too old to get into a fist fight for you, but I've got a good pair of ears to listen.'

Ned has long ears, pointy at the top, their lobes grown pendulous with age. I have to admit he is a good listener. I'm sure, if they could, his ears would wag like a donkey's to hear me the better.

I relent and tell him. 'They're letting Bruiser fight.'

'Ah. The thatcher's dog.'

'I've only just patched him up after last time. His leg won't stand it!'

I've grown fond of Bruiser. He's a soft thing when he's not going for the bull's throat. I saw his plague-sore of a master dragging him along Head Street earlier, doing his best to pretend he hadn't noticed Bruiser had a limp and one eye swollen shut.

'How's he going to fight like that? The dog can't even see properly!'

Ned's gaze flicks down to the fists bunched at my sides and he gives a twitch of his narrow shoulders. 'Ain't nowt you can do.'

As soon as the words are out of his mouth, his open hand comes up as if he wants to snatch them back. He knows by now that if he says I *can't* do something I will be sure to show him I *can*. He's told me plenty of times that it's perfectly normal for a fifteen-year-old to say white's not white and black's not black (except when we're playing merels). Fifteen is when youngsters need to test their wings, he says, and if that means telling their elders they're wrong – even if they aren't – then an old man like him should be old enough and wise enough to have learned a little patience.

'I can go to Maldon, *that's* what I can do.' I stand up.

He reaches a hand to stop me. 'No, Dela ... wait. It isn't safe for you.'

'It's not *safe* for Bruiser. I'll be just fine.'

He doesn't want to say what he and I both know he's thinking – that it isn't safe for me because some folk have got it into their heads that I'm different.

Before he can say anything else to make things worse, I run across the chamber, snatch my cap from the peg by the door, and slip on my shoes.

Ned pushes himself up from the settle. 'Dela ...'

By the time I reach the fullbridge that crosses the Chelmer, I have a blister on my heel and a stitch in my side. I pause for a moment, stooping over the rail to catch my breath, watching the dark waters move sluggishly towards the hythe, where the trading ships unload their cargo. As I imagine the river flowing towards the salty reaches of the Blackwater estuary, troubling thoughts circle my mind.

I think of Ned's saying 'I never want to see another fury rushing on you', and my stomach curls. What lurks behind the words is the memory of the day Mother died, when all those birds and animals flocked to our door and the fish wriggled and flapped their way up Goldhanger Creek. Plenty of girls my age fly into a passion, but that is not what Ned's scared of. He's fearful lest I work myself into a rage and it stirs up the animals again. He, like our friend Sal, believes it was something I did, but it's been two years, and nothing like that has happened since.

At quiet moments, fear bubbles up unbidden and I know with some inner instinct that what happened that day had everything to do with me. Some say I have a way with animals. They call it a blessing when I calm their horse or stop their dog from killing chicks, but Ned knows that a blessing like that can easily turn into a curse if folk get the wrong idea. Poor Ned. He told me not to go to the bull-baiting, and I'm doing just that. It's as if my feet have a mind of their own and there's nothing I can do to stop them from taking me there.

Ahead of me is Market Hill, so steep it is almost sheer, at the top of which is Maldon's main square. Even from here, I can hear the noise of folk jostling to get a view of the bull stake.

It is not long before I crest the brow of the hill. I'm already feeling faint from the climb, and when I make my way past the pie man's stall my stomach lurches, queasy at the smell of kidneys and onion. I push through a crowd still well-behaved, not yet full of ale.

The bull, when I finally catch a glimpse of him, is snorting and rolling his eyes. Tethered to the stake on a short rope, he bucks like a barge on a spring tide. As if a fine cord connects us, I can feel his heart knocking against his ribcage. His ears, like mine, hear the rumble of men's voices, their shouts of laughter, and he shakes his collared head from side to side to rid himself of the sound.

I continue to push my way through, cutting a path between the onlookers, shoving them aside with my arms. A few of them complain with a tut of the tongue, but at this stage of the evening little can break their good humour.

Now I have sight of the dogs. They strain at their collars, held between the knees of their crouching masters. My eyes scan the group, and it takes only a moment to pick out what I've come to find.

'*Bruiser!*' I'm too far away to call him – the word is but a roar in my head – and yet he turns. His blunt, scarred face looks to me, then back at the bull. Then to me again. His master's sharp face flicks round to see what has distracted the dog; he tugs hard at the collar, almost throttling him.

I push forward some more, heading for the bulldogs. *Don't do it! Leave the bull! Come away!*

Two more dogs turn their heads, ears pricked, as if waiting for a command. It's as if the words in my head have carried to them through the air.

A man moves forward and blows pepper from a pipe into the bull's nose. Enraged, the creature bellows and snorts, head ducking and surging. Horns lowered, he roars as the five dogs are unleashed.

All around me men are shouting, pumping the air with their fists: 'The nose, the nose, Bruiser!' ... 'Go, Blue! Get in there, boy!'

The bulldogs fan out, working as a pack, keeping below the jabbing horns. Bruiser makes the first dart, but he's clumsy from his injuries and narrowly avoids being gored. I see the quick stripe of red as a horn gashes his shoulder. He refuses to give up and makes another leap at the bull. His teeth catch the nose but fail to grip, and I hear his master's furious voice urging him on – 'Stick with it, damn you!' – but the dog bails out and backs away, hugging the ground.

Now the others rush in from the sides. One gets hold of an ear, and the bull shakes his head, bellowing his rage. The bulldog hangs for a moment, then is tossed to the cobbles on his back.

Watching is unbearable, but I can't take my eyes away from the bull's face, running red. A tide of horror rises in me and the strangest feeling takes me over. I'm burning inside, fixed to the ground like a candle in a lump of tallow. My body is ramrod straight, arms tight and stiff at my sides, fingers splayed. I raise my head to the skies and open my mouth in a silent scream, the same wide black hole that spewed forth a torrent of rage when my mother died. The air around me quivers, as if a thousand birds have just taken flight, and the rushing and the burning and the quivering consume me, distracting me from everything else around me. Then it dies down, and I'm vaguely aware of a group of boys near me nudging one another. A feeling of shame sweeps through me.

A shout goes up. 'The dogs! Look at the dogs! They're pullin' away!'

The bulldogs ignore their masters' cries and in a silent line they walk towards me, tails between legs. Gawping, the crowd parts to let them through. Another voice shouts:

'It's that girl! Look at her! What's she done to 'em?'

Then my body is my own again, and I run, desperate to get home to Goldhanger. Market Hill is empty, and as

I sprint down to the fullbridge I realise the dogs are running with me.

Then I'm out on the road by the marshes, a sobbing mess of mud, sweat and tears. My stockings are torn and bloody; I've lost a shoe. I turn to see that the dogs are still here. Why do they follow me? What is it that I've done?

They are waiting for a command.

'Get home!' I tell them, and one by one they turn and leave.

The next thing I remember, Ned is bending over me, rubbing my shoulder. He's found me huddled on the stable floor, my mare Bessie nosing round me worriedly. I barely know how I got there and I sit up, stalks of straw sticking out of my hair.

'Come on, Dela.' He picks me up in his arms and carries me across the yard and into the cottage, where he lights a taper and sees to my cuts and grazes. He doesn't say another word, but as his grey head bends over my bleeding foot in the glow of the rushlight, I can feel the fear eating away at him.

In the morning, when he asks me what happened, all I can do is shrug, unable to find the words to explain. I give him the bare facts, and they don't seem so terrible in the cool light of day. We sit over our bread and small beer and I tell him yes, I went there, and yes, the dogs became unsettled, I'm not sure how.

'I didn't do anything. Something happened, but it's not as if I called to them.'

We both know Ned won't leave it there; he's not my guardian for nothing.

'Seeing the state of you last night … we both know it was a bit more than that. I've been telling you to steer clear of the town, keep to my yard and the marshes.'

I open my mouth to answer back, then close it. After last night, all fight's gone out of me. I'll hide under a stone like a worm if he asks me.

He puts down his beaker and wipes his mouth on the back of his hand. He smiles when he catches me looking at his red and swollen knuckles. 'Getting old and creaky. You'll be putting me out to pasture soon.'

He means it half in jest, but I won't hear it … not today. Ned is like the hinges of the door or the rafters holding up the roof. I cannot think of going about my days without him.

'Don't say that.' My face is stiff, unable to return his smile.

'You mustn't mind what I say. My old pa worked the forge till he was eighty, and we lost count of the years after that. There's plenty of Methuselahs in my family. I'll be keeping an eye on your grandchildren, most like. I'm not going anywhere.'

Ned has always taken his role of guardian very seriously, as if he's studied for it all his life. I once asked him why he takes such trouble over me, since we aren't related or anything, and he said that some poor wight had to stop me doing an injury to myself.

We are saved from more talk by our good friend Saltpan Sal hallooing outside the door. She gives a knock, though why she bothers I don't know, for she clatters straight in. Tall as a giant, she makes her way to the table with a crookback to avoid the oak rafters.

'Hey ho, friends. I've come for Bridey if that's all right wi' ye? I've brought herring since ye won't take my coin.'

Sal works out on the mudflats at Goldhanger Creek, and Bridey is the carthorse who carries her salt to market. Sal spends her days raking the saltpans, shallow tidal pools that the wind and sun dry out to leave a white crust on the sand. She swears she'll live for ever, being as she's salted like a kipper.

Ned gets to his feet creakily and draws up a stool, onto which she carefully lowers her broad rump. He honours her with his slow smile. He doesn't give that smile to just anybody. 'Bridey's a right one for kicking a man when he's down,' he says. 'But I managed to pick out that stone in her hoof.'

Sal's carthorse has a knack for catching Ned with a flick of her fetlock just as he bends over to treat her. For all his sixty years, he is remarkably nimble at jumping out of her way. I think he allows the mare to do it on purpose, just to make me laugh, and he sticks out his backside so that it's within kicking distance of her hoof.

'She only does it to them she favours,' chuckles Sal.

'A fine way of showing it.'

I fetch Sal a drink, and she beams at me, taking the beaker from my hand. She has a large gap between her two front teeth through which she likes to suck her beer, enjoying the squirt of it as she takes it in. I sit down, feeling the comfort of her warm giant's body beside me. Her forearm on the table is as weighty as a flitch of bacon. She reminds me of a Viking – one of those warrior queens from the northlands – but instead of hair plaited into gold ropes, her cropped black mop stands up in spikes, stiffened by the salt.

She takes a close look at my face – the shadows under my eyes – and puts down her beaker. 'What's up wi' ye?'

Ned and I exchange a quick glance. I wonder if Sal's heard anything. 'I didn't sleep too well. Folk making a noise in the lane.'

I *will* talk to her about Maldon but don't feel up to it now.

'I hope Bridey weren't keepin' ye awake wi' her snortin'. I meant to pick her up last night, but Rob had one of his turns.'

'Is he all right?'

She nods. 'He's gone down to the jetty. He never lets it get him down.'

Sal's son Rob is known to be the best fisherman in Goldhanger. Folk give him the respect that goes with that and forgive him the fits, though they aren't above crossing themselves whenever Sal has to shove a spoon between his teeth to stop him biting his tongue.

'Did Rob say he saw any goings-on when he took the boat out yesterday?' asks Ned.

'He sailed right past that warship at the mouth of the estuary, if that's what you mean. Its cannons were pointing straight at Goldhanger, he said. He felt like giving the skipper a piece of his mind.'

I picture Rob's little beechwood boat next to the great warship and almost laugh, but Ned's serious face puts a stop to that.

He clears his throat to speak. 'I had a word with the carter. He says folk in London are full of it. The boy king's getting sicker by the day. The Duke of Northumberland ain't just pulling Edward's strings now – he's taken over. And it's him who sent that warship.'

'But why would he send it to the Blackwater?' I ask.

'Because he doesn't want Princess Mary getting the throne if Edward dies. A Catholic like her might make the duke and his cronies give back what they stole from the abbots.'

'So the ship's there to catch her if she tries to escape.'

'That's what they're saying in Maldon,' says Sal.

'See, if Mary were to sail off to her Spanish cousin, Emperor Charles, she might tell tattle tales to him,' Ned explains. 'And Northumberland doesn't want that. No, sir. The emperor might just send his fleet to make sure Mary gets her crown.'

'Why does Northumberland think she'd leave from here?'

'She's owns plenty of land round this part of Essex, as you know. Odds are she'd use the Blackwater to escape.'

Ned is for Mary – King Henry's first-born – and follows the old prayer book. A Catholic I was born, he says, and a Catholic I'll die. But he keeps this to his chest. He says that if you show yourself for Mary, the Duke of Northumberland – the so-called Lord Protector – will have you locked up quick as anything. I think of the ailing King Edward, a boy the same age as me, and quickly distract myself by imagining the princess waiting on the jetty at Goldhanger Creek, wearing her golden crown.

I am brought back with a crash when Rob bursts through the door. Taller even than Sal, he has to stoop right down to avoid the lintel. He is always wary moving about Ned's, as he's forever banging his head on the rafters.

'I thought you was down at the jetty,' says Sal.

'I was, Ma, but then I heard folk talkin' 'bout Dela.'

I give a start, and my arm knocks my beaker, trickling beer onto the table.

'Son, I told you, pay no heed to them janglin' fishwives.'

'It weren't them. Tom Sherrin was sayin' as how he was at Market Place last night and the dogs went mad. Just when their blood was up, they turned tail. He says they followed Dela, cringin' along on their bellies. Every wight's talkin'. Says it's her fault.' Rob meets his mother's stare and hastily remembers his manners. 'Beg pardon, Dela … Ned. Forgot meself.'

'Well, we might as well know what folk are saying.' Ned is grim-faced, as if he's been expecting this and thinks it's better to know the worst.

This time, Rob remembers his manners and tells me to my face, standing like a great tree trunk in the middle of the chamber. He has a strange way about him, but we're used to his bald way of speaking.

He fixes me with his slightly squint-eyed stare. 'Some folks is saying it's a fuss about nothin'. But Tom says it's a whole lot more than nothin'. He says thou stretched thy fingers and stared at the dogs, Dela. He says a bulldog ain't one to cringe. Not unless summat's not right.'

I feel a little faint, and Sal puts the flat of her hand on my back. 'Don't worry, my lovekin. You've friends here in Goldhanger.' She turns a sharp eye on her son. 'Thou stood up for her, son?'

''Course, Ma, what did ye think? Anyways, they all know Dela has a way with animals.'

Rob has rubbed his hair so hard that it sticks up in black spikes just like his mother's. I can see how the talk down at the jetty has got to him. He takes a breath to calm himself.

'I told Tom he should mind his tongue, considerin' as how Dela helped him with that mad old mare no one would give him a penny for.'

'Quite right.' Sal's gaze softens. 'Glad you told him, son. I'll wager it stopped his tongue.'

'It didn't, Ma.'

Ned prompts him, impatient to be done with it. 'Get it out, lad. What did that fool of an oysterman say?'

'He said as how folk were crossing themselves. Last night, the men wanted to ride out and get Dela.'

I let out a small bleat, and Sal clamps a meaty hand over mine, cutting in briskly: 'There's always some like to make trouble. Drink addles their brains. Best not listen to 'em, Dela.'

Rob moves from foot to foot, rubbing his hair. Ned catches Sal's eye, and she gets up from her stool.

'Come on, big barnacle,' she says to Rob. 'Let's get Bridey, leave these two in peace.'

Peace is not how I'd put it. Ned knows very well that I'm as shaky as jelly.

When the others have gone, he sits me down at the hearth. 'I'm not going to say don't worry, it's nothing,' he says quietly. 'I've known for some time it ain't safe for you. Not since animals and birds started following you about the place … as if they were doing your bidding.'

I can't speak – it doesn't seem right to feel shame for what I am, but I do.

Ned reaches out a knobbly hand and squeezes my arm. His gestures of affection, like his smiles, are given only sparingly and are the better for it. 'What you have is special, and I don't want you going about thinking it's wrong,' he adds softly. 'But it's Tallon that worries me.'

Tallon ... Just the mention of his name makes my stomach churn violently.

'Now that the duke has made him one of his lieutenants, things will only get worse. The power's gone to his head. He's busy levying any man who can hold a bow for his own private army, every one of 'em ruffians. Spying on innocent men ... arresting them. He ain't just keeping a watch on Catholics – he's got his eye out for gypsies, players, wayfarers ... anyone just a bit different. And there ain't nothing Tallon hates more than cunning folk. He never went after your mother, but he might just come after you.'

Ned pauses, and I think he's finished, but then he goes on: 'If things don't blow over soon, we'll have to find somewhere to hide you.'

I bring my hands to my hot cheeks, tears flooding my eyes. After everything that happened last night, it is all too much. 'Hide me? ... Send me away?'

This is my home, I've never known anything else. What would I do without Ned ... without Sal?

'Dela, lass. I didn't mean to upset you. There now.' He rootles around for his kerchief and hands it to me. It looks dirty, as if it's been used as a hoof-scraper.

'Why do you risk so much for me?'

'Caring for you, as your guardian ... well, that's something like a calling. That's how I see it.'

CHAPTER 2

My mother always said there are two things a woman needs to remember – that she's every bit as good as a man, and that there is nothing she cannot do if she puts her mind to it.

She put her mind to teaching me my letters, 'so that no lord or lawyer can ever stitch you up'. It seems to me that if my father hadn't been so clever with his letters he wouldn't have penned the pamphlet against land enclosures. And if there hadn't been a pamphlet, he wouldn't have been strung up at Colchester's town gates and left hanging there for weeks. There was nothing he could have done, even if he had 'put his mind to it', to stop the crows pecking out his eyes.

Sir John Tallon signed his death warrant. As keeper of Colchester jail, Tallon's always done whatever he pleases. As a young man, in King Henry's time, he grabbed every bit of Abbey land he could lay his hands on and set himself up in the hall at Tolleshunt d'Arcy. But he didn't stop there – men like him always want more. Very soon, he'd put up fences where they had no right to be, his sheep growing fat on marsh grass that should have belonged to us all.

It was once he started on the oyster beds that my mother had exploded like a firecracker. 'If he takes the saltings, what's to stop him saying the seabed's his as well?

Or the shoals that swim over it? There's some things a man *shouldn't* own.'

When my mother got fired up she was unstoppable, better than any preacher. My father loved her for it. Drawn to her fire, it was only natural he should catch her spark, and when one of Rob Kett's rebels came down to Colchester to spread the word, Pa wanted to do something to help the cause. *Stop the unfair land enclosures! Tear down the fences! Give back our commons!* – such brave words in his pamphlet.

Brave words that got him killed.

Tallon had never liked my father. What he *did* like was Pa's fine piece of land bordering the marshes at Goldhanger Creek. Tallon had wanted to get his hands on Barrow Farm the moment he'd laid eyes on it. My father hadn't stood a chance.

Thinking about these things makes my head ache; I can feel the tightness around my forehead like an iron bridle. I decide to go gleaning for shellfish on the tidal flats west of Goldhanger Creek. I'll dig out some cockles and see what else I can find for supper.

The tide is out when I walk down the slope of Fish Street, passing the tiny thatched cottages of Goldhanger's fisher families. Ahead of me is the almost empty wooden jetty, noisy with gulls circling for fish guts. The silvery clay of the marsh mud beyond spreads out like shining veins of trickling water across the creek, pale against the livid green of seaweed and marsh grass. Ahead of me, across the mudflats, the dark flat line of Osea Island stretches along the horizon, blocking my view of the southern shore of the estuary.

My spirits rise when I spot Kitty Henlake and her two children on the jetty, and I hasten towards them. The boy squats over a pail of shellfish, while his sister makes a tower of oyster shells. She nestles close to Kitty, who is bent over a fishing net, mending a tear in the hemp with a large needle.

The boy looks up from his pail, and his eyes widen when he catches sight of me. 'Look, Ma, it's her! The animal witch.'

At first, it's as if I haven't heard him. I have a smile on my face, ready to greet them. But then his flaxen-haired sister turns and stares at me too, huddling into her mother as if she thinks I'm going to eat her.

I expect Kitty to hush the children and greet me kindly – only last week she said I was a marvel when I trained her dog not to bite them – but she doesn't. Instead, she stuffs her needle into her apron pocket and clambers to her feet, grabbing her little ones to her. 'Come away. Don't look at her!'

I stand, frozen in shock, as she picks up the pail and hurries her children up the jetty in the direction of Fish Street. She takes a furtive glance back at me, and I'm shocked at how scared she looks.

Anger and shame swell inside me. If Kitty's like that, what will the others be saying? I never used to feel on the outside of things, but then my father was hanged for being a traitor and the animal gift grew stronger, and girls my age stopped coming by to ask me to join them in whatever they were doing. Now they group together on the village green and watch me, twirling their cap strings and smirking, and I blush scarlet, my eyes bleary with tears so that I can hardly see to walk. They've even made up a chant. I hear them whispering it at my back when I go past: *Dela, Dela, she'll never get a feller.*

But no one's ever called me a witch before.

As I pick my way along the marshes, a sea mist sweeps in to shroud the estuary, making it impossible for the sun to fight through. It feels a relief to hide in the thick, white wetness of it.

My mother told me that it's a fine thing to be cunning with herbs − Nature's own physic − but when a blight steals the crop or a sheep gets swallowed by quicksand on the flats, you can guess whom they point the finger at. I'm not the first in my family to have a gift with animals, nor the only one to get into trouble with it. I'm sure other women back in my mother's line had geese and cats following them down the street. It's my misfortune to be in the world just when Sir John Tallon and his men are itching to bag themselves a witch.

The mud and shingle are cold under my bare feet. It's hours yet till the tide turns. The curlews' piping sounds like an echo in the mist; then above the calling of the sea birds I hear a different sound. Someone whistling a tune. I nearly stumble into one of the fingers of water that fan out across the marshes. I've heard that song in a time before words, before I knew anything but the comforting arms of my mother. I listen, but my mind cannot grasp it − the words are tantalisingly out of reach. I head towards the whistling, but then I become confused, all at once thinking I hear the sound behind me, then to my right. It's eerie in the drifting fog; everything sounds muffled. I keep walking, and the tune seems to get bleaker with every step until it sounds almost menacing.

As mists on these marshes tend to do, this one lifts without warning, swept away by a sudden breeze from the sea. I realise I've wandered quite a distance, and not in the direction I thought. The whistling has stopped, but ahead of me I see the screens of a decoy pond and my eye catches a flash of movement through one of the gaps. It is Red, the sneaky fox-like dog belonging to Fowler, a man as sly as he is cruel. I'd best steer clear of the red-haired weasel: he's employed by Sir John Tallon, the very man whose iron fist is bent on crushing us Blackwater folk.

I've had my run-ins with Fowler before. He says he 'works' with animals – as gamekeeper, wildfowler, dog trainer, horse breaker – but if he can use an instrument of torture he will.

'Bend an animal to your will, it's the only way,' he assures anybody who'll listen.

I know what he does to them. Davy, a groom up at the Hall, brings me 'broken' horses that need fixing.

Ned was my first teacher when it came to horses. He explained that their first thought is to flee when they feel a weight on their back. 'They haven't got aught to fight with, just them long skinny legs to run away. When the saddle goes on, they think it's a wolf, see? Ready to sink its teeth into their neck.'

A horse tells you everything with its body. If it hangs its lip or rolls its eyes, that's its way of talking to you. It is easy to make friends with horses because they like company. All they want is to be with their herd, and if the herd isn't there, you're the next best thing. If you stand close and look at them sidelong, peeping from the corner of your eye, they like having you there. It's as simple as that.

Fowler doesn't care what a horse thinks. He ties up one of its legs so it can't run and rams in the bit, and when the colt arches its neck he whips it till it bleeds.

Because I know all this, my first instinct when I see the dog is to run. But I'm too late.

'Good day, young mistress.' Fowler arches himself, holding the small of his back as he stretches. I notice his hands, small and white, with pale, freckled skin. His long-ish hair is darker than Red's on account of the grease, making it not quite a match for the dog's rust-coloured fur. His smile is wide and snaggle-toothed, but there's a mean twist to it.

'Come to look at my pond, eh? There's plenty folk want to know how's I catch so many.' His voice is high, like a girl's. He snaps his fingers and Red runs to his side. The dog gives me a sidelong look and his upper lip twitch-es up at the corners, revealing a pair of sharp canines.

'Red here looks like a fox, see?' He nudges him with his foot. 'Now take a look at them gaps in the screens. There, and there.' He points to the large pool, shaped like a crab shell with channels running from it, at the end of which sit the basket traps.

'When duck fly down to the pool, see, they spy Red through those gaps. Think he's a fox come to snatch 'em. Then he steers them out the main pond into them pipes, and into my *trap*.' He raps his hand sharply against the wicker and it makes me jump.

He follows my eyes which have been drawn to a pair of tatty mallards drifting on the decoy pond. 'I'll let you into my little secret. Those two are mine. I bring 'em down in a basket. When I pops 'em on the water, other duck spot 'em, come down to join the fun. Oh, yes, we do have fun, eh, Red?' He gives the dog another nudge with his foot.

I cannot help asking, 'Why don't your ducks fly away?'

'I broke their wings. An' if they try to run, Red gets 'em back in the basket.'

My head is starting to throb again. I'm desperate to leave, but while he keeps talking it is impossible to get away. I avert my eyes from the ducks and fix them on the eastern tip of Osea Island. Beyond it, almost level with Stansgate Abbey on the far shore of the estuary, I can just make out the fat stern of the warship at anchor, like a great blot against the greenish-grey of the Blackwater.

'Know what it's there for, missy?' He is watchful, studying my face with sidelong glances.

I shake my head.

'So Princess Mary can't fly the coop. The Duke of Northumberland sent it to guard the estuary, see. And my master Tallon has his watchers out to help. Oh yes! He'll catch any scum who tries to help her, mark my words. You'd best tell the farrier to watch his self.'

Again the sharp glance to accompany the threat.

'There's a few papists here in Goldhanger. Can smell 'em, plotting against the king. You know all about treason, eh? The long drop. A kick of the legs, and snap.'

I shift awkwardly, a flush creeping up my neck. Fowler thinks to dig the knife in, knowing that my father was arrested for treason and hanged for it. But what has he got against Ned? What does he think Ned's up to?

'If Mary thinks to run whining to that lantern-jawed cousin of hers, it'll be the worse for her. That greedy Spaniard had better keep his paws out of our business.' Fowler spits a gobbet of phlegm on the mud. 'Stinkin' foreigners. It's all we need.'

Fowler's stupid if he thinks I'll talk to him – a weasel so close to Tallon's ear. Suddenly I have the urge to kick down his screens and rescue the miserable ducks. My hands clench into fists but I never get the chance to use them because at that moment there's the swish of birds' wings and five mallards fly over. Quick as a flash, dog and master raise their heads.

The ducks circle and fly down to the pond, immediately beginning to dabble, making supping noises with their yellow bills.

'Ah, missy, you watch Red now!'

It's a trap! Get out! Fly away! the voice in my head calls out to the ducks.

They have glimpsed Red now. Two fly off, and the others zigzag the pond for a moment in a frenzy of alarm. Confused by the screens and paddling as fast as they can away from Red, they head straight for one of the channels.

'Get in the pipe!' Fowler shrills, his round eyes popping. 'In the pipe, my beauties!'

It is then that the strange feeling comes over me, that same pulsing heat I felt at the bull-baiting. I cannot move, and it's as if an invisible thread connects me to the panicking mallards. The harder Fowler urges them into the pipe-like channels, the harder my mind tugs on that thread. *Come away, come away!* The ducks, half-running along the surface of the pond towards the trap, all at once turn and face us. For a moment I feel the penetrating stare of their brown, bead-like eyes, then they spread their wings and take to the air, flying close to my head in a triumphant swoop.

'What's going on, damn it?' Fowler squeals. 'Why didn't they heed Red?' He starts to bellow at his dog who dithers, running back and forth, then cringes, tail between legs.

Fowler's eyes narrow as they fix on me. His pale, freckled face grows blotchy.

'It's you. It is!' he hisses. 'I know witchery when I see it. You dare come here, put a spell on my ducks! I know what you're about, missy. I saw it with the dogs!'

Palms out to ward him off, I take a few quick steps backwards, thinking he might attack me, then I turn and run.

Behind me, I can hear him shouting, 'We'll hunt you down. Burn you! That's what we do to witches!'

Back at the jetty, I calm down as I make my way up Fish Street, hoping to see Sal seated on the wooden bench outside her cottage door. She is exactly the person I need to soothe my sore head.

She isn't at home, but by happy chance I spot her at the village square, fetching water at the pump opposite the Bell. I call to her, and her face breaks into a gap-toothed smile. She picks up her wooden yoke, pails at either end, and hoists it onto her shoulders. Then we walk back down Fish Street together.

Standing outside her cottage, I cannot help thinking it looks fit to topple over in the next storm, propped up by the one next door like a drunken sailor leaning on a doxy. Inside, though, it's neat and clean. Even Sal's two stools are polished to a gleam, though they are no more than a few bits of driftwood knocked together. Out back there's a lean-to, where a bread oven has been scooped out of the wall, but otherwise it's just a little square box made of rickety wood from wrecked ships stuck together with river clay. It's nowhere near as solid as Ned's, but it's warm and snug once the shutters are closed to the sea fog that comes seeping up the creek into Goldhanger.

She and Rob live in the one room, but as he's mostly out fishing they rarely get under each other's feet – which is lucky, them both being giants. Sal says he's never had a fit on the water – they come upon him only on dry land. That's why he mostly lives on his boat.

She stirs up the ashes on her hearth and adds some driftwood, then fills two beakers with apple cider and puts them to warm in front of the fire. I sit down on a stool and she pulls over the other to perch next to me, her broad backside spilling over the edge.

'How ye feeling after Sunday?' she asks, getting straight to the point. 'Still down in the dumps?'

I nod bleakly. 'It's just happened again, Sal.' It's hard to stop my voice from shaking.

She puts a man-size hand on my knee. 'What? More bulldogs?'

'Not this time. Ducks.' I give a rueful smile.

Sal chuckles. 'Ducks, was it? Well, all those aldermen and bailiffs and justices and whatnot had better shake in their shoes!'

'Fowler was trapping them in his pond.'

She clucks the roof of her mouth. 'That bladdersack should be put in the pillory.'

'He says they'll string me up. All I did was look at the ducks and wish they'd fly away from his trap. He was making threats about Ned, too. Don't know why.'

'I'd pay no heed to that son of a drab,' Sal says comfortably. 'Fowl by name, foul by nature – that's what I say.

And don't worry about Ned, my lovekin. He may be faithful to the old ways, but he knows how to keep out of trouble … Anyways, it's Fowler should watch out. One day those dogs he trains for Tallon are going to eat him up. All they'll find is a snaggle-toothed jawbone on the kennel floor.'

I laugh, feeling much better suddenly. My headache's almost gone.

Sal hands me the warm cider and I sip at it. She takes a long look at me, then shakes her head wonderingly. 'You look so like your ma. Two peas in a podlet. You've got her wild black hair and skin like a Spaniard, and those big thick lashes, though your eyes are darker than hers. She had a way with animals too. Though not half as powerful as yours.'

She raises herself from the stool, crosses the chamber in two giant steps and brings back a pair of muffins from her tiny bakehouse lean-to. Handing one to me, she settles back on her stool and carries on talking, all the while eating hers with noisy pleasure.

'Did I ever tell ye 'bout the day your ma and I went pickin' berries in Tolleshunt forest?'

I shake my head, though I have heard the story many times.

'Thou was just a babe, an' she left thee on a bed of pine needles, tucked up in a muslin. We got carried away – berry-pickin's like that. Anyways, when we came back there was a couple of wildcats standin' o'er ye. Your ma, she screamed and hollered … thought they was after eatin' ye. There she was, wavin' her arms like a mad thing, and them wildcats just stood there, archin' their backs an' hissin'. Well, she calmed down once she saw they was guardin' thee. She fixed 'em with such a stare …. An' guess what? Them cats marched up to her with their tails straight up. She thanked 'em kindly, and they nodded their stripy heads an' stalked off ...'

She swallows her muffin and grins. 'So what d'ye think of that, my lovekin? Ain't it just what I said? Two peas in a podlet!'

She pops the last bite of muffin in her mouth and chews a while, then sucks noisily at her fingers and smacks her lips.

'Do you remember that old grey raven your mother rescued from a drift-net on Osea?'

'Oh yes! What happened to him? He used to visit when Father was ploughing.'

'Your ma said he was as old as the isle itself. She said he was lonely for his wolf friends and that's why he hung about. In the old days, see, when the ravens called, the wolves came runnin'. That were before we hunted every last one.'

'Why did the ravens do that?'

'The wolves would rip open the carcass, and the birds would get the pickings. A fine friendship, if you ask me.'

I am silent a moment, thinking of the great bird of Osea with his stippled wings and grizzled head. 'What made you think of the grey raven?'

'I saw him in the churchyard this morning when I was putting marigolds on your mother's grave. He flew down and perched on her headstone. I were that surprised, I near fell over.'

'He remembers her!'

'That he does. But it's more than that. I think he's come to look out for ye ... He knows ye need a friend.' She reaches out and pinches my cheek. 'Call me soft in the head, but that's what I think.'

Chapter 3

A week goes by. I feel the heaviness in the air that comes before a storm, only it doesn't arrive and the ache behind my eyes sets up a constant, dull throb. Ned is preoccupied, and I get the feeling it's not just my situation that's making his shoulders so stiff and hunched. He looks older than his sixty years.

We are just finishing trimming a horse's hooves, working in silence. There's nothing unusual in that, but this time I feel his unease. At various points he seems about to speak: takes a breath, then thinks better of it. I can always feel the slightest change in Ned's moods, like a wisp of wind setting up a ripple in a wheat field.

We are washing our hands in the water trough when we hear something going on in the lane. The clinking of bits and bridles … a horse's whinny … men's voices.

Ned stills.

I look at his face, thinking, *This is it. They've come for me,* and I look from left to right, my head in a spin, casting about for the nearest hiding place. But it's too late for that, and Ned places a hand on my arm. We both know it won't look good if I run and the men see me.

Three riders enter the yard. They don't bother to dismount. Two are in uniform; I recognise their mustard

and dark-green livery. It takes me a moment to realise
that the rider mounted between them is Sir John Tallon
himself. His black horse is on a tight rein; it jerks its
head, the arch of its neck straining. I can see the steel bit
digging into the soft parts of its mouth. I'm puzzled as
to why a man like him would concern himself with a
fifteen-year-old girl and a farrier. It doesn't make sense.
He disdains ordinary folk – doesn't like to look at them
too closely – and is the sort who gets his henchmen to
do his bidding.

He doesn't have the swagger of a braggart; his power
has grown too great for that. His clothes aren't showy
either: he wears plain and sober black – the mark of a
keen Protestant. The only gleaming thing to catch my
eye is a pair of spurs on the heels of his riding boots. The
dagger-like points fixed to the shank look sharp enough
to do some real damage.

I raise my eyes to Tallon's face and it shocks me to see
how handsome he is. His features are just the right size,
each one sitting in just the right place on his head. He
has a broad, noble forehead, widely spaced grey eyes, and
a generous upturned mouth that looks as if it is smiling
even when it's not. But though the face might be lovely,
the flesh covering it is bloodless, with a curious bluish
sheen to it. His eyes carry no warmth at all, and when
they lock onto mine I give a gasp. His cool grey stare
burns me; I feel the pain of it as if I'm being held by
tongs near the blazing charcoal and he is bending me to
his will.

But I will not bend. *This is the man who killed my father
and took the farm.*

Tallon's nostrils flare slightly as if he's caught a scent. Sensing his master's mood, his horse stamps the hard earth of the yard.

Ned feels my tensed muscles ready to spring and he grabs my arm. 'Get into the house.'

I don't want to leave him to face the men alone, but nor can I suffer Tallon's burning stare any longer: a moment more and I think I would collapse. I stumble across the yard and into the house, where I stand inside the doorway, leaning against the wall. I leave the door open: it's better to know what's going on, in case something happens to Ned.

'What can I do for you, your lordship?'

'The girl, who is she?'

'Just an orphan, my lord. She helps in the stables.'

So Tallon hasn't come for me. I feel relief, but also puzzlement. Why, if I'm a stranger to him, did he stare so?

'Hear me, farrier. A man – a foreigner – was seen coming this way. What do you know?'

'I've been seeing to a horse, my lord. I rarely hear aught from the forge.'

A pause. 'What about the girl? Maybe she knows something.'

My heart thuds as Ned says, 'No, she was in with me, helping with the horse.'

I cannot help myself and peek through the crack of the door. Tallon seems undecided, then makes as if to dismount, but, before he can do so, the soldier to his right says something to which he gives a curt reply.

I see Ned's shoulders relax a little as the two soldiers start to bring their horses round. I realise I've been holding my breath and let it out in relief, but then Tallon calls to his men to wait and takes his feet out of the stirrups. He's dismounting!

He tethers his horse and walks over to Ned, his stride muscular and loose-limbed. Next to him, the farrier appears tiny, fragile.

'You underestimate me if you think for one moment that I don't know what you've been up to, farrier. I know everything that goes on. My watchers see everything. The foreigner, a spy, came this way looking for you – don't bother to deny it. Just tell me why he came and where he is now.'

'My lord, I know nothing of what you speak. I've been in my forge all day.'

'Are you sure about that?'

'Yes, my lord.'

Tallon strokes his neat black beard thoughtfully, then shows his even white teeth in a smile. 'I have a desire to see this forge of yours. Would you show it to me?'

Ned is white-faced, his ears as red as those of a young boy caught out in a lie. He knows something, I can tell. Rooted to the ground, he doesn't move.

Tallon places a gloved hand on his shoulder, and when he speaks it is as if he's merely passing the time of day with Ned.

'Heat, I find, is a remarkable way of working the truth from a man.'

I can guess what is coming next and want to yell *Stop it! Stop it!* and sprint across the yard to grab Ned away from him. *Run, Ned. Run!* But my feet are stuck with fear.

Ned has better control of his legs and manages to walk, leading the way. I crouch down, sobbing. No … please no.

They go across the yard, through the doorway of the forge and out of sight. I picture Ned heating the charcoal to a blaze with his bellows, then the pulsing white heat.

The screams when they come sound nothing like his voice. Then Bessie starts up, shrieking from her stall.

I don't know how I manage to get Ned into the house and onto his bed. He's conscious, but barely, with a lump on his head and a nasty cut. I can't be sure, but I think Tallon must have kicked him, catching Ned's head with his spur. The left hand, covered in weeping burns, is more worrying. I need to act quickly.

I see to his head hurriedly, then take out the mortar and make a paste with oatmeal and alehoof, carefully placing it over the oozing sores on his hand to draw out the heat. He gives a groan and his head falls forward. My heart jumps in my chest – is he dead?

No, still breathing, thank heavens. When I make to pull a blanket over him, he rouses himself and mumbles my name.

'It's me. I'm here, Ned.' I place my hand on his forehead and tell him to rest. 'Don't talk. You need to sleep. It'll be better in the morning.'

If anything, his attempts to speak grow more urgent. 'Dela ... listen.'

'I'm listening, Ned.'

'I didn't tell Tallon ...'

'Hush now ... Of course, you didn't.'

'St Mary's ... he's there.' He tries to push himself up with his good arm.

'Here, let me help you.' Soon he is sitting upright, his chest heaving from the pain. 'Ned, tell me. Who is at St Mary's?'

'The man Tallon's after ...'

'So you *did* meet the foreigner!' My mind reels. 'The one he called a spy.'

Ned's head dips forward, and I rouse him with a sip of ale. He chokes a little, and it spills down his chin. 'Dumont, the emperor's man ... I must take him ...'

'Where to?' I give him another sip of ale.

'To the princess ... at Woodham Walter ...'

The princess? My head spins. The Lady Mary is like a figure from a fairy tale to me, with no more substance than that. *Ned and the princess?* I realise he's been distracted these past days, but not for one moment would I have guessed such a reason. He's been quiet, yes. Secretive, maybe. But when he takes himself off sometimes, I've never been in the habit of asking him why.

I take a breath to collect myself. 'You're not well enough. If one of us must go, it should be me.'

He shakes his head. 'No. Too dangerous.'

Ned starts to shiver. He badly needs to sleep. I worry that infection will set in, and goodness knows what I'll be able to do about that. My mother was cunning with herbs, but I know only a little. He needs to keep warm and let Nature do her work.

'Please, Ned. Let me. I can get past the watch.' I realise I'm sounding like my mother, firm and practical. 'It's almost dusk. I know paths they won't even think of.'

My mind works rapidly. It's three miles to St Mary's, the church at the hythe, Maldon's quayside. And it's another three miles from there to Woodham Walter Hall, Sir Henry Radclyffe's moated manor. I know a good path through the woods. The hythe will be the dangerous bit because it's always milling with people – traders, sailors, customs men. I'm guessing Ned's put Dumont in St Mary's church tower. The curate is a friend of his, a man sympathetic to the old faith.

'By the time I get to St Mary's, it'll be nearly dark. Most folk will have retired to the alehouse by then,' I say, trying to reassure Ned as well as myself. 'We just have to hope no one wants to light the church beacon. We don't want your spy turning into a Michaelmas candle.'

Ned musters a smile at my brave attempt at humour, then he falls asleep, breathing evenly. I think he's made peace with the idea of letting me go. Spreading a wool blanket over him, I stoke the fire and quickly gather my things. I must go down to Sal's, as she'll need to sit with him. First, though, I'd better see to our mare, Bessie. I'm guessing the spy in the church tower hasn't brought his horse, in which case she will have to carry two on her back.

All is quiet at the hythe when Bessie and I get there. It's a chill May evening with clear skies and a full moon. The storm never arrived, and the air has lost its mugginess. I marvel how quiet it is now that the herring gulls have hunkered down, no longer wheeling in the air looking for scraps. I glance up at St Mary's standing tucked behind the quay. With its squat, square tower, the church looks broad-shouldered and dependable. I'm sure nothing can hurt me once I'm through its lychgate.

I tie Bessie to a branch of one of the yew trees that stand either side of the path and make my way to the porch. In the churchyard, the gravestones, silver in the failing light, throw their lengthening shadows on the grass. The colour has been bleached out so that everything is grey, black and white.

Suddenly I pause on the path, listening hard.

A sound, like a cough. Eyes watch me, I'm sure of it. I look around but see no one, then just as I lift the latch of the church door I hear a croaking cry and spin round, heart thudding in my chest.

'Oh, it's *you!*' My voice sounds loud in the still evening air. I give a breathless laugh.

Perched on a gravestone to the left of the door is the grey raven. In the dusk, the stipple on his wings gleams silver and his head looks almost white. He caws again and pauses, tilting it to one side as if waiting for an answer. His black eyes stand out against the pale feathers of his poll, and in the shadows he looks huge, the size of a cat.

'Thank you, grey raven,' I say, feeling a formal greeting is required. 'Sal said you'd come to help me. I'm grateful for it.'

He tilts his head the other way and gives another croak. I wave to him and lift the latch of the door. Hopefully, the bird will mount guard until I come out again. I feel safer having him here.

Inside the church, the moon casts its light through latticed windows. The stained glass has been taken down. The Protestants have made their mark here. A simple wooden table has replaced the altar; gone are the brass candlesticks and sanctus bell. Two niches in the walls, which once held alabaster saints, are now eyeless sockets that seem to watch me as I walk up the nave.

I climb the stairs of the tower, wondering if the man is up there at all. Maybe I have it wrong: he might have left for Woodham Walter already, having given up on Ned, or maybe he's been taken. One of Tallon's men might be on the roof waiting for me. My heart gives a flip, but then I think of the grey raven standing guard on his gravestone and feel reassured.

The man is standing in the shadows, hand on his scabbard. Stepping out of the gloom into the moonlight, he moves heavily. I can see that he is well past his youth, not built for swordplay. He looks hollow-eyed with exhaustion, and the fine cloth of his cape is dusty, his boots caked in river mud. I wonder how many hours he's been hiding up here.

'Where is the farrier?'

'Mr Dumont, I have come in his place. My name is Dela Wisbey.'

He curses in a foreign tongue. 'They send me a *girl*.' He kicks the ground in frustration.

I'm stung by his comment. 'I haven't been sent by anyone, sir. Ned is my guardian. Sir John Tallon burned him in the forge.' I raise my eyes to his face. 'Ned is the bravest of men. He told them nothing.'

Dumont doesn't care one bit about Ned or his bravery, that much is obvious. 'Tallon ... one of Northumberland's men,' he says, stroking his small, neatly shaped beard. 'What does he know?'

'That there's a foreign spy in Maldon. He thinks Ned's got something to do with it.'

He stares at me coldly. 'If Lady Mary's man, Rochester, had been here to meet me, we wouldn't have this problem.' He gives a snort. 'A farrier's girl, for God's sake!'

At this, I'm ready to run straight down the tower steps and back to Goldhanger, but, as if he senses he's gone too far, he says, 'Come, no more talking. We must be off. If we're stopped, remember this – I'm a corn trader from Ostend.'

Nothing about this man – his fine lace collar, soft hands and face untouched by wind and weather – marks him out as a seafaring trader. You barely need to look twice to know he's a foreign courtier. It's lucky he hasn't been questioned by a bailiff or customs man already.

He trudges down the winding stone stairs, breathing heavily. At the bottom, he coughs and brings a lace kerchief to his face. 'This infernal marsh! How can anyone live in this place?'

With difficulty, I swallow a retort. I'm doing this for Ned, I remind myself. All I need to do is get Dumont to Woodham Walter and I'll never have to see him again.

Outside in the churchyard, he reels back with a cry. The grey raven, still on the headstone, has his eyes fixed on the spy.

'What is that abomination?'

'The raven is my friend, sir.'

Dumont staggers a few steps away from me. 'Friend? It's the very devil! What sort of place *is* this?' He flaps his arms at the raven. 'Be gone, Satan!'

In my outrage, I forget my place. '*Don't* do that! Let him be!'

The grey raven looks on, unruffled, as Dumont's hand tightens on the grip of his dagger. I can guess what is going through the spy's mind. On the one hand, I can get him to Woodham Walter – he cannot go alone – while on the other, he probably thinks I'm in league with the devil himself.

The raven hops from the gravestone to stand in front of me, beady glare fixed on the spy. It is clear from the puffed-out feathers of his breast and shoulders that he is mounting a defence.

'Get rid of that raven,' Dumont hisses, pulling the dagger from its scabbard.

What on earth makes him think a dagger would be any use against a bird? This spy doesn't seem very clever to me. I cannot think why Ned was bothering with him. As if reading my mind, the raven gives another hop and opens his beak to make a rude sound. He turns his back on the spy and bends over, offering a vulgar display of the fluffed-out feathers beneath his raised tail.

'That bird is doing your bidding. Get him away!' snaps Dumont.

The raven chooses this moment to fly at the spy's head and, as a parting shot, knocks the feathered hat off it. Dumont screams shrilly and swipes wildly with his dagger, but the bird has already flown off. I swear his rattling call is laughter as he swoops his way up the estuary.

I untie Bessie and lead her to the mounting block outside the porch. 'She's strong enough to bear the both of us, sir.'

Dumont shakes with rage and the aftershocks of fear. 'You forget yourself, girl. *I* will ride. *You* will walk.'

CHAPTER 4

By the time we reach Woodham Walter Hall, I am foot-sore and thirsty. It has been a long day of shocks, and I'm dropping with exhaustion. I've had more than enough of Dumont, as has Bessie. Jumpy with nerves, he's been pulling on the reins until her mouth has become quite sore. I've had to watch her moving the bit around with her tongue, without being able to do anything about it.

At the gates, the spy becomes more confident. Woodham Walter Hall is clearly the kind of place he feels at home, but if the thought of hobnobbing with royalty comes naturally to him, for me it is the opposite. At the sight of the two rampant lions on the gateposts, I want to turn and run. But first I need to get the spy off Bessie's back.

A barking of dogs heralds our arrival. Through the massive wrought-iron gates the great manor looms, its crenellated roof and twisty chimneys outlined against the night sky. Then a square of light as the door opens, and two figures walk towards us, haloed in the bobbing glow of a lantern. They make an odd-looking pair: one extremely tall and thin, the other short and fat. Judging by their fine clothes, these are no lowly servants.

'Who are you? State your business,' the man says in a low voice. He has the rounded shoulders typical of the

very tall, and his blinking eyes dart nervous glances across
the deer park to the elms bordering the road.

Dumont gives his name, then purses his lips sourly when
the tall man introduces himself as Robert Rochester, Princess Mary's comptroller. We are ushered swiftly through the
gates and around the side of the manor into a stableyard,
where Dumont dismounts. A young groom, wearing a green
jerkin and breeches, emerges from the stables and walks
languidly across the cobbles to take the reins from him.

It is only now that anyone seems to notice I'm here.
The woman steps forward to peer at me. 'Goodness!' she
exclaims to Dumont. 'You've brought a girl with you!'

Dumont eyes me with distaste. 'No suitable guide was
available, apparently.' Then he lowers his voice and adds
something that I cannot make out, though I'm sure I catch
the word 'witch'.

The woman raises her brows and looks down her beak-
like nose at me for closer inspection. 'What is your name,
girl?' Her lips, when she pinches them together, disappear entirely, leaving her with nothing more than a slit for a mouth.

'Dela Wisbey, my lady.' Worried that Bessie will be
whisked off, I add, 'That is my mare, if you please.'

The languid groom, whose wheat-coloured hair hangs
half over his eyes, barely bothers to hide his amusement as
he glances from Dumont to me. I am surprised how little
deference he shows towards his seniors. Although he looks
a year or two older than me, he affects a world-weary air
that makes him seem more.

The woman gives him a reproving stare. 'See to the
horse, Master Fitzjohn, and take the girl with you. Ask one
of the cooks to find her something to eat.'

As I follow the groom, I look up at the great brick building with its twisty chimneys breathing smoke into the night sky and give a shiver. More than anything, I want to go home, but I dare not ask.

It is not long before we are both seated at a wooden board on trestles next to the pantry. A serving girl brings me a beaker of ale and a trencher of ham and bread, with a pickled onion. I'm so thirsty that I gulp down the ale in seconds and, once I'm calm enough, eat a little of the food. It is a long time since Ned and I sat down to our midday meal of bread and cheese. It feels like another life.

Tears threaten to spill over, but I am ashamed to let them.

The groom regards me, chin on hand, his eyes a strange and lucid hazel colour with bright gold flecks. He is neither friendly nor unfriendly, just curious. 'Where on earth did you come from, witch girl?'

'Who called me that?'

'The Flemish envoy. I heard him say it to Mistress Clarencieux, the lady-in-waiting.' He continues to gaze at me, intrigued. 'I think you must have terrified the poor man. *Are* you a witch?'

This doesn't merit a reply, so I merely glare.

He laughs, and I can't help noticing how white his teeth appear against the bronze of his face. 'All right, never mind. I'm sure Dumont is a fool. I just hope Lady Mary takes what he says with a pinch of salt.'

'There's plenty of that in Maldon.'

'Ah, a dry tongue. Excellent.' He grabs a piece of my ham and pops it in his mouth. 'You can call me Fitz.'

Just then, Mistress Clarencieux comes through the door. She moves with a curious, sweeping dignity, in spite of her wide girth, and I cannot imagine how it is that such a small person can bear the weight of so much cloth. Yard upon yard of it in her skirts, train and veil. A galleon in full sail.

She glances at me briefly. 'Good. The girl has eaten.'

'The girl has a name. It is Mistress Wisbey.'

I raise my eyes, doubly startled that not only has Fitz remembered my name but he dares to speak to the lady-in-waiting that way. I wonder if he's the son of some lord or other.

The tiniest glimmer of a smile flickers in Mistress Clarencieux's eyes, though her beak-nosed face doesn't lose any of its sternness.

'Enough, sirrah. Lady Mary wants to meet the girl.' She speaks without so much as a glance at me, still acting as if I'm not here. 'Bring her to the great chamber, *Master* Fitzjohn.'

As the lady-in-waiting sweeps out, my mind is left reeling. *The princess wants to meet me?*

It can mean only one thing, and my stomach gives a sickening lurch. Dumont must have told her I'm a witch, and she believes him.

I follow Fitz into the great hall and stop for a moment, frozen at the sight of the animal heads mounted on the walls. Tusks and antlers throw jagged shadows on the stone, and glass eyes follow us as we make our way to the far end. I've never liked hunting. Everything about it – the baying of dogs, the bugles – makes me want to run away. If ever I happen to catch the sound of hunters smashing through the stretch of forest below Tolleshunt d'Arcy, the back of my neck prickles in fear.

I avert my eyes from the animal heads and fix them on Fitz's back as he leads the way. His movements are athletic, precise; he takes steps as neat as a cat's. The more I look at the lad, the more I am compelled to watch him.

He stops at a door, which a liveried page opens, but when Fitz turns, beckoning me to follow, he takes one look at my frightened face and hisses, 'Whatever you do, don't answer back. And remember to curtsey.'

I nod dumbly. Dry-mouthed with fear, I can't imagine I'd manage to utter a sound anyway.

Inside the great candlelit chamber, a small group of nobles are huddled at one end: three seated ladies, and as many men standing. My eyes immediately pick out Dumont. He stares at me with the same baleful and accusing expression he has worn since meeting the grey raven in the churchyard.

Fitz leads me to a canopied chair in the centre of the group, in which a small red-headed woman sits staring at me intently. He bows with the same effortless grace with which he seems to do everything, but when I sink into a curtsey, taking my cue from him, my knees shake so much that I am afraid my legs won't be able to bring me up again.

'Thank you, Master Fitzjohn.' The woman's voice is deep, almost like a man's.

He steps back into the circle of figures, leaving me alone.

'Please rise. Let me speak to you.'

With quivering knees, I straighten up.

'Look at me, girl.'

I raise my eyes to the woman's face. I cannot help noticing that although she is richly dressed in blue silk, bright as a jay's wing feather, her plain square face appears sallow next to the brilliance of its hue. Deep frown lines tell of strain, but her eyes at least are bright, displaying both intelligence and determination. Fixed on me with a steady gaze, they draw me to meet them in spite of my fear.

'My, you're a wild-looking girl. Look at that hair! Its curls have quite escaped your cap.'

With trembling fingers, I try to stuff them inside the cloth.

'So … Dumont says you've a raven to do your bidding. Is it true?' No smile, just that same intent look.

I say nothing, unable to find my voice.

A woman seated to the right of the princess fills the silence. 'If I may speak, Lady Mary?'

I guess this to be the countess – Lady Radclyffe, mistress of the house. Her white powdered cheeks are painted with spots of vermilion, and her clothes are so gaudy they have a look of the fairground about them. Standing next to her chair, a man with a small head peers out nervously from his stiff, frilled collar. From his de-meanour, he seems not so much husband as whipping boy, shrinking into the lace ruffles of his collar when the countess speaks.

'I've heard of this girl,' she shrills. 'She's the one they've been calling the animal witch.'

My knees tremble. Lady Mary rubs her temples and her eyelids close for a moment as the countess screeches on, oblivious to her royal guest's irritation:

'Apparently, my lady, she spoiled a bull-baiting in Mal-don. The dogs never got to fight because this girl drew them away with her stare. Everyone's talking of it.'

I swallow, and lower my gaze. One word from the prin-cess and it will be the end for me. All I can think is: *who will look after Ned if I'm gone?*

I hear her sigh. 'I'm afraid, Lady Radclyffe, I rarely credit talk of witches with much truth. Maybe the girl has a way with animals – a gift. She wouldn't be the first.'

At this, Dumont cannot help himself. 'But that terrible raven – Satan's bird! Beware, my lady, the girl is the devil's spawn. You should have seen the way she spoke to it.'

'Why must it have anything to do with the devil?' snaps the princess. 'It could be a gift from God. Had you thought of that, Dumont? Look at St Francis … Daniel and the lions. The Bible is full of such things.' She smiles for the first time. 'I'm more interested in seeing if the girl really *can* talk to animals … whether they understand her.' She turns to her lady-in-waiting. 'Mistress Clarencieux, you're a practical person. How can we have the girl show us what she can do?'

The lady thinks for a moment, her lips doing their disappearing act. 'Maybe, my lady … if we could find the most difficult, untamed animal – a beast who hates people …'

'And show it to the girl!' I can see Lady Mary is taken with the idea. Her eyes brighten, headache forgotten. 'Countess, have you such a thing?'

Lady Radclyffe thinks for a moment, tapping her painted lips with a finger. 'I think we may have one such animal, my lady.' Beckoning her servant, a puny lad with pustules on his face, she asks, 'Is that dog still working in the kitchens?'

'The vicious one, my lady?' He gulps and clears his throat, darting nervous glances at the princess. 'I can't fetch him. He'll bite me, he's that dangerous!'

Lady Radclyffe ignores him and her shrill voice rattles on. 'The dog was trained to help in the kitchen, my lady. A kind gift from Sir John Tallon.'

I glance at her husband, the earl, who closes his eyes. Even I realise his wife has made a grand error with Lady Mary in singing the praises of the Catholic-hating Tallon. It's a shame the earl wasn't bold enough to stop her before she went too far. I cannot help wondering if he's more nervous of his shrill wife than he is of offending the princess.

At Tallon's name, Lady Mary's face darkens, and only then does the countess realise her mistake. 'Not that he's a friend of ours. No, not at all!' Her eyes roll wildly in her painted face, and she seeks quickly to distract the princess: 'Bring the dog!' The rings on her hands flash as she flaps her fingers at the manservant. 'Quickly!'

While they wait for the dog, the princess calls Rochester, the earl, and Dumont to her side and talks quietly with them. Every time Dumont says something, she ignores him frostily, the frown between her eyes deepening. I have the impression that whatever message the spy delivered earlier was met with disappointment. Maybe I've been called to the chamber as some sort of diversion – the witch girl from Maldon – but if I was, it doesn't seem to have worked. The princess looks miserable, and I guess her head must ache, as she keeps rubbing at her temples.

I continue to stand in the middle of the chamber awkwardly, wondering if I should move well away from the four of them and slide into the shadows. I dart a look behind me and catch Fitz watching, his expression impassive as his eyes meet mine. I cannot tell what he is thinking.

Finally, a storm of noise outside the chamber – growls and shouts – and the dog is brought in. Eyes bulging, he snarls and snaps his teeth, rearing and twisting violently, straining against his leash so that it almost throttles him. His wiry hair is filthy, pasted to his thin body in strands, and in places his fur has fallen out, leaving balding patches. As soon as I see him, a hot flood of outrage courses through me. *Of course he bites and growls. The dog is scared and angry.* Whatever they've done to him must have made him like this, and now they're going to torture him further.

'Go on, girl,' shrills the countess. 'Go up to the dog. Make him dance, like the players with their spaniels.'

I can tell she longs to see me bitten, and it is she who gets the full force of my rage as it spills over. My hands ball into fists by my sides, my eyes smarting with tears.

'No, I will *not*! Can't you see he's suffered enough? And now you want him to do *tricks*? What kind of people are you?'

The silence in the chamber is terrifying. No one speaks.

Then a strange thing happens.

The dog starts to walk towards me, leading the cowed manservant with him. His paws pad across the silk carpet, then he stops in front of me and sits down. I could swear he smiles when he looks up at my face.

The manservant lets go of the rope in astonishment. Instead of running away or whipping round to give his captor a nip, the dog stands on his hind legs, never once taking his small nut-brown eyes from mine.

He licks my hand. Just like that.

For a long moment, no one moves a muscle. Lady Mary stares at me and the dog, and her gaze makes me quail. What will she do to me? She's sure to think I'm Satan's servant now. I'll be burned! Fowler is right: that's what they do to witches.

The princess approaches, and I make a clumsy curtsey. She drops her gaze to the dog, and, as she does so, the corners of her mouth lift a fraction.

'On this dark day, I'm glad there has been one good moment,' she says quietly. 'I'm afraid I've had bitter news … my friends aren't keen to stand with me.' Her face falls for a moment into its tired creases before it brightens into a smile. 'But then you appear. A wild marsh girl. And you want to protect the ugliest, most bad-tempered dog I've ever seen … Dela, that's your name, isn't it?'

I nod, the lump in my throat stopping my voice.

'Well, Dela, I sense you're a trustworthy, truthful sort of girl.'

I bow my head, cheeks flushed, then the princess takes my arm and raises me up. 'Now, I believe apologies are in order. You helped the Emperor Charles's man. That surely deserves our thanks.'

I have been given a reprieve. A warm glance, kind words. But what of the dog? While I behaved like a moonstruck calf, lapping up the princess's attention, he has been returned to the kitchen, where whatever miserable treatment he has been given will no doubt be resumed. Sickened by the thought, I beg Fitz to take me there. He makes no comment, merely raises his straight black brows and gives a shrug, before once again leading me with the same languid grace back through the great hall to the kitchen. His unhurried stride frustrates me – he doesn't seem to care that I have an impatient need to see the dog – but at least he is willing to help me, and that's something.

Used only to the slow quiet life of Goldhanger as I am, the heat and noise of the kitchen overwhelms me the moment we walk through the door. There are two great hearths, one at either end, with fires burning in both. Scullions scurry back and forth, carrying piles of dirty knives and bowls.

I start to boil, as if I've been plunged into one of the cauldrons hanging from their great iron hooks, and I wipe my forehead on the sleeve of my smock.

In all the heat and din – barked orders and the clattering of pans – something catches my eye, a 'something' moving on the wall to the right of the hearth. I take a step closer. It's the dog, in a wheel-shaped cage barely bigger than him. As the wheel turns, so does the spit on which a headless boar is roasting. For a shocked moment, I watch the dog as he paces his prison on short, bowed forelegs, muscular as a mole's. Sensing our presence, he turns his terrier-like face towards us and fixes a pair of small nut-brown eyes on me.

A leering scullion with a lazy eye pauses in his work. 'Get on with it, Turnspit!' He turns to grins at us. 'I were in charge of the spit 'fore he came. Very near killed my arm.'

I stare at the wheel and the little dog inside it. 'It's the cruellest thing I've ever seen!'

If he notices my disgust, the scullion hasn't the wit to stop his mouth. 'He's a lazy so-and-so. We chuck burning embers in and that soon gets him moving.' He gives a snort of laughter and wipes his nose on his sleeve. 'He snaps if you go close. See?' Lumbering forward, he jabs his finger at the cage.

The dog bristles and snarls, his teeth snapping wildly at the snot-nosed scullion.

I am beside myself, so furious that I'm almost spitting. 'I can guess who made this horrible cage. Tallon's man, Fowler. He likes to break an animal if he can.'

'I wouldn't know,' Fitz says. 'We only arrived two days ago.'

'No, she's right – it were Tallon's man,' the scullion offers. 'The mistress was well pleased with her gift.'

'I'm sure she was,' murmurs Fitz under his breath. 'It's just the kind of thing the countess might like.'

I can sense he doesn't care for the wheel cage any more than I do. Maybe he could help me rescue Turnspit. It would be easier than having to manage it on my own, and I'm not leaving Woodham Walter without the dog.

I walk up to the cage. Instantly, Turnspit lowers his hackles and his fur relaxes its spikes. He presses his light-brown nose to the bars and his cobnut eyes meet mine in an oddly confident gaze. *I am yours,* he seems to be saying, *here to help you.* Which is strange, because it's quite clear that it is he who needs *my* help.

'Get away! You're slowing him down,' says the scullion.

Fitz gazes at the dog, wonderingly. 'You'd have thought this would have broken him.'

I am about to answer when we are interrupted by the spotty manservant from the great chamber who comes running into the kitchen.

'There you are!' he says to me. 'Lady Mary wants you. You need to come.'

As Fitz and I follow, I glance over my shoulder at the turnspit dog. *I'll be back to rescue you, don't you worry!* It is only a silent promise in my head, but I could swear his small brown eyes understand.

The princess is waiting for us in a tiny chamber lit by a single beeswax candle and the dying embers of a fire. Seated at a writing table, chin on hand, she looks up when I am brought in, and Rochester leaves his post at the window where he's been scanning the shadowy manor grounds. Both look ready to drop with exhaustion.

'Ah, here's the girl.'

I give a curtsey. 'Your loyal servant, my lady.'

She smiles and signals for me to come closer.

'I do believe you are. Loyal and true. And because of that, I have one more favour to ask of you … Dumont must be taken back to his ship at first tide tomorrow. Do you think you could you slip through again? Apparently, they're watching every path and creek.'

I nod dumbly.

'Rochester, have we a purse of silver we can give her?'

He bends closer to his mistress, and I can see in the curl of his tall frame how protective he feels towards her.

Before he can reply, unable to help myself, I blurt out, 'My lady – ' I hear my voice and it doesn't feel like mine at all ' – I don't want any silver, but there is something …'

'Yes?'

'I'd like to have the turnspit dog.'

She is surprised, then an odd sort of mirth takes her over. The sound she makes is one of whimpered bleats, and I can hardly tell if she is laughing or crying. After a shocked pause, Rochester joins in.

Finally, the princess wipes her eyes. 'Yes, you strange child. Of course. He is yours.'

CHAPTER 5

I can't believe I have a dog! Turnspit trots at my heels as
if he's been doing it all his life. I have the strangest feeling he is taking charge – that he feels himself in some
way my protector. Ever since he locked eyes with me
when he was in his wheel cage, I have had the sense that
I've been entrusted to his care, not the other way round.
He still wears an ill-tempered expression, though, and
after what he's been through I'm not sure that will ever
entirely change.

I say as much to Fitz as he shows us to the stables.

'I can't believe you prefer that snappy cur to a purse
of silver.'

'You'd be snappy if you were treated like that. Turnspit's earned the right to be disagreeable after all he's been
through.'

'I'm sure he's the most admirable creature,' Fitz says
easily.

I shoot him a sharp glance. This careless way he has
about him irks me. It makes me wonder if the boy feels
deeply about anything at all.

Still, Fitz is the closest I have to a friend at Woodham
Walter, so I'm not going to pick a fight with him. I've asked
if the dog and I can sleep near Bessie tonight, and Fitz

shows me to the hayloft, leading the way up the wooden ladder, holding his lantern with one hand. I scoop Turnspit under my arm and follow. Up here it feels snug, sheltered from the cool of the night, and there are bales on which I can lie. It is only a few hours till dawn, and I know I'll fare better here than on a straw pallet in the manor. The sweet fragrance of hay, the puffs of breath from the horses' nostrils, the noise of chomping mouths and swishing tails … they're the smells and sounds from home.

Fitz doesn't leave at once. Instead, he sits on a hay bale and leans against the one behind, fingers linked behind his head. His legs are stretched out in front of him, ankles neatly crossed. I don't quite know what to make of this relaxed and wordless attitude, and after a moment of awkwardness in which I remain standing, waiting for him to leave, I perch stiffly on a bale a few feet away. I cannot tell if the twist of his mouth, which is very like a smirk, is arrogance or just a smile – I really can't make him out at all.

The truth is I don't know what to make of boys, never having had much to do with them – and anyway, Fitz is nothing like a Goldhanger lad. He has a narrow frame, whippet thin – the very opposite of the beefy-shouldered farmhands who like to compare the size of their arms and wrestle with each other to catch a girl's attention. Fitz has a different sort of confidence that seems to require no effort at all. His hazel eyes watch me carefully, guarded enough as to be unreadable. He doesn't seem to care that we speak not one word to each other, and although I am squirming inside he seems not to notice my discomfort, or if he does I don't think he cares one whit about it.

I cannot help darting surreptitious glances at him.

Beneath his straight black brows his eyes are a striking green, brown and gold, and he has the longest, blackest lashes I've ever seen on a lad. With his grace and neatness, it would be easy to say he has something girlish about him, but he doesn't ... not at all.

All this while, Turnspit lies, hairy chin on my foot, watching the groom's every movement with his small brown eyes. Maybe the dog is having more success understanding him.

Finally, Fitz breaks the silence. 'Do you think he'll let me scratch him?'

'If you're genuine about it. Not if you're only doing it to see if he'll bite you.'

He gets up and walks the few paces to where I'm sitting, stoops and holds out his hand. He folds away his fingers, offering the part below the knuckles for Turnspit to sniff. 'Aha, he likes me.' He scratches him behind the ears.

Something in me doesn't want to admit Turnspit enjoys being tickled by Fitz – a sort of jealousy. After all, I'm the one who saved the dog.

'He tolerates you, that's all,' I say ungraciously.

Fitz smirks, and for a moment my mood hangs in the balance, poised somewhere between a sour sort of crossness and the heady relief that I am alive and Turnspit is not only safe, but mine. I smile, and feel myself unwinding like a spool of thread.

'All right, he does seem to get along with you. Don't know why, but I have to admit he does.'

'I like dogs,' is all he says.

Silence again, and this time I break it. 'Can I ask you about why you're here? ... Why the princess is here?'

'You can ask, but I won't answer.'

'Won't, or can't?'

He grins suddenly, and I think my crossness must seem foolish to him, and I don't like how that feels.

'Tell you what,' he says, 'I will let you ask two questions if I can ask two of you.'

I agree to his proposal, and he immediately sets about answering mine.

'I'm here because Lady Mary needs someone to look after the horses and she trusts me to keep my trap shut ... which is clearly a mistake,' he adds with his twist of a smile.

'And why is she here?' I repeat.

'Because the king might die, and if he does Northumberland will put her in the Tower. So she's trying to get help from Emperor Charles.'

'But she'll be Edward's successor, won't she? Surely King Henry made it so.'

Fitz forgets I've had my two questions and decides to go all in and explain. Maybe he feels it's only fair, since I've risked my life to bring the spy to the manor.

'You're right, but there are those who will refuse to have a Catholic on the throne – the Duke of Northumberland chief among them. He knows that Mary looks to her Spanish cousin for advice in all things, and that worries him. What if the emperor were to find her a husband? What if England should fall into the hands of a foreigner?'

'And Dumont?'

'The emperor's envoy. Lady Mary wrote to ask for her cousin's protection ... I shouldn't be telling you any of this ... Anyway, two years ago when she was at Woodham

Walter she nearly escaped in one of Charles's ships. I suppose you Blackwater folk got to hear of it.'

I shake my head. 'But does she want to escape now?'

'I don't know. That may be why we're here, but I think if she wanted to she'd have gone by now. I'm guessing she asked the emperor if he could send men and ships when the time comes, and Dumont didn't give her the answer she wanted.'

I remember the princess's words. 'She said friends weren't standing by her.'

'Yes, well ...' Fitz bends to scratch the fuzz of hair on Turnspit's head. 'Charles has got too much on his plate fighting the French.'

'So she's on her own.'

'Yup.' He sits up, folds his arms. 'Right, that's enough. My turn now.'

There is something in the way he scrutinises me as he delivers his first question that makes me uncomfortable, as if he's watching a creature in a rock pool, curious to see what it might do.

'How do you do that thing with animals? Are you really a witch?'

'That's two questions.'

'It's all one really. I can rephrase it ...'

I roll my eyes. 'Don't bother. I'm not a witch. And the other thing ... I don't know ... I sort of know how they're feeling. And because animals feel, not think, it means I kind of understand what they're thinking. Does that make sense?'

His black brows draw together in a frown. I can tell he feels cheated by my reply, as if he was expecting strong ale and received only milk.

'That's disappointing. I've never met a witch … In that case …' he says, opening his mouth in a giant yawn, '… I think it's time for bed.'

He gets up in a fluid movement and makes his way to the ladder. There he salutes me – a flick of a hand to his temple – and the gold flecks in his eyes catch the light of the lantern. A moment later, he has disappeared from view.

After he's gone, I find I'm too tired to sleep. I lie down and lift Turnspit onto the bales, so he can settle into the crook of my knees. He puts his head on my leg, watching me as I chew on Fitz's disappointment at my not being a witch and how my explanation was greeted with a yawn. I know it is contrary of me – I've been longing to be ordinary, like other girls – but just now I would like to be a little extraordinary.

'I'm glad you're here, Turnspit,' I whisper, and he gives a little grumbling sigh.

'You know, with the right food your coat will be springy in no time. You'll look quite handsome.'

I don't think he believes the 'handsome' part and he gives another gusting sigh. Ned always says that if people tell you you're nothing but pond scum you'll believe them. Especially if, like Turnspit, you've known nothing else since you were a pup. I decide to list his admirable qualities to help him feel proud of himself.

'Well … you are certainly *not* ordinary. You've got strength in your legs and shoulders, intelligence, loyalty … an unusual light-brown nose …'

I'm sure I see the sharp-toothed glint of a smile in the darkness.

Next day, the fog is back, and I'm relieved. The weather's on our side. Surely there won't be many watchers out in this, and, even if there are, hopefully we can slip by unnoticed.

Dumont and I are standing in the stable courtyard, readying ourselves for the journey. Just as we are preparing to mount our horses, Sir Henry Radclyffe joins us.

'Dumont's ship is moored off Stansgate, just where the estuary widens out,' he tells me.

I cannot help thinking that either the customs men will be crawling all over it by now or we'll get there and find that the skipper has weighed anchor and put to sea, leaving the spy behind. I'm sure that the same has occurred to Dumont, who fiddles nervously at the cuff of his glove.

'We've got to catch the tide! They told me I had to be back first thing, but look at this fog!' His eyes attempt to pierce the thick whiteness. 'How can we possibly ride in this? I can't see a damn thing!'

I notice how his shoulders droop this morning. Clearly the message he delivered to Lady Mary last night earned him little thanks — and no wonder. If Fitz is right, all it achieved was to let her know she's on her own.

Sir Henry ignores him, addressing his next words to me. 'You can leave Dumont's mare at Crabbe's Farm afterwards. The farmer's a tenant of mine. He has a small landing stage at a little inlet off Southey Creek. Limbourne, d'you know it? The east bank. Do you think you can get Dumont there?'

I nod a little doubtfully, my eyes on the spy. 'I know the marshes across from Northey well enough, my lord.'

'Do you think you'll catch the tide?'

I nod again.

'I've sent a man to the hythe. A small boat is moored there with two of Dumont's crew. By the time you get to Crabbe's Farm, they should have rowed to meet you, all being well.'

The earl, in command of the situation, seems so different from last night when he let his wife take the upper hand. He looks at me kindly as I prepare to mount Bessie, then stoops and scratches Turnspit behind the ear. 'The Lady Mary and I will take Mass this morning. In a quiet way, of course. We'll pray for you, Mistress Wisbey. You've served the princess bravely and well.'

Blushing, I duck into a curtsey, then make to scoop up Turnspit, thinking he might prefer to squat between my hip and the pommel of the saddle. He wriggles free, making it clear he wants no such thing.

Dumont and I set out through the deer park, Turnspit trotting ahead of us, his bowed and stocky front legs stepping out with the confidence of an army scout. I find myself putting my trust in the little dog: doing so feels like the most natural thing in the world. He seems to know exactly where he should be leading us.

Behind us, Dumont is perched on a piebald mare who is already looking cross at having her mouth tugged. I can't wait to be rid of him. What I want, more than anything, is to get back to Goldhanger – but first we have to get to the inlet across from the little isle of Northey.

I always avoid the island. The causeway is a death trap if you don't watch the tide, and who'd want to go there anyway? A sad and unforgiving place crowned with a few thorn trees, it nurses its memories of defeat, sucked up and stored in the mud of the saltings. My father told me the

story of the battle with the Vikings that raged on its causeway, when the whole marsh had run purple with Saxon
blood. Sal says she fancies she can hear their cries, but I
tell her it's only the curlews and not to let her imagination
run away with itself.

I shake myself free from thoughts of blood. The shock
of seeing Ned's wounds still ripples through my body;
I can't think clearly if my mind keeps skittering with the
horror of it. I need to be alert to every sound. It's hard
enough with Dumont's sniffing and coughing. When he
moans about catching a marsh ague, I want to throttle him.

We run into trouble where the lane meets the London
road. We're no more than fifty yards from the junction
when Turnspit halts. Bessie, who's been following him step
for step, comes to a sudden stop, but, behind us, Dumont's
piebald mare is so confused by his yanking on the reins
that she shies. He slithers from the saddle, and it is his
startled cry – not the fact he tears his breeches in the fall
– that is our undoing.

'Who goes there?' A shout from the end of the lane.

Dumont tries to catch the reins of his terrified mare.

We don't have time for this! I can hear two voices, and
they're getting closer.

'Stop! In the king's name!' These aren't just any watchers. Tallon's got his guards blocking the lane to Woodham
Walter. We're trapped.

Dumont manages to haul himself back in the saddle
and attempts to pull his mare round. Before I can do the
same with Bessie, Turnspit gives a short bark and runs
towards the guards. After several yards, he takes a few steps
to the edge of the lane and whines. What is he doing?

There's no way through the impenetrable thicket of black-thorn and brambles.

But then I see him disappear into it.

'Wait, sir!' I call in a low voice to Dumont. 'We must follow the dog.'

I don't bother to check if he's behind me; there's no time for that. Bessie, needing no instruction, leaps the ditch and plunges headfirst into the thicket.

I was wrong. The way isn't impenetrable. Turnspit glances over his shoulder then darts forward, weaving his way through clumps of furze and bracken, looking like a swimmer fighting the swell as he ploughs through a great sea of brambles which snag and catch at his fur.

Behind us, I hear another shout. 'They've left the road! Don't let them get away! Follow them!'

I pray they haven't got a hound. With the fog, we might be able to get away, but if they can track our scent we're done for. I look over my shoulder to check on Dumont. He is barely managing to stay on his mare, who blunders into saplings and bushes, her eyes rolling wildly. *Please keep following*, I will her. What would I do if I lost the spy?

We are relying entirely upon Turnspit. By now I have no idea of our direction, but follow blindly as the little dog ducks and weaves to find a way through – one that's wide enough for the horses to manage. It feels as if we'll never get out.

I can no longer hear the men's voices: that's something, though they may guess which way we're headed and try to block us further down. What if they're waiting for us?

Just as I reach the point of despair, Turnspit leads us onto a road. I look left and right. Where are we? Then I spot a rickety bridge with missing planks. Clever dog! He's got us to Fambridge Road, and this here is Limbourne Brook.

'Which way?' demands the spy. His hat is askew, cape and britches in tatters.

Turnspit crosses the road and takes off down the side of the brook.

'Keep to the road!' Dumont's shout comes out as an enraged squeal. Turnspit pauses, forepaw raised. He glances at us, then back to the brook. The ground is boggy. I can see the dog wants to head east – and rightly so – but maybe the spy is right and we should keep to the road, then head towards Southey Creek once we have firmer ground.

Turnspit gives a sharp bark.

'Call your hound! He's not taking us into this mire.'

Turnspit gives another bark, more urgent this time. And, just then, there's a clinking and the thud of hooves … men's voices heading this way. They're not far off, coming from the direction of Maldon.

I don't hesitate. In a moment, Bessie steps off the road into the reeds. Dumont's mare follows, ignoring her rider's tugs at the reins. Once again, I bless the fog for shielding us from men's eyes. With the noise of the brook masking the sound of our horses, we may yet escape the guards.

The screech of gulls is welcome. We can't be too far from the saltings. Cautiously we pick our way, taking care to avoid the boggy patches among the rushes that threaten to suck in unwary limbs. Bessie shadows Turnspit, step for step; the dog seems to have a knack of knowing where it's safe for her to tread. The piebald mare tries her best to follow, but she is continually at odds with her rider. I hear a whinny and look round to see that her front leg has sunk into the wet mud, almost to her fetlock. Instead of waiting for her to free herself, Dumont urges her on, kicking her with his heels. He raises his whip.

'Don't do that! She'll break a leg!' Until now, I've managed to hold my tongue – the servant girl doing her master's bidding – but this is too much!

Dumont's face twists in fury – 'I will have you hanged, witch!' – but he stays his hand, and the mare tugs herself free of the mud. After that, we progress in sullen silence.

Then we're clear of it, and ahead of us is nothing but the mudflats leading to Southey Creek. We can't see Northey isle or the main channel through the fog, but the brook has widened into a creek. We haven't far to go. The landing stage Sir Henry mentioned, the one that belongs to Crabbe's Farm, can't be more than fifty yards ahead.

The tide is already going out, the retreating water pulling on the marsh mud like an old crone sucking her gums. I am relieved to see that the causeway, away to our left, is still well covered. Now that we're nearing our destination, Dumont becomes alert, almost as if he thinks that the closer we get, the more likely it is that all will be lost – like a child having to forfeit a sweetmeat just as it touches his lips. At the piping sound of the oystercatchers he jumps, thinking it's the whistles of the constables.

Two figures appear out of the mist. Could they be Dumont's crew? I find myself watching Turnspit for his reaction. He looks no more than a brown lump, caked in wet mud from head to tail – a tail that, I'm glad to see, is held aloft triumphantly, a little wagging pennant. He trots up to the two men, head high, sniffing the air. They speak in a language I don't understand and laugh when they catch sight of the dog.

Dumont almost upsets the rowing boat, such is his desperate desire to be gone. He bends almost double to steady himself, grabbing the gunwales on each side. His crew try to stifle their laughter when they catch sight of the torn seat of his breeches, which reveal a plump expanse of mottled flesh. A few moments later, with a slosh of oars, they are away, bearing their ill-tempered passenger with them.

They let the tide take their boat, following Southey Creek as it bends round the sad little isle of Northey, then Osea, before joining the Blackwater.

CHAPTER 6

The mist has cleared by the time we arrive at Goldhanger. My heart lifts with my first glimpse of St Peter's tower. 'Nearly home,' I tell Bessie. Most times on rounding the bend into Head Street she takes off at an untidy canter to get to her manger. Not so now. Her head droops almost to her fetlocks with exhaustion.

Turnspit marches along happily. He's used to walking for long stretches on his wheel, I suppose, though it's never got him further than the kitchen wall. I washed the mud off him at Crabbe's Farm, and he looks almost presentable. I cannot wait to tell Ned how I freed the strange little dog.

'You'll like Ned,' I tell him, and Bessie gives a snort on hearing the farrier's name. 'He'll be impressed when he hears how you helped Lady Mary.'

Goldhanger is quiet – too quiet. As we walk down Head Street, the shutters are closed. What is going on? It feels as though a plague has struck the village; I almost expect to see crosses chalked on the doors. As we cross the square, we see one of the fishwives, Maggie, at the pump. I head towards her, thinking that she'll know why it's so quiet. Instead of waving when she catches sight of me, however, she hastens to get away, tipping and clattering her buckets so that the water sloshes over the sides. Does she think I'm a witch – is that what this is about? She certainly looks scared enough. But she's known me all my life.

Even the benches outside the Bell are empty. Not one of the old fishermen, who usually nurse their mugs of ale, resting their bones in the sun, is here.

None of this makes sense.

When we get to Ned's, the gate is swinging on one hinge. Nothing in the yard looks any different, but the broken hinge worries me. I take Bessie to the water trough while Turnspit runs about sniffing. Something more important than the need to slake his thirst bothers him. His head flicks round continually to check on me as he circles the yard. Like me, he can smell trouble.

No smoke from the chimney. I leave Bessie at the trough – she'll have to wait to be fed and rubbed down – and Turnspit follows me into the cottage. It is quiet but not cold, the embers in the hearth still warm. The room is in disarray: the bench on its side, the merels board knocked to the floor, its black and white pebbles scattered everywhere. I call Ned's name, but there is no response. I know something bad has happened here and need to find out where he is. It is possible he's at Sal's.

I run out of the house, across the square and down Fish Street, Turnspit at my heels. Sal must be watching out for me, because her door flies open and she hustles me inside so quickly that the dog only just escapes having his tail caught.

'Have you been home?' she asks. I notice the purple swell of a bruise on her cheek.

'Ned's not there.'

'Tallon's men took him.' She clasps her hands tight to stop them from shaking.

'I should have been there.'

'They'd only have taken you too.'

My words tumble over themselves. 'Where have they taken him? What are they going to do?'

She sits me down. 'You need to have something, then we'll talk.'

When she brings a bowl of pottage, I have a sudden yearning to be fed like a baby, to have Sal spoon it into my mouth.

'Here.' She hands me the bowl and puts a mug of milk on the floor next to my stool. 'You eat. I'll talk.'

She speaks gently, so I know it must be bad.

'Ned's been taken to Colchester jail. They took him a few hours ago.'

I let out a yelp as if I've been scalded.

She puts one of her huge hands on my arm. 'Don't you worry. A little shaking and shouting, that's all. It'd take a lot more than that to finish him off.'

All I can think of is Ned in the castle dungeon, a lightless, terrible place. My father spent his last days there, alone and desperate. The thought of the farrier in that same cell squeezes the breath out of me.

'We'll get him back.' Sal stoops and hands me the mug. 'Here, get this down you. I've added a little summat.'

I take a few sips. Whatever she's put in the milk steadies me. 'Sal, what will Tallon charge Ned with? What does he think he's done?'

'There was talk of a ship taking off with the tide. From what his men were saying, it sounds like Tallon is hopping mad.'

I give a nod. That makes sense. If the rowing boat slipped past them in the fog, it's no wonder he's furious.

'They were making out Ned's been plotting against the king,' Sal says. '"A nest of papists, we'll smoke 'em out like rats." That's what they said.'

'Did Ned tell them anything?'

''Course not. And take others down with him? He's not a squealer!' She touches her bruised cheek, testing the sore place with her fingertips. I sense she is reliving the violent scene in Ned's house.

'Does it hurt? Should we put something on it?'

She brushes me off. 'Nothing to fuss about, child.' Then she catches sight of Turnspit, who is sitting quietly, his back resting against my calf. 'Mercy me! What is that you've got there?'

'He's called Turnspit.'

'I must say, he's a funny-looking thing. You rescued him, did you?'

'We rescued each other.'

'And now the three of us must do the same for Ned.'

She tells me she's hatched a plan, and I'm not surprised to find it involves salted herring. It is doomed to fail, but at least it means going to Colchester Castle right away. I know that without Sal's cart it would be impossible – Bessie is too tired to take another step.

Sal stands up and ties the strings of her cap. 'You go home, see to Bessie. I'll pack the cart.'

Not long after, she picks me and Turnspit up at the gate and helps us into the back.

'When we're clear of the watchers you can join me up front. Try to sleep, though.'

Tallon has ordinary folk keeping an eye on the comings and goings in every one of the estuary villages. Now that

Ned has been arrested, I will be a person of interest too. Sal doesn't need to say it. I know it's on her mind.

She gives my shoulder a squeeze. 'That's why folk's been behavin' like hermit crabs. You can't blame 'em for not wanting their shells bashed to bitty-bits. And that'll happen if they're seen talkin' to thee.' She spreads sacks over me and the dog until we're completely covered. 'If your friends close their shutters, it's 'cause they don't want to spy on thee.'

With a click of Sal's tongue and a jerk of the cart, we're away. Bridey heads out of Goldhanger at a fast trot, sensing her mistress's impatience. Allowing for some stretches of walking, I reckon we'll manage to cover the twelve miles in little more than two hours.

Under the sacks, beside Sal's basket of salted herring, the tears finally come. Turnspit wriggles until he's tucked into my side. I feel the better for crying. Once I've got it out of the way, I know I can be strong for Ned.

I wake with a jolt, not knowing where I am. The rocking of the cart has stopped. The next moment, I see a blue patch of sky and Sal's face framed in it as she peels back one of the sacks. Turnspit growls.

'Don't you grouch at me, dog,' she says. 'While you rested your paws, some of us has been hard at it.'

'Where are we?' I sit up and rub my eyes. Without sleep last night, I'm feeling as if the world's turned over. I woke expecting to find a dark sky, but it's still light.

'We got through Head Gate by the skin of our teeth. We're now at Bury Field. 'Tis the best place to wait with the cart.'

Colchester Castle stands brooding over the town, its thick grey walls pierced by a few tiny arrow slits. Raised up over the flat land, it looks vast and unbreachable, its keep a reminder to the townsfolk of Colchester that they are not only being kept safe but also watched. As children, we were told that if we didn't behave we'd be thrown into the dungeon, and we all knew that no one who goes in ever comes out alive.

Sal's plan is a simple one. It relies on her belief that no one in God's world can resist her salted herring.

'All you need to do is take the basket, walk into the castle, and bribe 'em with my fish. A girl with a basket covered with a cloth is a sight for sore eyes if you're a garrison soldier on duty.'

I regard the wrapped parcels doubtfully. 'I just hope they'll get me past all the guards. And what about when I get to the jail?'

'That's when you'll have to sweet-talk the jailer – persuade him Ned's better off with you than with him.'

I nod as if I credit the plan with a chance of success. I'm not fooling myself. Herring or no herring, the best I can hope for is to be slung out of the gate by my hair.

'I'll come with thee.'

'It's better you stay with the cart. You've done enough getting me here. Anyway, you've got Rob to look after. I've got no one but Ned, so what have I got to lose? At least there's a chance I might get to speak with him. I've got to try.'

I get through the gate in the bailey wall without a problem. A lazy soldier guards it, a man more interested in scratching the seat of his breeches than hearing what I have to say. A fifteen-year-old girl and a small, miserable-looking dog pose no threat in his eyes. I don't even need to waste one of Sal's parcels of salt herring.

So far, so good.

We cross the bailey, heading for the keep. It looms in front of us, so tall that it throws its shadow over a vast area. Feeling like an ant next to a giant foot that is about to stamp on us, I force myself to press on, but a voice in my head shouts, *Run away, run away!*

Ahead of us, the great stone barbican gapes like the mouth of a whale, iron portcullis ready to snap down on intruders. It is crawling with guards and sentries; getting through will be an impossible task.

Turnspit shows none of my faint-heartedness. He walks tall, his little tail standing proudly. I look up at the keep. A white flag with a big red cross flaps from the battlements and, together with Turnspit's pennant-like tail, it helps to stiffen my resolve. I remind myself I'm doing this for Ned, whose fight is mine now. Courage, Dela!

A helmeted guard steps forward, barring my way with his pike. 'Your business, girl?'

'Salt herring for the kitchens, the finest in all Blackwater.' Sal said to lay it on thick, and I try my best.

I lift the cloth and remove one of the parcels of fish. 'Perhaps you and your friends would like to try some?' I give my most winsome smile.

Turnspit gets up on his haunches, forepaws begging, and it breaks the ice. Two guards join the first and they stand leaning on their weapons, laughing.

'Just look at his pale nose wifflin' in the air,' one of them, a round-faced man, says. 'What a funny little fellow!'

'Looks downright ugly to me,' says the other.

'Aw no. He's a great little dog,' Beaming, the round-faced man turns to me. 'What's his name?'

'Turnspit,' I say. 'You'd best take the fish quick. He's a terrible thief. Leaps so high he can snatch it just like that!'

Once the parcel has been handed over and I'm safely through the gate, we make our way quickly through the barbican to a flight of wooden steps at the end. At the top, the studded oak doors of the keep are set at quite some height in the wall. I start to climb, but soon realise that Turnspit isn't following. He stands, tail drooping, staring at the wooden steps with fear. What is it with him? Sometimes the simplest of things seem to hold such terror for a dog. I climb back down quickly and scoop him up under my arm.

Soon we are standing at the great doors of the keep. In each there is a square opening, barred with iron. As I approach, a face appears.

'What is your name? Who sent you?'

Where the bailey gate guard was lazy, this tight-faced man is the opposite. I haven't given any thought as to whether I should use a false name, so I give him mine and say that the cook is expecting me.

He doesn't open the door.

'You'd best let me in,' I say, trying and failing to give a dimpling smile. 'Sir John Tallon's man, Fowler, sent me with salted herring from Goldhanger.'

Now that Turnspit is safely up the steps, he fixes me with implacable brown eyes.

'It's all right,' I whisper. 'I'm not going to run away.'

With a heavy, metallic scrape, the bolts are drawn back, then the doors creak open and we are inside.

If I feel small, Turnspit must feel even smaller. The walls are so high that on glancing upwards I immediately feel as if they're going to fall on us. The tight-faced guard hurries me along.

'Follow me,' he says. 'You're expected.'

My heart knocks against my ribs. I try to persuade myself that everything is going to plan, but the dog knows we're in trouble. His hackles are up, shoulders hunched.

The guard grabs my arm; Turnspit runs ahead and turns to face us, bristling and barking, trying to tell me not to go any further. But I haven't a choice. I call him to me, terrified he'll get skewered on a lance. 'Turnspit! Heel, boy!'

We're taken up a winding stone staircase to the first floor, emerging at one end of a great chamber where the garrison's soldiers are eating their supper. I catch only the briefest of glimpses — a few heads raised from their trenchers, curious to see a girl and her dog in the castle — before I am led briskly by the guard to a door. He takes my basket from me and knocks. When a quiet voice bids us enter, Turnspit's growls grow louder. He tries to tug at my kirtle, but then we're through the door.

My eyes take a moment to adjust to the gloom. The chamber is a nest of shadows. At a table in the middle, a dark-clothed figure sits illumined within a small pool of light provided by a beeswax candle. He is bent over a parchment; I can see only the top of his head, the waves of thick black hair. Then he looks up, and his cool grey gaze meets mine and brightens. Tallon. A flash of even white teeth, above the neatly trimmed beard, almost dazzling in the darkness of the chamber, then he pushes back his chair to stand. He seems the very picture of elegance and good breeding, but not for one moment am I fooled by his attempt at charm. He is as sleek and dangerous as a stoat.

'Mistress Wisbey. I hoped you'd come.'

I feel a prickling at the back of my neck at his cool, even tone. I know I am defeated. The herring and the sweet-talk have been for nothing. All the time Tallon has been waiting for me, and here I am – a sprat swept along by the current straight into his net.

He sits back down in his chair, smooths his hair with a hand. 'I think it's time you and I had a talk, don't you? Your farrier friend is in a good deal of trouble and I hope you'll be able to put a few things straight.'

I wait for him to continue, to say what he has to say. The flesh of his face with its curious, pale, damp sheen has the look of a stone after a wave's washed over it. There are no crow's feet around his eyes, no doubt because the smile never reaches them. His bright gaze slices into me, anatomising me as coolly as if he's gutting a fish. He twists a gold signet ring on his little finger. Set with a black stone, it is engraved with a heraldic beast, some sort of hunting mastiff. I've seen the crest before, carved into the gatehouse of his manor.

'You look very like your mother. I didn't make the connection when I saw you in the farrier's yard, though you seemed familiar.' He pauses, waiting for a reaction.

I am a stone, giving him nothing.

'She came to me, you know. To beg for your father's life. We knew each other of old, from childhood days. She thought to play on my softer feelings.'

Softer feelings! I cannot think my mother thought she had any hope of awakening such things in Tallon. She was desperate, it's true, but I can't imagine her bending to him. She and he were bound to clash. If she'd known him of old, she must have known what she was in for. She'd have done better not going at all.

His eyes are fixed on my face, his expression difficult to read. 'It is strange to think she sat there, where you are now, pleading your father's case.'

I shift uneasily in my seat, painfully aware of that same thing.

'She laid out her arguments like a lawyer, put up a masterful fight,' he continues. 'Marian always stood out from the common crowd. You have that same spirited look about you.'

'She just wanted to save his life.' My voice comes out in a croak.

'The good farmer Wisbey.' His face hardens. 'He should have known better than to have his head turned by traitors and thieves. Your mother was foolish to waste her breath on him.'

I squirm in my chair, clenching and unclenching my fists. The image of her seated here four years ago, valiantly presenting her case, torments me.

'Your father wasn't worth it. He didn't deserve her.'

I don't think he means to goad me, but he does. 'He was a *good* person. A man of principle. You wouldn't know what that is!'

He steeples his fingers, pleased that I have been drawn out from my stubborn silence. 'You're wrong about that. Being principled has nothing to do with dying for a hopeless cause. It means sticking hard to that which gives you power.'

I open my mouth to reply but then close it tightly. I cannot begin to argue with that kind of thinking.

'I'll tell you who is the most principled of men. My master, the Duke of Northumberland.'

My words come out in a splutter. 'Principled! He slaughtered three thousand men in cold blood, just because they were protesting the loss of their commons.'

'Of course, you take your parents' view. It is commendable that you do. But it is time you opened your eyes, young lady. I'm going to give you a chance to help our cause. You must understand that the duke is the one we must follow if we are to build this country into the greatest of nations. We need that sort of calibre in our statesmen. A man who has proved himself. A soldier … a hero.'

'A soldier, yes. Hero, no.' I screw up my mouth, as if there is bitter wormwood on my tongue.

I can sense that Tallon, having wanted to draw me out, is starting to wish he hadn't done so, but he continues, nonetheless: 'A hero, who trusts *me* to purge Essex of its traitors. Though it's not all about purge and punishment, absolutely not. I am keen to reward hardworking citizens who uphold the Protestant cause. I can be generous when a person deserves it, as I'm hoping you'll find out.'

I think of the ruffians he has taken into his retinue, the ones he has trained to be a brutal fighting force. Such men do not deserve a leg-up in society, but he has honoured them – and disdained decent, ordinary folk. His even-toned arguments bear no relation to what is really going on. He tries to paint a picture of a fair and ordered society, and yet it is nothing like that.

I see no reason to speak. He doesn't really want a debate, just likes the sound of his own voice, wants to bask in his power. I don't know why he has sought to persuade me anyway. Why bother with a fifteen-year-old girl? What does he think I know?

'We're working towards a nation that doesn't let men thieve and cheat and pull down fences. And it's not just disorderly countrymen we have to worry about. What do you think would happen if we let foreigners and their spies creep in? We'd have papist influencers corrupting everything that's good in English society. That is why I've had to arrest your farrier. He left me no choice. But maybe you can help me, tell me what you've seen and heard.'

Tallon is behaving as if he's an officer with a new recruit, one he can shape and bend. Surely, he cannot believe that I would ever side with him? I shudder, and on seeing it something shifts in him. Up until now he has been gazing at my face, but he peels his eyes away and looks down at his hands as they straighten his already immaculate papers.

His voice is distant, suddenly. Clipped. 'I can tell I'm wasting my breath.'

'Please sir, let me see Ned.'

'Fair enough.' He turns to the tight-faced guard. 'Take her to the dungeon. Put her in with the farrier.'

The man salutes. 'Yes, sir.'

Tallon stands, with the same show of politeness as before. 'We can offer you a bed, but I'm afraid you won't be getting board. If you get hungry, I suggest you eat your dog.'

Turnspit growls. Tallon flashes his white shiny teeth, the way a highwayman might open his coat to display a dagger.

'I hope you will get the farrier to talk, young lady. You have till morning; then we'll hang him. What happens to you and your canine familiar depends on what you give us.'

CHAPTER 7

Ned sits on the floor, head tipped forward to his chest. His dressing is stained brown, and he cradles his burned hand in his lap. He doesn't look up when I'm thrown into the cell. He's either asleep or unconscious, I don't know which.

Turnspit bolts in behind me, tail tucked out of harm's way, but the guard's foot catches his hind leg anyway and sends him rolling on the filthy rushes. The man laughs, and I can hear the sound of it fading with every tread of the winding stone stairs as he leaves the dungeon.

The cell has a foul stench, a midden of human waste and rotting cabbage, with the sharp reek of rats. Its walls run with green slime; it has the dank chill of a sea cave that's never seen the light.

I rush to Ned and squat down, my hand on his back. 'Ned, it's me. Dela.'

He raises his head with difficulty. 'Dela … you shouldn't have come.'

'Of course I should. Sal brought me. She had a plan.'

'I guess it didn't work.' He manages a flicker of a smile.

'Not quite. Though it brought me to you, so that's something.'

I help him to sit up, so he can lean against me. Turnspit tucks the other side, and together we offer the warmth of our bodies. I wonder what I can do to help Ned, my guardian who has fed and clothed me, tended to me patiently day after day. He has been mother and father to me. What can I possibly do to save him?

Our warmth revives him little by little.

'You've a dog … that's good.'

'This is Turnspit. I rescued him.'

'Rescuing is what you're good at.' He pauses, clears the phlegm from his throat. 'Did you get Dumont to Woodham Walter?'

'There, and back to his ship.'

'Good girl.' He motions to a pot of water on the floor in which stands a wooden ladle.

I reach for it, bring it to his lips. 'I didn't say anything to Tallon.'

The name causes Ned to splutter, the water dribbling over his chin and onto his chest. 'He didn't hurt you, did he?'

'No. He mostly just stared at me. Talked about my mother.'

I put back the ladle. His body relaxes as he leans into me again.

'Ah.'

'What do you mean, *Ah*?'

His eyes rest on my face. 'You look very like her. I saw the way Tallon stared at you in the yard.'

'He told me he knew her from before. So when she went to beg for my father …'

'Oh yes, he knew her. Marian's father was a tenant on one of their farms. Young Tallon couldn't keep his eyes off her. Kept coming round, hanging about the farmyard.

He didn't have friends of his own, you see. Not surprising, mind you.'

'I'll wager she tried to be kind to him.' I try and fail to imagine a young Tallon. 'I cannot believe he refused to help her when she came begging for Pa's life.'

'I'm not saying he was a decent lad. He wasn't. He had a polecat – white with red eyes – he'd had from a kit.'

'Trust Tallon to have one as a pet.'

'He took it everywhere with him, liked to set it on folk's chickens. If someone vexed him, next day there'd be a foul stink from his polecat hanging about their hencoop, and nowt but a heap of feathers on the ground. I heard he set it on a litter of kittens for his sport.'

I shudder. 'Sounds like Tallon. It seems strange, though, that he should be drawn to Ma. She was so fierce when it came to right and wrong.'

'It was her fierceness he was drawn to – and she was the best-looking maid around. There were plenty others keen to have Tallon, believe it or not, but he didn't notice. Your mother was an itch he had to scratch. And she only had eyes for a certain Farmer Wisbey. Lucky she did, or you wouldn't be sat here now.' He gives a cough and I can hear a rattling in his chest as he tries to master his breathing.

I circle my arm closer, hugging him to me. I'm surprised my mother never told me any of this, though I suppose she always did refrain from talking about Tallon. I know I should let Ned rest, but I can't help myself asking for more. 'What happened then?'

'Well, as I remember it, when your pa came a-courting, Tallon went mad. He must have thought "I'm well-to-do, handsome, how come she's chosen that farmer over me?"

Anyway, once your ma's hand was promised to Wisbey, it was all-out war with that polecat. Your grandpa lost flock after flock of chickens. Ducks and geese too.'

'Didn't he do anything about it?'

'Did he heck! If young Tallon was bad, his father was worse. Your grandpa would've been kicked off the farm if he'd so much as peeped. Anyhow, once your parents moved to Goldhanger, it all stopped.'

'Why was that? Surely Tallon isn't a man to give up. Not when he has a score to settle.'

'His father was appointed one of King Henry's henchmen, sent out to burn the monasteries, throw the monks out on their ear. Young Tallon got stuck in too, got an even bigger taste for bullying and blood than he had before. And he was well paid for it.'

I think of the great castellated manor he built, in which he lives alone. 'He never married, did he.'

'There were rumours he kept a woman, though not at the Hall. But I don't think he ever cared for anyone but himself.'

'And the polecat.'

'That came to a sticky end. Before your ma went to Barrow Farm as a newlywed, she brought that grey raven back with her from Osea and nursed it better. You know the first thing that clever bird did?'

'No. What did it do?'

'Killed Tallon's polecat. Stabbed his beak into one of its red eyes.' Ned gives a chuckle that turns to a cough.

I wait for him to recover, my hand rubbing his back between his shoulder blades. Through the cell's gloom, my eyes pick out the humpback shadow of a fat rat moving along the opposite wall, unhurried as it noses through the greasy rushes. One bright eye fixes on Turnspit who gives a low growl.

'That reminds me, Ned. The grey raven's back. Sal saw it on mother's headstone. I did too, at St Mary's.'

He pauses a moment, taking it in. 'Aye. He's come to look out for you ...'

'Funny. That's exactly what Sal said.'

'That raven always reminds me of a song Marian used to sing when you were a youngun. An old song from these parts. Do you remember it?'

I'm about to say that I don't ... but then it comes back to me: the haunting melody I heard Fowler whistle at the decoy pond. Ned starts to sing in a voice that is barely more than a croaking whisper, and after a bit I take the song over, aware that I'm cradling him in my arms as my mother used to cradle me.

'The great wolf howls on the marsh beside the sea,
Hey, ho, the grey waves a-rolling.
The raven cries from the isle of Osea,
Hey, ho, the east wind's a-blowing.

There's a girl with the wolf on the marsh beside the sea,
Hey, ho, the grey waves a-rolling.
Salve Regina, *we follow Mary,*
Hey, ho, the east wind's a-blowing.'

Ned is quiet. After a while I start to worry that he's fallen into a faint. I'm about to whisper his name when he says, 'That song, it talks to me. It never did before.'

'What do you mean?'

'It's not just the raven. There's the girl and her wolf. I picture you as the girl.'

'I certainly haven't a wolf.'

Turnspit makes a gruff sound in his throat.

'*You*, Turnspit?'

He turns his back, offended, and sets to work nipping at a flea on his hindleg, ignoring me.

Ned repeats the last verse of the song in a creaking plainchant. '*Salve Regina*, we follow Mary ... know what that means?'

'It's praise to our holy Mother. *Salve Regina* ... hail Queen.'

'Well, that verse has been playing in my head, and it's another Mary running through my mind, the one who would be queen if they let her. That's what I meant when I said the song speaks to me.'

'Oh ... I see what you mean.'

'There's the raven, the girl, the wolf, and Mary. And you know what my next thought is?'

'No. Tell me.'

'Well it's my thinking – and I know you'll think I'm cracked – that you might need to help her win her throne.'

'*Me*?'

'You and Turnspit.'

They come for him at dawn – two guards, the tight-faced one and the man who was kind to Turnspit. I cling to Ned and won't let go. The mean guard grabs my arm and slaps the side of my head, making my ears ring, but the round-faced one pushes him away, his hands gentle as they peel me off my guardian.

'Come on, lass, let him go. You'll only make it harder for him.'

Ned's limbs have seized up so they have to hoist him, each taking an arm. His legs bump and drag along the stone flags, but he's still conscious enough to whisper, 'Look after yourself, Dela. Don't fret about me.'

Left alone, I pace the cell, arms wrapped around my body. Turnspit waits at the bars, keeping an eye out for rats. I can't believe Tallon will carry out his threat. Why would they hang Ned? He's done nothing they can pin on him. A spell in the pillory maybe. The other was just a threat to make me talk.

But then Turnspit and I are led out to the bailey where Sir John Tallon stands with five soldiers. They are staring at something; I can't see what, as they're blocking my view. Tallon is in his usual black, athletic in riding breeches, boots polished to a rich shine. My eyes glance at the spurs on his heels, then at his face, as perfect as if chiselled by a master craftsman. It wears an expression of intense concentration.

Then I see it. Something ... somebody ... swinging gently back and forth. Bootless, his feet past kicking. Now a breeze stirs and plays with the body at the end of its rope, gently, so that it twirls like a dancer. I give a bleat of pain and raise my hands to my mouth. I think of all those times I've seen Ned's grey head bent like this – over his merels board; holding a hoof with gentle hands; taking a splinter out of my foot after I've run barefoot back from Sal's; saying his prayers on his knees, asking God to watch over him while he sleeps.

But he's not sleeping now. And if God is watching, how could He let this happen? I raise my face to the cool, pale heavens, and all at once the sky shivers and grows chill. The shrieking of gulls and starlings stops, quite suddenly, and a silent trembling takes its place. The raucous sounds of market day – drovers herding their cattle, carts trundling over the cobbles – grow quiet in an instant, while a breathless horror sucks the life out of everything.

A stirring. A breeze, which grows in force and becomes a wailing windstorm. It picks up whirlwinds of dust as it howls its rage, swinging Ned's body violently at the end of its rope. My shriek when it comes is guttural and raw, echoing and bouncing off the grey stone walls of the castle.

I hurl myself at Tallon, a screaming banshee, a hurtling ball of fury. He rears backwards, shielding his face with his arms. Turnspit, snarling, tears at the boots and hose of the soldiers who leap away in fear. For a moment we have the upper hand, the benefit of surprise, but then the balance shifts, and the soldiers' strong arms recapture us.

They hold me back from Tallon, who recovers himself, keeping his distance as he watches me with a kind of fascination as I writhe and spit. A man with such icy control, hysteria repels him. My back arches and bucks as I strain to reach him, but it is no good. His soldiers have my arms pinned behind my back. One of his men – a giant with thick, roped forearms – holds Turnspit by the scruff, taking care to keep the snarling, snapping dog at arm's length.

'Take the cur.' Tallon has to raise his voice above the din we're making. 'Throw him from the battlements. I want to hear every bone in his body snap.'

At this, Turnspit fights even harder, kicking with clawed feet as he dangles from the man's grasp. I shriek his name, but he cannot break free – his captor's grip is like steel. The man sets off in the direction of the keep, and soon I can no longer see them, though I can still hear the dog's furious barks.

With Turnspit gone, all fight leaves me. I hang my head, limp in the soldiers' grasp, just wanting them to get on with it and kill me too. I hear the clink of spurs as Tallon takes two steps closer. He clears his throat. I refuse to look up, staring instead at his boots.

'You might want to listen to what I have to say, Mistress Wisbey.' His tone is pleasant, no more threatening than if he were a churchgoer in the pew next to me.

I neither look up nor make any sign that I've heard him.

'I will spare your life on one condition.'

Still I'm silent.

'You will go to Lady Mary. I know you've helped her before – don't bother to deny it. You will join her household, be our spy.'

Finally, anger flaring, I look up. 'Go ... to ... hell.'

He speaks distinctly, his grey eyes returning a cold fire. 'Hanging is too good for you.' Then he gives his order to the men who hold me. 'This one I will deal with myself. You know where to take her.'

Before anyone can take a step, a ghoulish and unearthly screeching fills the air. From over the castle battlements a black storm cloud looms, moving at speed to shadow the bailey beneath, casting us in darkness as it blocks out the pale morning sun. The swirling ink-black mass hovers a moment, then descends sharply, violently, and there is nothing but flapping and shrieking and men's voices shouting in terror.

Like black ants swarming over a honeycomb, the ravens attack Tallon. His arms wrap around his head as he tries to protect his eyes from their beaks. All I can see are wings and claws and currant-black eyes. Like a living feather cloak, they cover him until no part of his body is visible.

Transfixed, I cannot move a muscle, until one of the birds separates from the rest and flies to me. Grey head and stippled wings. The raven of Osea.

He stares at me, and I can hear him, though he makes no sound. 'Fly, Dela, fly!'

So I do. My feet run so fast to the gate in the bailey wall that I'm gone before anyone thinks to stop me. There's no one at my heels calling halt, no sound other than the terrified shouts of the soldiers. In seconds, I'm through the unguarded gate and sprinting along the High Street.

In a doorway I stop, bent over with a stitch, panting with shock and rage. My thoughts are scattered, formless, but I know if I am to live, it depends on my making a plan. But I can't do it, don't have the will for it. Even if I could, I can't run all the way back to Goldhanger. It won't be safe for me there now. Hopeless, I hang my head, until suddenly I am distracted by a commotion in the street, headed my way.

Low to the ground and moving at speed, a brown shape barrels along, ears flapping madly.

'Turnspit!'

He takes a great leap into my arms and covers my face and neck with licks. Then, just as quickly, he struggles to get down.

'Where shall I go, boy? You know, don't you.'

He heads down a tiny alley which cuts between the stalls and shopfronts, then turns left into a street that runs parallel to the first. He's heading back towards the castle, I think with a jolt. Then I realise Bury Field is just ahead of us. I can't believe Sal will still be there. Not now. She wouldn't have sat in her cart all night, surely.

Turnspit barks and barks and barks. And there she is, holding the reins of her horse, Bridey. They're coming up the road at a lick, her cart rocking from side to side.

CHAPTER 8

We take the Maldon road, both too shaken over Ned to say much. Sal hands me a flagon of ale, and I take a long drink.

'Where will ye go?'

'I can't go home. Will you look after Bessie?'

''Course. But what will you do?'

Sal knows nothing about the princess or the spy. 'It's best you don't know.'

'They'll be straight back to Goldhanger questioning us, that's for sure.' Her mouth is set in a grim line. 'A pecked face isn't going to stop Tallon, more's the pity.'

I nod. His face won't be a pretty sight. The man's over-weening vanity will have been sorely pricked, and I doubt he'll forgive or forget any time soon.

Just before Heybridge, Sal slows the cart, and before I step down we hug, long and hard.

'You look after yourself and that odd little hound of yours. I'll make sure Bessie's all right, don't you worry.' She hands me a parcel wrapped in muslin. 'Put this in your pocket. Bread and cheese for later.' She tightens the reins and clicks to Bridey. 'If Tallon's lot ask, I'll tell 'em you got a lift with a carter to London.'

I thank her, and with a jolt the cart starts to move. I watch it getting smaller in a swirl of red dust as Bridey takes it left onto the Goldhanger road. It's as though every loving face I've ever known is gone.

'We've only got each other now, Turnspit.' I bend down and tug on his ear. 'How about we go find the princess? It's what Ned would want.'

I don't feel capable of helping myself, let alone anybody else. But, at the very least, Lady Mary might provide a port in a storm. She owes me a favour, and I don't have anyone else who can help me now that I cannot go back to Goldhanger.

It never occurs to me that the princess might not be at Woodham Walter. Turnspit takes me along overgrown paths, through woods and swampy streams, and I follow blindly, numb with grief, so exhausted that I hardly know in which direction we're going. Nor do I care very much.

It is afternoon when we reach the deer park and the wrought-iron gates. The spotty servant who brought Turnspit to the great chamber walks across the gravel, arms folded across his chest.

'Get lost, you two. Lady Radclyffe wants you off her property. Right now. Or she'll get the constable.'

Turnspit snarls, snapping at the man's legs so that he dances backwards, protecting his white hose.

'I mean it. Beat it!' He flicks the fingers of his gloved hand.

'Please. Lady Mary will want to know we're here.' I can't bear begging to this noserag, but I try to hold my temper. Turnspit has no such qualms and takes another snap at the dancing legs.

'You're out of luck. She's gone.' He slips back inside the gates and shuts them with a clang.

'Please. Wait! Where's she gone?'

Already walking away from us, he doesn't deign to turn his head, but at least he gives us an answer. 'New Hall.'

I know of King Henry's great palace, of course I do. It's one of the things of which we Essex folk feel most proud. He called it Beaulieu, which means 'beautiful place'. My mother told me that they built it where the old manor stood just before Lady Mary was born, when Henry was happy with his Spanish queen, Catherine. The princess was adored, as much as any little girl ever was. She had her very own nursery wing, and never was there a child so spoiled. I used to imagine the young king tossing her in the air, laughing in his red beard.

Then everything changed for the Lady Mary. The spoilt king spurned poor Queen Catherine, breaking her loyal heart. His fancy had been caught by the dancing feet and dark eyes of Anne Boleyn, who, once she had power in her grasp, bullied the young princess. She turned the king against his daughter and had her shut in a bare room. Worse still, they never let the girl see her poor mother again. I think of Mary now: the haunted eyes, the frown lines grooved into her forehead. I doubt she can shrug off all those bad things that have happened since she was that little girl dandled on her father's knee. Not when they're etched in her heart.

No one calls the palace Beaulieu these days, not since King Henry died. The name never stuck in the heads of local folk. It was called New Hall back when Anne Boleyn's father owned the manor, before he sold it to the

young king, and it will always be New Hall to us. I fancy
the princess may still call it Beaulieu, though. I'm sure she
cherishes the few good memories she has.

I don't like to think what will happen if Lady Mary
turns me away. I haven't the strength to come up with
another plan if she won't take us in. Instead, I concentrate
on how we will get to her palace at Boreham. Turnspit
and I have two options. The first is to take the lane up
to Hoe Mill and the Chelmer, where we can follow the
bends of the river, splashing through the shallows so that
bloodhounds can't follow our scent. Judging from his
happy muddy countenance yesterday when we followed
Limbourne Brook, I can guess this is the option Turnspit
would go for. But I'm tired and aching, and, after his
attack by ravens, I'm sure Tallon is in no state to send out
his troops to look for us. So I tell Turnspit firmly that
we'll take the easier route, a perfectly good track through
the woods to Little Baddow. The village is on the way
to Boreham, and it's not too far. There'll be somewhere
we can shelter, I'm sure. We both need a night's rest,
and if we leave at first light we can be at New Hall by
midday tomorrow.

I'm putting one foot in front of the other only out
of duty to Ned. If it weren't for that, I wouldn't mind if
the devil took every one of us. Then I glance at Turnspit's
face. He looks as miserable as he did on the wheel, if that's
possible. His wiry fur hangs limply and his ears are bent
flat, mouth turned down so that his whiskers droop.

'Don't worry, Turnspit. Maybe once I've slept I'll feel
better.' I give my best attempt at a smile. 'I know – let's
share the bread and cheese.'

I hardly think I'll be able to swallow anything, but I take out the parcel and unwrap the muslin. The poor dog hasn't eaten since I gave him the last of my pottage at Sal's. Nor have I, for that matter.

The ewe's cheese reminds me of Barrow Farm. It tastes of salt and hay and carries a whiff of dung and sea lavender. In my mind's eye I see my father and his dog at the sheep fold, my mother feeding peelings to the geese in the yard.

I was right. After the first mouthful I cannot swallow it down, but at least Turnspit has regained his temper, his tongue doing a good job on his whiskers, tail wagging, pointing skywards. You can tell so much from a dog's tail.

If he senses my low spirits he doesn't show it, seeming happy with the decision to go to New Hall. Not for the first time, I take my lead from him. I haven't the energy or will to do anything else.

2

IN SERVICE OF
THE PRINCESS

CHAPTER 9

New Hall, Essex, May 1553

My body shakes, dripping sweat, head roaring like a furnace. I feel a cool cloth wipe my forehead, my neck and shoulders. Where am I? I cannot see. Just a red haze. Vague forms, fuzzy at the edges. Did I dream the great palace, its diamond-shaped windowpanes hurling the sun's rays, like lances of fire, to split my head in two? Was it a dream that Fitz took me in, carrying me in his arms while I thrashed and fought him?

Other pictures come and go. Nightmares and strange fevered wanderings. Ned hanging, spinning on his rope, his face winking and grinning at me. Another time, I am with him in the forge, sweat beading my skin from the heat of the flames. His grizzled, narrow head hangs over tongs that slowly bend before my eyes, soft as beeswax, to become a lobster's pincers. 'Ned,' I call. 'Ned! The tongs!' But then he turns, and it isn't Ned at all. The stippled grey of his hair is bird feathers, and a hooked beak stabs at my face till it runs with fat drips of blood.

I hear the deep voice of a man – 'She's clear of the fever, Rosie. A couple of leeches should do the trick' – but I cannot see or speak. When he's gone, I feel the touch of a tender hand as it wipes my body with a cloth and lifts a spoon of broth to my lips.

As day merges into night and back into day, the man visits less. His voice sounds bored, as if he's keen to be gone. 'It's no disease I can name. The girl is suffering from an excess of black bile. Melancholy's a humour given to dampness. Keep the fire burning, Rosie. Day and night.'

My mother would have explained it more simply. I can hear her voice now, as clearly as if she were sitting beside my bed. 'You're grieving, my little one. Sick at heart. There's nothing physic can do for you. When you've lost what you hold most dear, your body finds its own way to help you make peace with that.'

But I have no peace. I've grieved before, but this time it feels worse. The pain of losing my parents strikes me again, the stab of it sharper and deeper than anything I've ever felt. Because now I've lost Ned, too.

It's as if my mother is telling me in her quiet, implacable voice that I must sweat this new loss through every part of me till I can once more stand a world that doesn't have him in it.

I cannot do it. Haven't the strength for it.

Stifled by the heat of the fire, I long for the breeze off the Blackwater. I'm aware, now and then, of a rasping against my hand: a touch, insistent and gentle, that brings me back to myself – the tongue of Turnspit.

'Rosie, please. I feel well enough to go outside. I can't lie here for ever.'

My small whitewashed chamber is beginning to feel like a prison cell.

The round blue eyes in Rosie's plump face blink. 'But Dr Scurloch … I'll need to check with him.'

'He'll be pleased to see the back of me. You know he will.'

The tiny window slit of my chamber gives onto a yard they call Stable Court. I can hear the horses' hooves on the cobbles outside, the lively calls of grooms and riders. I want to be out there with my face in the sun. I know I'll feel better in no time.

Rosie is a girl entirely given over to the desire to please. Sometimes this causes indecision, as she worries she might offend someone – in this case Dr Scurloch – while doing her best to please another. She rocks on her toes for a moment, then gives a dimpling smile. 'Let's get you outside, then. Lady Mary will be pleased you're better.'

It still amazes me that not only had the princess taken me in, but she'd had her physician tend to me.

'Mistress Clarencieux was only checking on you this morning.'

'I don't think she likes me very much.'

Rosie is too kind to agree, but she and I know it's true. I haven't set eyes on the lady-in-waiting since Woodham Walter, but I've heard her sour, disapproving voice outside the door to my chamber. So has Turnspit, who gives a low growl whenever his ears pick up the sound of her clipped footsteps.

Rosie finds a small bench and stands it against the courtyard wall. She leaves me there with Turnspit, and I raise my face to the sun, wishing to soak it up, spread my petals like a flower. My world has shrunk to the simplest of wants.

Turnspit sits with me for a short while. He twitches and scratches and gives the odd gusting sigh, every so often opening and shutting his mouth with a smack. I can tell he is not content to stay in one place. He itches to explore, and after a while he leaves my side and trots out of Stable Court without a backward glance. It makes me smile to see him busily sniffing the air as he sets out to investigate the palace. I am sure he will give the kitchens a wide berth, though.

When he returns later he is not alone. I may have fancied being a gillyflower against this redbrick wall, shrinking from meeting anyone, but Turnspit clearly has other plans for me. A lad and two girls follow him, making a good deal of noise as they enter the courtyard. I watch the trio with curiosity in those few moments before any of them notice me.

Fitz is one of the three. I haven't seen the groom since he found me collapsed at the gate after Turnspit started howling loud enough to raise the dead. I blush to think how he held me in his arms while I moaned and flapped like a mackerel. What a fool I must have made of myself. I look at him now and he seems different from the guarded, arrogant young man I remember from Woodham Walter. Alight with mirth, his expression displays none of the world-weary carelessness I noticed then. Instead of the languid, loping tread, he strides freely, as if released from some kind of restraint. *It is because he is with friends*, I think to myself. And what a strange pair they are.

A flame-haired girl, not much older than me, dances along in a pair of red breeches, dragging with her a bald girl in a lavishly embroidered grey silk gown. As they draw closer I realise that the shaven-headed girl isn't a girl at all, but a grown woman. I can see why I mistook her for a child: she has the openness of expression I've only ever seen in children and simpletons. It's as if everything she sees is new – as if a whole world is born with each step – and she gazes at it in wonderment.

The girl in breeches spots me first. 'Aha! There she is!' She pulls along the shaven child–woman, who moves with a slowness that is so different from her friend's acrobatic darts and skips. Fitz follows a few steps behind, and on seeing me he seems to lose some of his playfulness: gone is the grin that split his face in two. Now that he is guarded again, I feel a little disappointed, as if a window had been opened to reveal a beguiling view, only to be closed again quickly. Doesn't he like me? Is that it? I wonder. Is he wary of me, thinking I'm an unnatural sort of girl? And then it pains me with a twinge that I should care.

'You must be Dela,' the flame-haired girl says. I notice that she speaks with a foreign lilt.

'Yes, I am. And this is my dog, Turnspit.'

'We know that. Fitz can't stop talking about the pair of you. We wanted so much to meet you.'

So Fitz has been talking about me. And not in a mean way, or the others wouldn't want to meet me. I am hit by a sudden spike of gladness and try to restrain my mouth from grinning.

Fitz colours at the red–headed girl's words and it earns him a nudge from her. 'Wake up, shy boy. Introduce us, *per favore.*'

'Glad to see you're better, Dela. This is Lucretia. She's Italian, from Florence. A tumbler.' He flashes her a look. 'As well as a royal pain in the backside.'

She grins, and I notice that one of her front teeth cross-es over the other, adding to her roguish look.

'And this is Jane Foole,' Fitz adds.

'The kindest, sweetest, most huggable person in the palace!' says Lucretia, slipping her arm around Jane's waist.

'You're pretty,' Jane says, reaching out to touch my cheek. Then she stoops to study Turnspit. 'Your dog isn't.'

He turns a humped back on her. I don't know how, but he has an uncanny knack of understanding folk.

'I'm afraid he's thin-skinned,' I explain. 'He doesn't care to have his looks remarked upon.'

Jane eyes immediately fill with tears. 'Beautiful. Turnspit is beautiful. I meant *that*.'

'I know you did, *tesora*,' Lucretia assures her quickly. 'No one loves animals more than you. You don't even mind if they're ugly and mangy.'

At this, Fitz glances at Turnspit. 'I think you've just add-ed insult to injury, Lettie.'

It is true. Lucretia's words haven't helped Turnspit's temper in the slightest. The way she said 'ugly' and 'mangy' has hurt his feelings all over again. I wonder if her lack of tact is something shared by all Italians. Maybe in Florence they let their tongues run away with them, and they're used to that there.

Lucretia hops down into a squat and tickles the curly tangle on Turnspit's head. 'You need to toughen up, *piccolo*. Mary's ladies want to meet you.'

My heart sinks. 'They don't really, do they?'

'*Si*. Both of you, when you're feeling strong enough. Fitz can bring his dagger to guard Turnspit from their nasty, snappy spaniels.'

Fitz glances at my shocked face. 'She's joking. The spaniels are comforter dogs. The ladies use them to keep their
stomachs warm.'

'I can't see Turnspit being on anyone's lap,' says Lucretia.

Fitz stoops to scratch the dog behind his ear, then
turns to me. 'Don't worry. Just greet them and curtsey.
Once they've done with their smirking, they'll show you
out again.'

I wonder to myself if I'll get to meet Lady Mary again,
and whether she'll let me stay here now that I'm better.
What if she's heard about what happened at Colchester
Castle? I'm sure to be asked to leave if she has. As anxious
thoughts take over, suddenly I wish I was back in my little
white chamber.

Two days later, Turnspit and I receive our summons from
Mary's ladies. Lucretia and Jane take me to their bedchamber to dress me. It has a huge feather bed in the middle with
a carved headboard and damask hangings. Jane, as Mary's
favourite fool, has been honoured with a bedchamber in
the privy apartment. Lucretia, as her minder and friend,
sleeps on a truckle bed at the foot of Jane's four-poster.

A massive, silvered looking glass hangs on the wall
above the fireplace. I find it hard not to study myself,
wonderingly, in the glass, and I rearrange my features
self-consciously. Ordinary folk in Goldhanger only ever
see their reflections when they're caught in a marsh pool
on a still day.

'Does everyone in the palace have a job of work to do?'
I have only recently left my sickbed, but it has started to

trouble me that I am without a role in the household. I am used to working from dawn to dusk, and this idleness sits uncomfortably with me.

'I have several,' says Lucretia proudly. 'Tumbler, fool, minder.'

'Whom do you mind?'

'Jane,' she says, as if it's obvious. 'She's a "natural". Always tells the truth. And that God-given gift has earned her this fine bedchamber. In case you wondered, she's not the sort of fool who tells those *buffone* when they're being ridiculous – that's for me to do. Someone has to keep those fathead nobles on their toes.'

While Lucretia's tongue runs like quicksilver, Jane stands the other side of me, docile and blinking. She's taking an age to lace my chemise, but I don't mind: there's something soothing in the slow movements of her hands.

Lucretia says, 'I also look after Lady Mary's gloves. In my family some of us are tumblers, others are leather workers, the finest in Firenze. I came to England to join my uncle, Alfredo. The best glover in the world.'

'Does he live at New Hall too?'

'In London. He likes to be near the skinners, where the Walbrook flows into the river. He has the peltry just north of him, where they store the skins, and the tanneries the other side of the river in Southwark. No man wants to live too close to the tanyards. *Il puzzo* – the stink!'

'If he's the best glover in the world, does that mean he makes the king's gloves?'

'*Naturalmente*,' she says simply. 'Edward's, and his father King Henry's before that. *Grosso*, the fingers of that fat old man. Like *salami*.' Lucretia screws up her freckled nose and hushes her voice to a stage whisper. 'I'll tell you a secret, Dela. Alfredo says that the first gloves King Henry asked him to make were a special pair. Designed to hide a mole on the hand of the-queen-who-mustn't-be-mentioned. Some say she had an extra finger, but she didn't. Not the mark of the devil either. Just an ugly mole.'

I remember everyone in Goldhanger jangling on about Anne Boleyn being a witch. For simple folk, even a mole has the stink of witchcraft to it. The thought gives me a bleak little shudder, and I quickly move the conversation on. 'And what about you, Jane?' I ask. 'Do you have a job other than fool?'

'I'm a minder too, aren't I, Lettie?'

'You are. You mind the geese,' Lucretia says, adding for my benefit, 'She's been at court for years. As far back as Anne – ' she corrects herself quickly ' – the queen-who-mustn't-be-mentioned.'

'I looked after Queen Catherine's geese, too.'

'After King Henry died. At Chelsea Place. Yes, you did.'

'The angels took her … and her babe, didn't they, Lettie.'

As Jane's eyes brim with tears, I wonder what strange things she must have seen in all those years of telling truths to courtiers.

Seeing her friend cry, Lucretia seeks to distract her as she would a child. 'Your geese adore you, *carissima*. I have the softest feather mattress in the whole world thanks to your birds.'

We fall quiet for a while as she and Jane use countless pins and laces to truss me up. Caged in a prison of boned linen, I wait, trying not to fidget while layer upon layer of wool is added to my finery. After the chemise comes a farthingale, a hooped undergarment stiffened with withies – how am I meant to sit wearing that? – followed by a green embroidered kirtle, to which separate sleeves with little shoulder puffs are pinned. Finally, when I'm weighed down by yards of heavy cloth, Lucretia pulls a dark-blue damask gown over it all.

While she's engaged with that, Jane busies herself primping the scratchy bobbin-lace of my chemise, which peeps out at the cuffs and neckline: the finishing touches to a horrifying instrument of torture.

I step away, almost panting with the need to fill my lungs and stretch my limbs. The stiffened bodice of my chemise and the tight pinch of the slashed sleeves are driving me mad. I want to pull everything off to get rid of this infernal itching. Suddenly I long to run on the saltings, breathe the sharp air, feel the soft wet mud between my toes.

'*Un momento*! We are not finished!'

Lucretia drags me back and helps me step into a pair of embroidered green slippers, while Jane pins a French hood to my braided hair, after which she claps her hands together.

'She looks beautiful, doesn't she, Lettie?'

Lucretia steps back to admire her handiwork. '*Che bella*! I envy you your long lashes, Dela. Like a fawn with your big dark eyes. Desperate to run away – not that I blame you, *carissima*.'

She studies me closely, hands on hips. 'At last we can see your face without those curls getting in the way.'

I feel quite naked with my hair braided and pinned back. There's nothing to hide behind, and I don't like the feeling one bit.

'You know,' she adds, 'there's a sculptor – *molte, molte famoso* – called Michelangelo. His studio's near my *nonno's* workshop in Santa Croce. This sculptor, he pays good money for models with a head like yours. Look at those cheekbones! *Drammatici!*'

I blush, and Jane leads me to the mirror by the hand. I cannot believe the girl looking back is really me. I feel like a cat which, confused on seeing its image in a pond, reaches out a paw to touch the water.

Lucretia watches my reflection with a half-smile, then darts me a sideways glance I cannot read. 'Fitz won't recognise you.'

I can feel the heat spreading over my collarbones. It is silly, I know. It's not as if I'm sweet on him. Lucretia gives me a penetrating look, but I am saved from further comments by a knock at the door.

One of the princess's chamberers pokes her head in. 'They're ready for you in the withdrawing chamber.'

Lucretia's eyes sparkle. 'This is the moment. Can you imagine Mistress Clarencieux's face when she sees you?'

Unfortunately, I can. The princess's lady-in-waiting has already made it perfectly clear what she thinks. When she came to tell me that Lady Mary wanted me to entertain her ladies with my dog, I could see the thought of it made her blood boil.

'She hates me.'

'Of course. You're a commoner going up the ladder, *cara*.'

'But I don't want to go up the ladder.'

'Then you're in the wrong place.' She gives me a little flick on the arm with a glove. 'Courtiers are curs, you know. And Susan Clarencieux is just one more bitch scrapping over a bone.'

I slump my shoulders miserably. Talking of curs, I do fear that taking Turnspit to the withdrawing chamber will turn out very badly indeed. I wish he could stay behind and guard our things. Dogs like to have a job; they never chew slippers if you give them something to do. Mind you, he has done little else but sleep this past week, so 'doing' has mostly involved chasing conies in his dreams.

I put him on a leash, which immediately annoys him. He likes to walk free, proudly at heel, as if to say, 'I choose to follow. No man owns me.'

'I have no choice,' I tell him. 'The ladies will expect it.'

They may have other expectations too. He's not the kind of dog who likes to do tricks, thinking that type of thing beneath him. I fear, too, that they will make light of his appearance. If there's one thing Turnspit hates more than anything, it's being criticised for his looks. Months spent treading his wheel – rib-thin, his hair coming out in clumps – has done nothing for his temper. If the ladies make so much as one jeering comment, I'm certain he'll go off like a powder-keg.

Lucretia leads us through a string of chambers belonging to the privy apartment till at last we reach a door. Next to it stands Fitz in a slouch, arms folded. Turnspit pulls at the leash, surprising me in his eagerness to greet the groom who immediately loses his air of indifference and drops into a squat.

'Hey, Turnspit! There's a boy!'

He ruffles the little nest of fuzz on the top of the dog's head, then glances up and sees me properly for the first time. As he does so, his eyes widen in astonishment.

This makes me prickle with irritation. It's bad enough that I have to bear the pinch of these scratchy, ridiculous clothes without having to be stared at. 'Didn't your mother tell you it's rude to stare?' I snap.

Fitz flushes and turns away quickly.

'*Bene, ragazza*,' says Lucretia. 'Keep the naughty boy in his place.'

'Enough of your cheek, tumbler.' He recovers himself smartly, but I notice that his eyes avoid me, and he quickly turns his attention back to Turnspit, bending till he is nose to nose with him. 'Just remember, dog, don't let those ladies with their naughty spaniels get you down. Give them a good nip if they're badly behaved.'

'They can forget about him doing tricks,' I mutter crossly, still feeling at odds with him. 'You know, I have a bad feeling about this.'

'You have surprise on your side,' he says. 'They're just as awful as you imagine, whereas they'll have no idea what to make of you.'

Unsettled, I don't know whether this is praise or a put-down, but it's too late to think about that.

CHAPTER 10

Turnspit and I follow Lucretia and Jane into the with-drawing chamber. As I stand inside the doorway, all I see at first is a blur of colour, illumined by shafts of light as the sun streams through two enormous bay windows. I feel like a mole who's just scrabbled up a tunnel and popped out its head, blinking, into the light.

Above the wainscot, fat pink cherubs float in a pale-blue sky tufted with clouds, and over my head the ceiling panels are carved in a colourful tangle of shapes – fig leaves and roses, dragons and portcullises – every inch of them painted and gilded.

'Bring them over here where we can see them.'

I'd know that hard voice anywhere.

Mistress Clarencieux is with a group of four ladies seated on cushions beneath one of the windows. Above their heads, in a gilded cage, a drab nightingale hunches on a perch. Of the princess there is no sign: the canopied chair is empty. Jane sits down next to the ladies, bending to retrieve her needlework, while Lucretia stays at my side. The pair of us curtsey, though the tumbler – scornful of anyone who tries to curry favour – offers no more than the tiniest of bobs.

I can almost feel the gentlewomen's eyes roving over my body while I keep my gaze lowered. Their perfume tickles my nose with its sharp reek of civet-cat musk, and I dare not breathe in case I sneeze.

Two of the four women have small comforter dogs in their laps, silky little spaniels who seem content to nestle there, peering out with almond-shaped eyes. Mistress Clarencieux doesn't have one – no surprise, as she doesn't strike me as a dog-lover – but instead fingers a small leather prayer book which hangs from a gold girdle chain at her bulging waist.

'Her skin's a bit brown. She looks swarthy as a sailor,' says one of the ladies with a dog in her lap, a sour-looking woman with a face caked in white powder. 'That won't do at all. Maybe a chamberer could lighten it with lemon juice.'

My skin crawls under their scrutiny. Now I know how the bearded lady must feel in her booth at the fair when folk pay to see her.

'Is this really the common marsh girl who helped the emperor's man escape?' asks a quiet-voiced woman with a large black cross around her neck. 'Where is Lady Radclyffe's turnspit dog we've heard so much about?'

Turnspit peers out from behind my skirts, and the gentlewomen study him closely. I don't know quite what they are expecting to find, but I sense their disappointment.

The woman with the white face purses her lips, causing her face powder to crack into furrows round her mouth. 'What an ugly tufty thing. What does he do? Can he perform?'

'He's a working dog, my lady. He doesn't know tricks,' I answer tightly.

Lucretia, sensing I might be about to disgrace myself with an angry outburst, steers me by the elbow to sit down at the edge of the group. Thankfully, the talk moves back to Lady Radclyffe, and for the moment we are forgotten.

'The countess has earned Lady Mary's displeasure for being so thick with Sir John Tallon,' says the woman with the crucifix pendant. 'Isn't that what you said, Susan?'

Mistress Clarencieux gives a murmur of assent with a sideways glance at me, her thin lips disappearing into the slit in her face. I can tell she doesn't think it fitting to be discussing such matters with a marsh witch in the room. I hardly care, for I feel faint-headed at hearing mention of Tallon's name.

A laughing-eyed girl with thick auburn hair bends forward to catch Lucretia's eye. '*Euch*, that man! I know plenty of women swoon at his feet, but he's like something they've brought up from the bottom of the Chelmer. His shiny skin's like a newt's. I don't know how Lady Radclyffe can flirt with him. *Euch*! He once raised my hand to kiss it, and it was like being wrapped round by an eel.'

This earns her a glance of reprimand from Mistress Clarencieux, though the girl seems to be oblivious to it. I sense that she likes nothing better than to try the lady-in-waiting's patience.

'That one is Mistress Dormer, the favoured lady of the bedchamber,' Lucretia murmurs in an undertone. 'She likes to tease. You mustn't mind what she says. None of them knows your history with Tallon.'

In the past day, Lucretia has gleaned from me the details of my life as painstakingly as if she had been drawing a winkle from its shell with a pin. I tell myself that this is what friendship is – telling each other everything – but I cannot help but feel a bit exposed.

My ears pick up more of the conversation. The ladies haven't yet done with Sir John Tallon. Hellbent on ridding the country of Catholicism, he has earned their scorn, but behind that I detect fear when they talk of him.

'He's not coming here, I hope,' the pious lady twitters, fingering her crucifix.

'I'm sure he's not, Mistress Arundell,' says the laughing-eyed favourite. 'By all accounts, he's hiding away in his hall with a scabbed face. There are all sorts of rumours as to how he got it.'

Mistress Clarencieux casts me another meaningful glance, and Lucretia makes a rude face at the back of her head the moment she turns away.

'It's strange he should live in that great dark mausoleum of a place on his own,' says the woman with the heavily powdered face.

'You'd have thought he'd have found himself a wife by now, even if he is like a newt,' admits Mistress Dormer.

'Not everyone knows it, but he did have a woman tucked away in Colchester. Not a doxy – a yeoman's daughter who should have known better. The sort who's scared of her own shadow, a pale wisp of a thing who kept to her chamber with her shutters closed.'

'It doesn't surprise me,' Mistress Dormer says with a dramatic shudder. Her eyes sparkle like those of a child hearing her first ghost story, and I fear she will not let go of her subject any time soon. 'Men like that enjoy bending an insipid girl to their will. One day we'll hear she's faded away to nothing, till she's no more than a piece of string. Or, worse still, she'll die and no one will hear of her passing. It will be as if she never existed at all.'

'I'm sure I heard that she *did* die. No surprise, as they say he treated her worse than a dog,' says the powder-faced woman. 'Now I think of it, wasn't there a son? I'm sure there was. A nervous, pale little thing, very like his mother. Tallon bullied him almost as badly.'

'Poor boy,' murmurs Mistress Dormer. 'Imagine having *him* as a father.'

I wish they would move onto something else.

Lucretia casts a quick look at me and another at the door. Then, with a tact remarkable for one who is usually so blunt, she swiftly changes the subject: 'Your comforter looks well, Mistress Arundell.'

The pious-faced woman blinks a pair of limpid, short-sighted eyes at her. 'Bread and milk, tumbler. You should never give a comforter meat. Isn't that so, Mistress Browne?'

The powder-faced lady casts a glance at Turnspit, who is minding his business, scratching an ear gently with his hind leg. 'Quite right. Give a comforter meat and what do you get? An aggressive dog. Like that mangy turnspit animal.'

'I did tell you all,' says Mistress Clarencieux smugly. 'The girl and her dog aren't fit to be in the palace, let alone the privy chamber! But would you listen?'

I am half aware of Lucretia casting me worried glances, but it is too late. It is one thing being unkind to me, but why should Turnspit suffer their insults? I struggle to my feet, while she hangs on my arm in an attempt to restrain me.

'He *isn't* aggressive. And he *doesn't* have mange!' My voice sounds loud to my ears. 'We didn't ask to come and meet you. Where I'm from, you treat a stranger kindly. That's how I was brought up.'

Hearing the anger in my voice, Turnspit draws back his upper lip and his hackles rise. *Grrrrr.* A throaty growl rumbles round the barrel of his chest.

The ladies stare at us in horrified silence, while on his perch above them the miserable nightingale fluffs out his feathers. Then, taking everyone by surprise, the two comforter dogs rear forward – the noblewomen hadn't thought to restrain them – and leap to the floor. They bark madly, making a dash at Turnspit like two jousters hurtling for the quintain.

I drop the leash, and in the same moment they go for his neck with their sharp little teeth and hang there like bulldogs. I hear Turnspit's yelps, somewhere amid the snarls of the comforters and the ladies' screaming, and feel his hot spikes of pain as if they were my own.

And that is when it happens. The wave of heat rises in me – familiar now, but no less shocking – and my arms grow stiff and straight, fingers splayed. 'Leave him be!' My voice can't be heard over the noise of the ladies and dogs, but the spaniels pause and cock their heads.

Straightaway, they let go of Turnspit. Slope-backed, tails tucked under, they back up to the skirts of their mistresses. Not once do their eyes leave my face. Openmouthed, the ladies sit frozen, stunned into silence.

I look down to check on Turnspit. Now the immediate danger is over, he is coiled round, attempting to nurse the cuts on his neck. His fur, which had been growing back so well, is a scattering of wet tufts and bald patches. Shaking, I pick up his leash, ready to flee, but when I raise my head again I see the squat figure of Mistress Clarencieux advancing on us, brandishing a fire iron. In her eyes, there's hatred, as well as fear.

'Witch! Begone Satan!'

I run from the chamber as fast as I can, dragging Turnspit after me. Fitz, who had been squatting against the wall outside, jumps up, startled. I can hear his footsteps behind me as I race down the long gallery, almost throttling Turnspit on his leash. I despise this place and everyone in it, including Fitz. I want to put a fist through every one of the smug painted faces of the kings and courtiers hanging on the walls. When Fitz grabs my arm, I shrug him off. I don't care what he thinks of me: he's one of them, after all. I wouldn't be surprised if, behind that careless gaze, he's as mocking of me as the rest.

I run to Stable Court. He's still on my tail as I enter the tack room and rip the French hood with its foolish veil from my head. Throwing it to the ground, I pull my hair free of its pins. He stares, but whether his eyes hold horror or fascination I neither know nor care. The pinch of my stiff bodice makes me want to tear every stitch of borrowed finery from my body.

Shaken, he begs me to stop. 'Wait here. Don't go anywhere. I'll get the girls.'

I collapse onto a bench and hide my face in my hands. Where can I go? I'll never be allowed to stay now ... and would I want to, even if I could?

Fitz returns with Jane, who's brought my clothes from her chamber. She says that she'll take me back to mine, and even in my frenzied state I can sense Fitz's relief at not having to deal with a crazed girl. With this realisation, my humiliation is complete.

Back in my chamber, I don't mind that Jane takes ages to unlace me and tidy away the pins. Her slow hands help bring my anger in check.

'What are they saying?'

'Mistress Clarencieux has gone to Lady Mary.' She speaks in her slow way as if she's laying down words like pieces on a merels board.

My shoulders slump. Turnspit gives my fingers a lick, and I take his head in my hands, holding it steady while I check his neck. 'What will they do to us?' I grab a linen cloth and rub at my face and shoulders before putting on my smock. All I want is to collapse on my straw pallet.

Jane pulls the sheet over me and puts a cool hand to my forehead. 'I don't know. We've never had a witch here before.'

Turnspit sidles over and settles into the crook of my knees.

I'm woken by Lucretia shaking my arm.

'Get up, Dela. The princess wants to see you.'

In a moment, I'm pulling my kirtle over my smock. With shaking fingers, I do my best to tidy my hair and tuck it into my cap. I have my summons, but I so wish it could be different. If only the princess had asked to see me to find out how I am after my illness and I could thank her for her generosity. Instead, I am sick with fear and bitterness, cursing her ladies and the gift that always seems to bring so much trouble on my head.

Lucretia takes me through the princess's privy apartment and we come to a door, next to which a page is standing. A moment later, I am ushered through it. I glance back at Lucretia, who returns a worried look.

The princess is at a writing table under the window, bent close to a document and holding a goose-feather quill. It occurs to me that she is near-sighted, which explains the intent, frowning way she has of looking at a person.

Like the withdrawing chamber, the room is richly decorated, but it is smaller and more intimate: a closet where the princess can work and read in peace. Through the open casement I can hear blackbirds singing. The early-evening light, yellow as custard, lends a warm glow to Lady Mary's face and hands. I smell lavender and the musky scent of beeswax.

I almost have to remind myself that this thin, small person is King Henry's first-born sitting in that chair, a princess by blood. It strikes me that had this mild, undistinguished-looking woman been in ordinary clothes, I could have imagined her scrubbing a hearth on her knees or calling the children inside for their supper. But then I remember with a sickening jolt that she has the power to change my life. And she's about to make it very bad for me.

It is only now that my knees begin to shake. I walk a few steps into the room and curtsey.

'You and your dog have caused a deal of trouble.'

'Yes, my lady.' I keep my face lowered. The best I can hope for is that she'll let me leave the palace without any other punishment.

'Look at me, girl.'

I raise my eyes to hers. She assesses me with a cool gaze while she slowly turns the quill between thumb and forefinger. 'You dared to raise your voice. You insulted my noblewomen. But worse, they're saying you used witch-craft. Do you understand the gravity of your offence? Mistress Clarencieux wants me to call the constable or at least have you whipped and thrown out.'

I nod dumbly, waiting for the axe to fall. A golden shaft lights the princess's hair a rich, burnished red.

She puts her quill down and makes a steeple of her hands under her chin. 'I heard about the ravens at Colchester. Sir John is nursing a scabbed face by all accounts.' She continues to study me as if I'm an insect pinned by its wings. 'I didn't credit those tales of your being a witch. But I do now.'

I stare at the granddaughter of Isabella, the Castilian queen, who roasted witches as soon as looked at them, and hardly hear her next words.

'I know you have a power. But I also accept you might be useful. You've helped me before and may do so again. Having you with me must be safer than if I make an enemy of you.'

'Thank you, my lady.' I hate being called witch, but this is no time to argue.

'I've decided to keep you close, but there will be no more mixing with my gentlewomen.'

She makes it sound as if I'm desperate to be in their company again. I'd rather eat my own hand.

'I was wrong in letting them use you for their amuse-ment. Mistress Arundell is a delicate soul.'

I nod, thinking that no one gave the slightest thought to my delicate feelings, nor to those of Turnspit.

'You and the dog may stay in your Stable Court cham-ber. I hear you're good with sick animals.'

'I am, my lady.'

'In that case, you can be my animal physician and work with the horses and dogs. You can find what you need in the physic garden. If you require a place for a mortar or such things, ask my steward. I'm sure you can find a corner of one of those chambers off Kitchen Court to call your own.'

'Thank you, my lady.'

'Good. I'm glad that's settled.'

I bob another curtsey, but she's already returned to her document. I pause a moment longer, shocked that my fate has just turned on a sixpence.

The princess raises her head. 'But no more witch-craft. If I hear of it, the consequences will be severe. Do you understand?'

'Yes, my lady.'

CHAPTER 11

As May draws to a close, three weeks into my stay at New Hall, the weather grows hot and dry. The pinch in the air has gone, and with the coming of summer the gentlewomen have discarded the heavier wool layers of their clothing. Even so, they stick to the leafy arbours and shaded walks, protecting their white faces, rarely daring to venture into the open to smell the damask roses or wander beside the beds of gillyflowers in the knot garden.

Lucretia has had a letter from her uncle with the latest news from London. In this swelter, the boy king is rotting away, he says. Covered in sores, hair and nails falling out, Edward's feet and tongue are black, and the sputum he coughs up from his lungs is putrid and stinking. She reckons we're in the calm before the *tempesta*. It won't be long before the king breathes his last, and, when he does, the duke will lock up Mary, or worse, thereby blocking her rightful succession. And it won't be just her, so it's no wonder that the ladies upstairs nervously finger their rosary beads.

Lucretia and I are in the orchard with Fitz, soaking up the sun. Lying on our backs in the shade of a medlar, hands behind our heads, we stare up through the branches to a cloudless blue sky. Beside me, Turnspit has his eyes closed, chin on paws. His ears flick, so I know he's awake, and occasionally his pale nose twitches.

I prop myself on an elbow and look out across the orchard. Scattered clumps of primroses stretch their yellow faces to the sun, little clumps of brightness that catch the eye. My mother used to liken them to gold coins that have slipped through a rich man's pocket.

'Poor Jane.' I cannot bear to think of her stuck inside, sewing in the privy chamber. 'How can she stand it?'

'Oh, she's happy enough, I imagine,' says Fitz carelessly.

'With her shaved head, she'd only get sunstroke,' says Lucretia. 'I'm an Italian, you're a sea witch, Fitz is a *vagabondo*. We *need* the sun.'

Fitz is not a vagabond, but Lucretia likes to tease him for being a travelling player. In the old days, players happily roamed from town to town, but not now. If they can't prove they're part of a nobleman's troupe, they are picked up for being vagrants. Fitz owes his place in Lady Mary's household to Lucretia. That much she's told me.

'How did you two meet?'

'At Tilty Abbey,' Fitz says, sitting up and crossing his legs.

He gathers three windfall medlars and juggles with them, and as the sun filters through the leaves it makes the gold flecks in his eyes glitter. I haven't entirely lost my awkwardness around him – if he were to throw me a medlar right now I would be all fingers and thumbs, unable to catch it – but the tension eases whenever Lucretia is with us.

'I was there with my troupe, Christmas two years ago.' He tosses one of the medlars at her. 'Lettie wagered I couldn't walk the length of the hall on my hands.'

'And did you?'

'Of course.'

'No, you didn't,' Lucretia says, laughing. 'You were good in that masque, though.'

She explains how the princess and her cousin Lady Jane Grey were friendly with each other that Christmas at Tilty, like sisters, exchanging little smiles and gifts, but that things have changed since then.

'Lady Jane likes to play the perfect purse-lipped Protestant. She's not alone in that. Mary's half-sister Elizabeth is just as bad. Mary thinks both of them wear black just to irk her,' she explains. 'I know you liked that Grey moppet, Fitz. But *santo cielo*! You'd think every day was a funeral the way she dresses.'

'She seemed playful enough,' says Fitz, 'considering how everyone bullied her.'

Lucretia makes a little face at me. 'He flirted like mad with her.'

'That's a lie!' He hurls another windfall.

'Oh yes you did. You showed off the whole time, even on stage. The players were quite vexed with you.' Then she adds for my benefit: 'Fitz was one of Oxford's Men.'

I've heard of the famous troupe of players belonging to John de Vere, the Earl of Oxford. A powerful man with many acres of Essex land and a town house in Maldon, he has a love of the chase – girls as well as game. He is close with Tallon. I've heard the pair of them like nothing better than to ride out together with their mastiffs and tear a hind limb from limb.

Lucretia must have noticed dread creeping over my face; the tumbler can be clever in the reading of other folk's feelings when she wants to be.

'I know something that will cheer you up, Dela. Did you know there's to be a *festa* next week? Dancing and a play. We've got to perform something, haven't we, Fitz?'

It seems an odd time to have a celebration, when we're all waiting to hear if the king is breathing his last, and I say as much. But when I discover that the feast will be on Corpus Christi – the day in the religious calendar most hated by the reformers – I'm shocked.

'That's the point,' says Fitz. 'Mary's thumbing her nose at the Lord Protector and his Privy Council. She wants to show the duke that she'll celebrate the day no matter what he says. Even if she gets arrested for it.'

I marvel at her boldness and say so.

'Thing is,' says Lucretia, 'her ladies are sour about missing out on that Grey moppet's wedding feast on Whit Sunday. The princess thinks they're owed a bit of fun.' She jumps up, eyes sparkling. 'And I, for one, cannot wait!'

She begins to turn cartwheels in a great circle round our medlar tree. Wearing linen slops to make her tumbling possible, not for the first time I marvel at her daring. I'm sure no other girl in Mary's household – or anywhere else, for that matter – could get away with wearing breeches.

I ask Fitz what he thinks will happen to us. He looks at Lucretia while he answers my question. I've noticed he finds it easier to talk if he doesn't have to meet my eyes. I still wonder if it's all the talk of witches that has made him wary of me.

'Things are quiet. Too quiet. The princess knows Northumberland's up to something.'

'How?'

'He's being nice to her. That's enough on its own to terrify anyone.'

This, I realise, is one of the first times I've been with Fitz when he's being neither offhand nor teasing. His face almost always wears a crooked smile, and I'd thought the boy incapable of taking anything seriously.

'It's no secret he's been building a war chest. Now he's made himself Treasurer, he can do what he likes with the country's gold. Easing himself into position. He just has to make sure Mary and Elizabeth don't succeed their brother. Why do you think he arranged for his son to marry Lady Jane Grey, a girl of royal blood?'

I turn his question over in my mind. I'd thought it strange that Lady Jane and Lord Guilford should have been married in an unlucky month. Everyone knows the rhyme Marry in May, rue the day. 'I did wonder why they'd chosen May to have it. A holy day, too.'

I don't add that nobles always seem to do as they please – the laws of the land are nothing more than straws in their fists to be broken.

'That's just it. The duke was rushing it through. He has a taste for kingship after pulling Edward's strings. He wants the throne … for him or his son. It doesn't take a genius to work out what's going on.'

The edge of scorn in his voice – though not aimed at me – is enough for the talk to dry up between us. I'm not used to conversations that concern royalty and affairs of state. If I were to ask Fitz any more questions, I'm afraid he'd only think me a simpleton. I think of Goldhanger, where a debate rarely reaches beyond the size of the day's catch.

I wish Lucretia hadn't left us to do her cartwheels. When she's with us, silences have no chance of growing. I can't tease and flirt like her – in that easy way where the words carry no great meaning and everything can be taken lightly. Now the silence is like a taut wire between me and Fitz, and I'm on the point of jumping up and brushing off my skirt – anything to break it – when Lucretia rejoins us. Relieved, I pass the burden of conversation onto her, and ask when she first learned to tumble.

'I was *una bambina*, of course.' She laughs happily at the memory. 'My *nonna* turned her back and, quick as a stick, I climbed out of my cot. Head first, *ovviamente*. Every Pisanelli tumbler starts out with a flip. Lands on its bottom, claps its fat hands together.'

'Tell Dela about your first act.' Fitz turns to me. 'You'll love this.' He grins crookedly, and I notice, not for the first time, how white his teeth appear against his tanned skin.

Lucretia beams, never happier than when she has our attention. 'We were famous … Lucca, Pisa, Siena … we performed in every grand piazza. *Il torre pendente di Pisanelli* our act was called, after the tower in Pisa that leans sideways. Have you heard of it?'

I say that I haven't.

She goes on to explain how twelve men of the Pisanelli family would climb onto one another's shoulders to form a tower – four men high, three wide. 'I'd climb up like a monkey and stand on the shoulders of the middle one at the top – *mio papa*. I held a red pennant in my teeth – the flag of Pisa. Oh, the cheers … you should have heard them!'

'I wish I could have seen it. How brave you must have been.' I try to imagine a tiny Lucretia scaling the wall of brothers and uncles and cousins till she stood victorious at the top.

'Pah! That was the easy bit,' she says. 'The next was the hard part. We had to make the tower lean to one side. The tumblers had to get the angle just right or they would fall and break their heads. I was lucky, of course – always land on my feet.'

'Like a cat,' Fitz says fondly.

I look at her and realise that she does remind me of a dainty little cat – a mother cat watching over Fitz, to be precise.

'If you were so happy, why did you come to England?' I ask, because the idea of living in the bosom of a big, noisy Italian family, tumbling together like puppies, is captivating to an only child like me.

At my question, the tiniest cloud flits over her countenance. 'I grew too big to be the pennant-waver. My sister took over.' She shrugs, as if to say: that's how the world goes when you're a Pisanelli. 'I'd always been a favourite with Alfredo, and he was happy to have me. So I tumbled my way into a court masque – and the rest you know.'

'Your father taught you well. You'll never be short of a patron,' says Fitz, and his kindness earns him a smile.

'Did your father teach you, too?' I ask him. Lucretia has described how he can stand on a horse's back while it gallops.

I have obviously said the wrong thing. His face snaps shut like a book, impossible to read. Lucretia swiftly changes the subject, rescuing him from having to speak.

I catch sight of Fitz later as I kneel beside my basket in the physic garden. Standing at the arched opening in the wall, he doesn't see me at first, because a low hedge of lavender screens me from sight. I wave to him.

He feigns surprise at seeing me here and makes out that he is on an errand. I cannot imagine what business would have brought him to the herb garden. And in any case, he seems in no hurry to leave.

'What are they for?' he asks, sitting on his heels beside my basket of chamomile and knitbone.

'A cooling poultice.'

'Is that what you give to your suitors? I'll wager there's a kennel hand or two who's in hot pursuit of you.'

I flush scarlet at his clumsy attempt at a jest. What did he go and say that for? I think he realises his mistake as soon as the words are out of his mouth. One look at my frowning face, and he quickly changes the subject.

'Who needs a poultice?'

'Rosie has a bad scald.'

Rosie, the maid who tended me when I was sick, is a shy girl who allows herself to be bullied by the scullions.

'I heard about that. It's her fault for being so easily pushed around. She should have told them the pot was too heavy for her.'

'Surely you aren't blaming her?' I ask, aghast.

His straight black brows draw together in a frown. 'Girls like that annoy me. Why couldn't she stand up for herself?'

'You think because she doesn't push herself forward that she's weak?'

'Well she could learn a thing or two from you, for a

start. When I saw you take on Lady Radclyffe, sticking up for Turnspit like that …'

'I can't think why you should blame Rosie,' I repeat stubbornly, ignoring his attempt to placate me. 'As if she's some pathetic creature who asks to be the victim.'

Scowling, he tears the buds off a lavender stalk. 'I just think women need to help themselves.'

I scramble to my feet and pick up my basket. 'Had it even occurred to you that she might simply be a kindly girl who wants to help others?'

He follows me as I stalk off. Turnspit runs ahead, blithely unaware of the tension between us as we skirt the redbrick wall of the kitchen garden in silence.

Fitz eventually breaks it. 'I expect you've never seen anything like New Hall.'

'Can't say I have.'

I have to admit that with its orchards and vegetable beds, fishponds and deer paddocks, I cannot get used to such plenty.

He turns to look at me, the better to catch my expression. 'It must be strange for you.'

I scowl at him. 'Not that you'd understand.'

'Wouldn't I?'

I stop, red-faced, hands on hips. 'Your sort have no idea!'

He reels back. 'Hold on. What do you mean, "your sort"? You know nothing about me!'

I don't mind that I've offended him. 'Do you even care that folk are starving? They're eating horsebread, for heaven's sake. Acorns.'

I'm sure he wants to say 'And what do you think I can do about it?', but he holds his tongue.

Meanwhile, mine continues to run away with me. 'Yes, I *do* feel strange at New Hall. What did you think? The rich just get richer. Gobbling everything, like locusts.' I jab a finger at his chest. 'And I don't know about you, but I wasn't brought up to think that's right.'

Oh why can't I hold my temper! Fitz stares at me, and I cannot tell whether it's disgust he's feeling or anger.

We enter a cobbled yard, on all sides of which are workshops: carpenter's, sawyer's and the forge. When I hear the familiar ring of a hammer on steel it reminds me of being at Ned's, and all at once I feel the anger fizzle out of me.

Fitz notices my moistening eyes. 'Look, I'm sorry if I offended you. Can we be friends?'

I nod, swiping at the tears with the back of my hand.

'It must be hard. You've lost your home. The farrier too.'

I nod again, thinking how different he sounds. Reacting to the softness in his voice, I find myself telling him what has been playing on my mind. 'Bessie, my mare, will be wondering what's become of me and Ned. It's not as if Sal can explain it to her. Bessie doesn't know he's dead, or where I've gone ...'

'I'm sure Sal is looking after her.' He pauses, and I wonder if he has grown uncomfortable again and will find an excuse to leave. But then he says, 'Come. I've got something for you ... a present.'

He leads me to his chamber, which he shares with two other grooms. I've never seen the inside of it before. It smells of boys – of sweat and hay. I stand awkwardly in the doorway while he goes over to a wooden box beside one of the three straw-filled pallets. He lifts the lid and

removes a sheet of paper from a pile of others and hands
it to me. It is a delicate charcoal drawing of a colt, whose
muscles and sinews have been picked out with such accuracy that it almost seems to move across the page. The
artist has captured the horse in subtle tones of light and
shade, legs stretched out in a spirited canter, as if it has just
entered an open stretch and has been given its head. But
it isn't just the accuracy of the drawing that astounds me.
Whoever has drawn it has managed to capture the joy of
the colt – swift, young and free – with a few magic swipes
of charcoal and chalk.

'Is this for me?' I ask, shocked and delighted.

'I thought it might make you miss Bessie a bit less.
But it was stupid. A picture won't help.'

'Oh, but it will!' I exclaim. 'I think it's wonderful. Did
you draw it?'

He nods, embarrassed.

'What a talent you have.'

Red-faced, he turns away, moving back to the box to
close its lid. As he does so, I catch a glimpse of another of
his drawings. He moves hastily to block my view; it is clear
he doesn't want me to see it. But he's too late.

It is of Turnspit, sitting obediently, just as he is now,
though in the drawing he is thinner and more scraggy.
His pale nose reaches out to somebody's hand, which he
is on the point of licking.

That somebody is me.

Chapter 12

As Corpus Christi approaches, my homesickness only gets worse. It doesn't help that I have hardly seen anything of Lucretia and Fitz. Busy all week with the players, they've practised a few scenes from a Chester mystery play, which they're to perform the day of the festival on a pageant cart in Chapel Court.

At supper, I notice an edge to Lucretia's teasing. Her jests are off-key, and it is painful to watch them falling flat. She and Fitz, who are to be Noah and his wife in the play, have lost their easy closeness. It's as if she's pricking him with a needle, looking for a reaction. He ignores her, but Lucretia needs to be noticed, so she won't give up – and the more he is silent, refusing to meet her eyes, the more she pricks away at him.

Noah and his wife are quarrelsome in the play. Mrs Noah, busy with her gossips, thumbs her nose at him when he tells her to come aboard the ark. I know Fitz's words by heart; I've watched him rehearse his lines:

'The flood comes in fleeting fast,
On every side it speedeth full fare.
For fear of drowning I am aghast,
Good gossip, let us draw near.'

The audience will laugh to see the scene, I'm sure, especially when Noah's sons have to carry Lucretia, struggling, into the ark, but this ill-humour between the couple, devised to entertain us, seems to have spilled over into the lives of my two friends.

Fitz asks Lucretia to pass the bread. She rolls her eyes. 'I'm not your *wife*, so don't order me around.'

He turns away, ignoring her.

After an awkward pause, where I pass the bread – thinking how childish they're being – we continue to eat in silence. It is not fair of them to poison the air like this.

Jane, trying to mend things, puts a gentle hand on Lucretia's arm. 'Don't be like that, Lettie. Be kind.'

How apt it is that Jane Foole – the gentle peacemaker – is to play the dove in the scene. She has shown me her costume: white satin with trumpet sleeves and feathers to stick to her bald head.

As Lucretia spars and sulks, I find myself missing the playful way it was before. Her green eyes follow Fitz, especially when he talks to me. My mother used to tell the story of a dragon curled under a tree of golden apples, its gaze ever watchful. The tumbler is no fire-breathing dragon, but she has a fierce longing for the lad. I see that now.

A worm of guilt uncoils in my stomach. Can I really pretend I have played no part in this? … That I haven't watched Fitz … and watched him watching me, my stomach tightening in that breathtaking game where our eyes play hide and seek – taking turns to take a surreptitious glance while the other looks quickly away? And when we do it, I've felt the flush spreading from my thighs to my stomach, my chest, my neck, and into my flaming cheeks.

The next day he is gone. Lucretia finds me in the stables and asks me if I've seen him. It's the day before the feast, and they still have to rehearse the play.

'No one saw him go,' she says, biting her lip. 'He must have left before dawn.'

'Turnspit's gone too. I've been calling and calling. Maybe they've gone off together.'

I've been growing more concerned by the minute; the dog never strays far from me, but now I try to put my worries aside. With so much to do today, I haven't time to fret about either of them. We can gather a search party later if they're still not back.

Lucretia finds no such relief. All day she paces, chewing her thumbnail. Sharp-featured, head thrust forward, she walks back and forth, eyes scanning every inch of the palace like a cat who's lost her kittens. It's a hard thing to witness; everyone is on edge.

Meanwhile, preparations for the feast continue. The servants dress the hall with silk hangings and blossoms, and above Mary's chair at the high table we fashion a canopy made of cloth of silver. We wind creeping vines, sweet pea and honeysuckle around the doorways and windows, threading in herbs to add to the scent, and it's as if we've brought the summer inside. Opening the windows wide, we let in the breeze, sweeping away the stale air and, with it, the brooding tension that has inhabited the palace these past weeks.

Jane comes down to report on the activity upstairs in the privy chamber. Rosy-cheeked and out of breath, she describes how the ladies are practising their dance steps. Their hair, sticky with gum arabic, is wrapped around clay curlers. Jewels have been chosen, perfumed gloves removed from silk wrappers, robes and trains laid out ready for the morrow.

She tells me that Lucretia is sitting slumped in her bed-chamber, staring at the wall.

Just before suppertime, when there is still no Turnspit – and no Fitz either – I pull on my boots, preparing to set out to search for the dog. I've grown accustomed to him following like a grumpy shadow at my heels, and it feels strange not having him here, as if I've lost a part of my body. But then I hear a whinny coming from Stable Court. I'd know that sound anywhere.

'Bessie!'

I look out through my slit of a window. It is Fitz, leading Bessie next to his horse. I rush out to meet them, thinking as I stand with him at the water trough how tired he looks and wondering how far he has gone. But when he sees me bury my face in Bessie's neck, breathing in the smell of her, he wears the satisfied look of one who knows he's done well.

Turnspit is no less pleased with himself, his head held high, whiskers bristling, tail straight as a maypole. Yesterday, as he snoozed in the sun, he grumbled at me when I tried to shift him with my toe. I can hardly believe it's the same dog.

We set off to find Bessie a stall. I cannot help myself firing question after question, but Fitz bids me wait, and it is only once we're seated on the bench in the tack room and Bessie's in her new fancy stall munching on a nosebag of hay that he tells me how he and Turnspit brought the mare here.

The first part I find hard to believe. He tries to make out that he was on an errand and just happened to pass by Goldhanger. I bite my lip to stop myself smiling. The village isn't on the way to anywhere. He can't admit he's done all this for me.

'Turnspit led me straight to Sal's door. She wasn't in, but then he took me down to the salt pan.' He bends to ruffle the dog's ear. 'Not a bad little scout, are you?'

Turnspit rolls on his back and offers a pink, freckled stomach to be scratched. His head is thrown back, lips peeled back in a grin, and his mouth gapes like a pike's. I watch Fitz's hand as it tickles the silky belly and, for a mad moment, want to reach out and touch his fingers, but I tug my gaze away.

'It was lucky I had Turnspit or Sal mightn't have talked to me,' he says. 'When I set off this morning, next thing I know, there he is, trotting ahead of my horse. Took us right there, didn't you, lad? A born navigator.'

Spreadeagled on his back, Turnspit gives a grunt of pleasure.

'How was Sal?'

'Missing you, but she's fine — better once she knew you were safe at New Hall.' He bends to take a parcel out of the oilskin bag at his feet. 'She sent you this.' He holds it to his nose and inhales deeply. 'Given what I've been through to get Bessie, I think we should share it.'

We make a good supper of Sal's salted herring. Fitz has a flagon of ale in his bag, so we have everything we need.

When we pass it from one to the other and brush fingers there's little awkwardness, no covert glances to bring a hot flush to my face – just my unbridled joy at having Bessie back and his satisfaction at having been the one to bring her.

To my shame, I never once think of Lucretia alone in her chamber, staring at the wall.

Corpus Christi brings with it a peerless sky, bright as the Virgin's mantle. Jane and I get up early to dress the pageant cart in the Chapel Court, and while we do it Turnspit lies on the cobbles, soaking up the sun.

All of a sudden, he jumps to his feet, nose forward like a pointer. The princess and her attendants are filing past on their way to Mass. He's spotted Mistress Arundell's comforter spaniel, I realise. Clasped in her arms, the dog cranes her head round, following Turnspit with almond eyes.

'Stay, boy!' I command in a low tone, fearful he'll draw attention to us.

Jane looks from one dog to the other, beaming. 'I think they're sweethearts. They are. Look!'

Incredulous, I have to admit she's right. Mistress Arundell's spaniel, showing no hint of aggression, peers out of her mistress's bosom with an expression that can only be described as a simper. And the more she simpers and makes eyes at Turnspit, the more he stands tall, bristling with manly pride. He takes a few strutting steps forward.

'Stay, boy!'

To his credit he does, though the spaniel – forward little miss that she is – tries to wriggle free of her mistress's arms.

Jane claps her hands in delight. 'She loves him, look!'

'Well she may.' I catch Turnspit's eye. 'Sorry, dog. She's above your station.'

Tonight, along with the fools and players, I have been invited to join the nobles in the main hall. Jane and Mistress Dormer have persuaded the ladies to give me another chance. I wish they hadn't. Turnspit isn't the only one who should know better. It is never wise to mix with folk above you in rank, everyone knows that.

'Now you can dance with us,' Jane says, as we wash our hands and faces at the pump after we've finished work on the pageant cart.

'I can't dance. I've never been taught.'

To my embarrassment she fetches Fitz, who's hard at work polishing leather in the saddle chamber.

Jane is insistent, like a child. 'Teach her to dance. Ple-ease! She needs to know the steps.'

Fitz colours.

Laughing with embarrassment, I say, 'Go back to your saddles,' but he has already made up his mind.

He holds out a hand, tucks the other behind his back, and bows. 'Mistress, if you please.'

The thought briefly flickers across my mind that I'm glad Lucretia isn't here. Then I'm holding his hand, and this time his touch scorches me. He looks at me with hazel eyes, and I can think of nothing else.

He tells me where to place my feet, but I end up stepping on his toes. I can tell he's trying not to laugh: the corners of his mouth twitch, then he throws back his head and gives in to it.

Wiping his eyes with the back of his hand, he says, 'It may take an age to make a dancer of you.'

I don't care that he doesn't flatter me with fine words and sonnets, because I've seen how he looks at me. When he has to clasp me close, I can feel his breath on my face and neck and it is torture. I want to be closer, to rest my warm cheek against his chest and feel his beating heart. I watch his laughing mouth, and the brightness of his teeth dazzles me. He is saying something, but I am so entranced at the movement of his lips that I have no idea what words they have formed. His right hand has mine in its grip, and when his thumb strokes my palm I can tell he is as acutely aware of my skin touching his. At some point during the dance we both stop talking, laughing, or jesting. We feast on each other's eyes, unaware of anything else.

Except once, when I glance up to see Jane standing by the pump, a new truth dawning in her simple blue eyes.

When you fall head over heels in love with someone who comes from a different world – a world that would spit you out like a rancid nut – you're too far gone to do the sensible thing: turn tail and put all thoughts of him out of your head.

So, with a mind that has lost all reason, I watch the play on the pageant cart. Barely able to follow the story, all I see is Fitz. Only him. He moves with cat-like efficiency, never overacting. I'm used to Lucretia's jesting but never realised he could have everyone in stitches like this. Even Lady Mary in her canopied chair cannot hold back her mirth. She makes an effort to maintain her pious countenance, but it isn't long before it cracks.

Mistress Clarencieux watches Fitz, a small smile lighting her features and a softness to her eyes. A moment later, her gaze moves to me, narrowing, her mouth becoming its usual slit. She's noticed that I'm moonstruck, I know she has. After all, it can't be very hard to detect. My eyes have been stuck fast to Fitz throughout the play.

Earlier this afternoon, knowing I'd be nervous, Lucretia explained the plan for the evening's festivities. After the play, she said, we will go our chambers to change our clothes. Then the highest-ranking nobles will repair to the privy chamber to dine with Mary. Jane will go with them, while the rest of us will feast in the great hall on boards and trestles that will be cleared away afterwards for the dancing. Lucretia insisted that she would fetch me from my chamber and escort me to the hall. I think she feared that I might hide away, otherwise, and fail to come.

I am standing in my chamber when I hear her knock at my door. Ever since Rosie finished dressing me I haven't dared sit down in case I crease my silk skirts.

On entering, Lucretia asks, a little sharply, 'Are those clothes Jane's?'

Earlier, I found the kirtle and robe on my bed and, beside them, a goose feather – Jane's way of letting me know the clothes were from her. Loose and simple, pleated and gathered to give a fullness without the need for a farthingale, they are made of fine, shimmering stuff, soft and light for dancing. The leaf-green robe parts below the waist to reveal a claret-coloured kirtle, sewn in a diamond pattern with seed pearls.

I can't help noticing Lucretia's smile is a little forced, her green eyes narrowing as she looks me up and down.

At first, I wonder if she's cross because she thinks I've taken advantage of Jane's sweet nature – we all know she'd give her last groat if someone asked for it – but then the real reason dawns on me. Lucretia is dressed in green, as am I. And our two greens look ill together.

I have stolen the wind from her sails, that's what she thinks. I've acted in a way that is far from being sisterly. Her eyes are telling me that I'm not a girl she can trust.

As we walk to the great hall together, lifting our skirts clear of the dust, I'm aware that I keep apologising for everything: 'You shouldn't have put yourself out. I could have walked over on my own.'

And when I can't think of anything else to apologise for, I resort to praising her: 'You were exceedingly good as Mrs Noah.'

Each plangent attempt to bring her round is greeted with a tight smile which she flicks across her face like a dusting cloth before resuming her stony expression.

Finally, as we walk through Fountain Court, making our way to the studded oak door of the great hall, I tell her the truth. 'I'm sorry I'm wearing green, too. I had no idea …'

'But you *know* I always wear green!' And, at last, her grievance voiced, she softens and links her arm through mine.

Fitz has saved us places at one of the trestle tables and stands up when he sees us walk through the door. He is wearing a short-skirted doublet of russet satin, slashed at the sleeves, and matching hose. When I take in the broad, straight cut of his shoulders, the stiff, standing collar, the feathered cap and the dagger at his side, all I see is a young man who *isn't* Fitz. This one seems to walk taller as he comes towards us, with a slight swagger of the hips, and it is only when my eyes drop to his feet in their soft, slashed-leather dancing shoes that I remember the other Fitz, the one I know – the player, the acrobat, the teasing Fitz. Not this straight-backed, muscular *man*.

At first our formal clothes make us shy, constrained by a new stiffness, as if these new tailored garments hold our manners in a vice. He greets us courteously, remarking on how well we look.

'Though not *together*. We don't look good *together*,' Lucretia puts in, referring to our greens.

This makes him smile, which only irks her, though not as much as the way he keeps staring in my direction. As his eyes rove over my silk-clothed body it makes me lose my breath, and a flush steals past my collarbones to my face. I'm all at once excited and embarrassed ... and more than a little fearful of Lucretia's tight-lipped reaction.

We sit down to eat and drink ... and I'd like to say make merry, but there is a constraint between the three of us. I've seen Lucretia like this before, talking fast in a brittle way, her eyes watchful, her laughter false and jarring. She is not herself, but then nor are we.

I find myself stammering, and very soon open my mouth only if I'm forced to answer a question one or the other has directed to me. My self-consciousness is only made worse by my rich clothes. After a lifetime of wearing smocks and kirtles in earth colours, the brightness of the dye makes me feel awkward. I'm sure folk will think I'm getting above myself – a drab little hedge sparrow trying its hardest to be a kingfisher.

I shouldn't be worried because when Lady Mary enters the hall with her nobles, their clothes outshine mine a hundredfold. Flanders lace, Venetian velvet, silk from Bruges ... in every colour of the rainbow. Gemstones wink with the light of a thousand candles – not just set in jewellery, but sewn on slippers, sleeves, French hoods and gloves. Even the ladies' hair twinkles from the seed pearls threaded through their nets.

The musicians tune their instruments – trumpets, viols, sackbut, pipes and drum – preparing for the dance. At a nod from Mary, her noblemen head to the lady of their choice, jewelled scabbards clinking at their sides. A smile and a bow, a gloved hand held out. With a train over their arm, the ladies move into line with a swish of perfumed skirts.

I feel a hot wave of panic. I don't belong here. I'm in the wrong place, in the wrong clothes, with people who aren't my kind. To make it worse, Lucretia grabs Fitz's hand, dragging him off to join the lines of dancers. I sensed that he was about to ask me – his eyes seeking mine, brows raised in a silent question – and maybe that is why she can't help herself pull him away. But when he doesn't so much as glance over his shoulder at me, I am filled at once by the whole idiocy of thinking there might be a match between us. What on earth was I thinking? He is nothing like me – the whole world is littered with simple country girls led astray, their eyes dazzled by a man dangerously above them in station. They used to come to my mother's door, begging for a love potion or wanting to rid themselves of a child quickening inside them. I'm not stupid, so how could I behave so stupidly? I used to scorn those girls drunk with love, unable to eat or think straight, and now it is me. I've been caught by the same sickness.

I cannot bear to watch Fitz and Lucretia but can't help myself. As I stand against the wall like a gillyflower, I am tortured by her green eyes laughing up at him. I stand awkwardly for a few moments as the lines of men and women surge back and forth. The noise of the pipes and trumpets cuts through me; the whirl of coloured silks, of flashing teeth and jewels, brings on a faintness. And then I can take it no longer and slip outside to the courtyard.

I stand in the shadows of the Fountain Court, watching the light stream from tall windows, glittering on the fall of water that patters into the basin. I knew this wasn't for me. I should have trusted my instincts and refused to take part.

I hear light footsteps and shrink into the shadows, not wanting to be seen.

'You left.' He stands beside me, close but not touching.

I say nothing.

'I wanted to dance with you.' His voice has a thickness to it, like honey off the comb.

I don't move or say a word.

Then I'm in his arms, and his breath is hot on my neck … and he kisses me.

CHAPTER 13

The day after Corpus Christi, the household is quiet. I lie on my straw pallet in a daze, thinking of Fitz's kiss. Nothing can spoil it for me if only I can stay here under my linen bedsheet, cocooned like a grub in an apple while the morning sun floods through the window slit of my chamber.

But thoughts come crowding in, and I'm the one who goes and spoils it for myself. Yes, he kissed me last night, but I tore myself loose from his embrace. He looked up, eyes drunk with passion, wondering why I'd broken away, and I couldn't speak – not a word. All I could do was run, stumbling in my velvet slippers, tripping over my green and claret-coloured skirts. I could hear his voice, slurred and confused, behind me: 'Dela, wait!' But I didn't look back.

The coward in me didn't want to have to see Lucretia's face. Even now I cannot bear to think how she'll react if she finds out. I groan and pull the bedsheet over my head. Inside, a quiet battle rages between the reasonable Dela and the headstrong one. Reason tells me that I will be a good deal safer if I do the right thing and spurn Fitz in a gentle way that won't hurt him. But then reason isn't a match for the ungovernable feelings that burst through, unstoppable. I don't want to give him up … and to hell with the consequences.

I've just finished getting dressed when I hear a tap at my door. I open it and my heart gives a lurch that feels very much like fear. Fitz stands in the arched frame of the doorway. I cannot meet his gaze.

'Dela, look at me.'

He doesn't make any move to touch me. When I raise my eyes, I am afraid they betray too much and it shames me, but then I catch the longing in his and it almost makes me gasp.

'Will you come riding? You could take Bessie.'

I nod, unable to trust my voice.

He lets out a breath, relieved. 'Good. Fine … I'll meet you in the tack room.'

Everything feels right again once I'm on Bessie's back. I watch Fitz slide his foot in the stirrup and spring into his saddle, marvelling at how he moves with such effortless power. Thankfully, the strange fluttering feeling, which makes it hard to breathe whenever he's near, has gone.

Turnspit is equally happy, especially when Bessie dips her head to nuzzle the back of his neck, gently huffing through her large, round nostrils.

Fitz turns to me, checking my face just to be sure that I'm not having second thoughts at spending the day with him, and gives a dazzling smile. 'I persuaded a scullion to give us leftovers.' He taps his saddlebag. 'There's plenty.'

'Did you hear that, Turnspit?' It makes me laugh to see the dog sit up straight as an altar boy beneath Fitz's stirrup, twitching his nose to catch the scent from the oilcloth bag. Tilting his head on one side, he tries his best to be winsome.

'Go away, dog,' Fitz says, tapping his horse with his heel. 'You can have the scraps later.'

It is not as hot as yesterday, and there is a light breeze. We start out side by side and, although I had worried that we would have nothing to talk about and that we'd squirm in awkward silence, Fitz begins speaking of horses, a subject we're both comfortable with.

'Bessie's doing well. She looks happy.'

I nod, patting her neck. 'She's got company.'

'It must be good not to be alone.'

Like me, Bessie's found herself in a different, unfamiliar world, but it is clear she likes it. No matter that she doesn't share the fancy bloodline of her new friends.

Fitz pats the neck of his stocky little grey. 'I'm fond of these Barbary mares, they're not too high-strung. They learn quickly, too. It's what you need if you want to teach them tricks.'

Without being the most elegant of horses, his mare is, I can see, built for endurance, with a powerful chest and front legs. She has that in common with Turnspit.

'What can you do with her?'

'Stand on her back while she canters. I've managed that. She'll dance, too. Take side steps, that sort of thing.'

I am about to ask him if he'll show me, but at that moment we come to a wide woodland ride and he lets out a whoop.

'Beat you to the end!'

He takes off at a gallop. Bessie does her best to keep up, and I'm proud of her for trying. Life is much slower if you're a working horse from Goldhanger. She's not used to being given her head.

Fitz pulls on the reins, bringing his mare to a standstill. As soon as I catch up, he gestures with his thumb back along the ride. Turnspit is bowling along, tongue and ears flapping, his bowed forelegs working hard to keep up.

'We'd better let him have a rest,' Fitz says, trying not to laugh. 'He looks ready to explode.'

He leads the way to a birch glade where the sun filters through the leaves to dapple the ground.

'Let's tie up here,' he says. 'I bet you're hungry. Turnspit certainly is. Just look at him!'

Ever since catching us up, the dog has trotted directly below the dangling saddlebag. Now he waits with quiet desperation, his tongue flicking out to lick his chops every two seconds.

'You'll just have to wait, Turnspit,' I tell him. 'Begging will get you nowhere.'

We tie the horses, and Fitz stamps down some bracken to make a springy carpet while I unpack the saddlebag and lay out bread, gammon, ewe's cheese and pickled onions. Fruit loaf, sliced thick and spread with yellow butter, will serve as pudding. We tuck in, munching in comfortable silence, every now and then passing the flagon of ale to each other. Turnspit has plenty of food, though I'm sure he thinks he isn't getting his fair share.

Fitz tosses him the fat off his gammon. 'He'd eat the lot if he could.'

'You need to watch him. He's not above thieving.' Affronted, the dog turns his back on me. 'Sorry, Turnspit, but you know it's true.'

Fitz reaches forward and tugs one of his ears. 'Don't sulk. It's in your nature, that's all she means. She's sorry to cause offence, aren't you, Dela.'

'I won't be if he grabs the gammon out of my hand.'

When we've finished eating, we lie on the bracken and look up at the sky through silvery leaves. I can hear a woodpecker's laughing call and catch a flash of green as it flits across the glade. We're close but not touching, and I have the taut feeling again. It's as though everything in the wood is holding its breath and listening – trees, birds, insects – waiting for something to happen. Then his hand reaches for mine and we twine our fingers.

Hesitantly, he asks, 'You're not sorry about last night?'

'No,' I say quietly. 'You?'

He turns on his side, leaning on an elbow to watch my face. 'Of course not.'

'What about Lucretia?'

'She'll get over it.'

I don't say it, but I'm not at all sure she will.

I'm relieved when he doesn't break away from my gaze. We need to be honest with each other. He could have in-sisted there was nothing in it – that he hadn't noticed the tumbler's feelings for him.

'I never toyed with her, you know,' he says. 'We jested, that's all. Like siblings, nothing more … I didn't know her feelings went deeper.'

He reaches out and takes a stray curl in his fingers, then touches my face hesitantly, stroking a forefinger across the slant of my cheekbone. I dare to turn my head and meet his eyes, and when I see the expression in them it occurs to me that the artist in him is trying to memorise my features, the planes of my face. But then his gaze deepens to one of longing: the same scorching need I had seen in his eyes when he came to my door earlier. It seems as if he wants to consume me, and it scares me just a little, but then the warm glow builds in my stomach and rises to my throat, and it is nothing like fear. He moves towards me, and I close my eyes, waiting for his kiss …

Turnspit, however, has other ideas. Clearly feeling left out, he inserts himself between us to lie his full length, using his strong forepaws to burrow a passage until we are forced to let go of each other's hands.

I flush, embarrassed, thinking how silly I must have looked with my eyes closed and lips puckered for a kiss only to be slavered over by a *dog* … but then Fitz throws back his head and laughs. I can't help but join in, and, although the moment we had is quite broken, this new one is just as good.

He scratches the little crown of hair on the head of Turnspit who gives a gusty sigh of satisfaction. 'I think he considers it his duty to act as chaperone.'

And that makes us laugh again … and kiss, reaching across Turnspit … then laugh once more when the dog gives a sigh.

'You know,' says Fitz afterwards, 'sometimes I think he has an extraordinary understanding for a dog.'

I scratch Turnspit's back and he rolls over, offering his belly. 'It's been like that from the start. I've had this strange feeling that he's always known me. And I'm sure he does understand things folk say. Don't you, Turnspit.' This is met by his pike-like grin, but that is only because I'm tickling his stomach.

Fitz hesitates, choosing his next words. 'I know you don't like to speak about it, but do you think your thing with animals is some sort of magic or just a talent you have?'

I remember how defensive I was on first meeting Fitz, when he asked me if I was a witch. Now that I trust him, I no longer feel prickly at the question.

'I suppose I've always had an instinct with them, so it makes it easier to see when they're ill or just trying to tell you something. If a dog is barking, most folk don't know if it's from anger or from fear ... or if it's warning you or just plain hungry. I've always known, you see. And animals know that I know. Which makes them simple to train and much easier to treat if they're sick.'

Fitz watches me avidly, his face bright with curiosity. 'I see that, but how do you get dogs in a pack to do what you want? Or a flock of birds? That's well out of the ordinary. Beyond anything I can understand.'

I hesitate, realising I have been avoiding that part of it. 'I can't *make* them do anything. What happened those few times really frightened me. I'm terrified it'll happen again. I can't control it.'

'Why do you think it happens when it does?'

'I don't know ... but it seems to be when I'm scared and furious. That's the mix of feelings that seem to stir them up. And sometimes, too, when they're being hurt and I'm upset about it.'

Fitz grins. 'So there you have it. Nothing to be fearful about, really. You just need to remember that it only happens for the very best reasons and ignore any mean-spirited types who want to punish you for it. Don't ever let them make you feel ashamed.'

Relieved, and thankful for his comment, I move on. 'Enough about me. My turn now.'

He groans, remembering our bartering of questions at Woodham Walter Hall.

I realise I know very little about Fitz. And, because of that, the questions tumble out of me: 'Where do you come from? Do you have parents? ... brothers? ... sisters?'

'All right ... Let's get it over with. I was born in Sudbury. My parents are dead. I'm an only child.'

'Like me.'

'That's right.'

'You must have had plenty of time on your own. No wonder you're so good at drawing.'

He frowns, ignoring my compliment. 'My mother didn't go out often. She kept me in my chamber much of the time.'

I wait, without trying to probe further. It's as if the lid of a chest has opened a crack and been put down again firmly. And while I want to share things – as sweethearts do – I understand that some feel safer keeping their tender feelings to themselves, locked away safely. Maybe, being a lad, he has grown a habit of strengthening the walls around his heart – fearing that should he show weakness he will be the lesser for it.

Fitz breaks the silence, moving to safer ground. 'Tell me about Goldhanger. I liked what I saw of it. Were you born there?'

I tell him about Barrow Farm and the years before I was eleven – years that seem like a dream now. I realise as I unpack these memories that they have been filtered until they are a trickle of rich sweetness, full of sunshine and good things. I can tell that Fitz is entranced, and it pleases me.

Like an idiot, I move onto more painful ground, even though I know it will break the mood. But I want no secrets between us. I broach the subject of my father's involvement with the yeoman farmer, Robert Kett. That summer of the rebellion four years ago is a memory fraught with pain, but I need to know Fitz's reaction to it. I am not ashamed that Pa wrote the pamphlet or that he stood up to be counted with Kett's men. Indeed, I'm *proud* of him for doing so, though it cost him his life. But I've realised that there will always be those who wish to shun me for being the daughter of a man executed for treason.

He tries to stop me when I begin to describe my mother's desperate attempt to gain clemency for my father. 'You don't have to do this.' He fidgets with a stalk of bracken.

'But I want to. It's better to tell you how it was. Then we need never speak of it again.'

He nods, a blankness to his face, and I continue, braving it out.

'She knew it was hopeless going to Tallon, but she went anyway. He hated my father ... thought he could get his hands on Barrow Farm.'

Fitz stares up at the sky, still as a stone effigy, hands linked behind his head.

Without knowing what he's thinking, I continue with my story, telling how Tallon let my mother make her case, all the while knowing he had signed the warrant for Pa's execution.

Fitz gets up suddenly, brushes the leaves off his breeches, and starts to pack away what is left of the food. 'We'd better go,' he mutters, without meeting my eyes. 'I'll get the horses.'

The sun retreats behind a cloud and a chill whisper of wind ruffles the birch leaves. The change in Fitz – so quick – and his rejection of me just when I reached the most painful part of my story is strange and hurtful.

'Fitz, wait! What's wrong? Something is, I know. It's Kett, isn't it.' I hate how plaintive my voice sounds, but I can't stop myself. 'You're disgusted that my father was in the rebellion, is that it?'

He continues to untie his mare's reins from a birch branch.

I sink my forehead to my knees when he doesn't answer, but a moment later he crouches down next to me. I raise my head, searching his face.

'It's not that.' His voice is gentle but remote, as if he is not connecting with his words. 'Your father was a brave man. You're lucky to have known him.'

We ride back in silence. I recognise bleakly how different it seems from the wordless contentment we shared when we set out this morning. Turnspit – often a weathervane when it comes to people's moods – detects the strain between us and hangs back, following a short distance behind.

We dismount in Stable Court and see to our horses, then Fitz follows me to the door of my chamber.

'I'm sorry,' he says awkwardly, his leg twitching as if he's desperate to run off. 'I know we need to talk. Not now, though. Tomorrow.'

I nod, wordlessly, thinking that by then an ocean of ice will have opened up between us.

The following afternoon I'm hard at work when Fitz walks into the bottling chamber, a small, cool space next to the dairy where I've been given a corner of the work-bench for my mortar. I see him at once, my eye catching the wheaten brightness of his hair just as I pour a little water from a green earthenware jug into my mixture. My heart starts to hammer, and there's anger as well as shame in the flush that creeps into my cheeks.

I hate the thought that he must have been dragging his feet with dread, knowing that he'd promised to explain himself – and to do it today. He's probably fearing I'll make a scene.

He walks to my workbench, and I am relieved not to see any sign of dread. His smile is apologetic, but his eyes light up on seeing me and there is nothing feigned in that.

He starts by telling me that Lady Mary's gelding is on the mend. 'The princess is pleased. I said I'd let you know.'

I've picked peppermint and chamomile from the physic garden for her colicky gelding. The horse – a grey – was King Henry's last gift to his daughter, and the prin-cess is picky about who's allowed to treat him.

'Thank you.' I can be as sparing with my words as he was yesterday.

He clears his throat, making no move to leave. 'Dela … I'm sorry.'

I nod, raising my eyes briefly from my mortar. He proceeds to explain his actions, and I sense he has the script learned by heart.

'I do not believe your father was anything but honourable, I want you to know that.' He puts a hand on my arm, and my skin shivers at his touch. 'It was a shock to hear how your family was treated. That's all it was ...' His voice tails away.

I raise my eyes to his and feel at once as if I'm being swept away, like a twig dropped from a bridge into a swift-flowing stream.

'Forgive me?' he says, giving his twist of a smile. 'Can we forget that it ever happened?'

I gaze up at him, already lost. 'Yes.' I breathe the word in a whisper, then, before I can say anything else, he bends to kiss me.

Later, a little voice in my head – an insinuating worm – tells me I'm a coward. *Admit it, Dela. You know he's still keeping something from you.*

But I don't want to think about that, so I choose to pretend everything is all right. I tell myself he'll share his secrets when he's ready.

CHAPTER 14

A storm breaks the spell of hot weather and for the next three days it rains so heavily that most of the household stays indoors. The horses whinny from their stalls, complaining at the lack of exercise, and upstairs in the privy chamber Mary and her ladies wait out the downpour, fractious and nervous by turns.

I'm pleased to be out of the fetid palace with its windows firmly closed against the wet. Splitting my day between the kennels and the stables, I nip out occasionally to pick herbs in the short breaks between showers. Fitz and I meet when we can, like a couple of poachers watching out for the gamekeeper. Neither of us has admitted anything to Lucretia, and I know we both feel shame in that.

Turnspit, who views our growing intimacy with approval, has moved from self-appointed chaperone to warner. Whenever we manage to steal away to our bench in the tack room the dog takes up position outside the door, giving a sharp bark if anyone approaches.

On the morning of the fourth day, the household bestirs itself. A messenger from Baron Rich of Leez brings word that he and a party of guests would like to pay their respects to the Lady Mary. The men are staying at one of Rich's hunting lodges, not far from New Hall. Everyone in Essex knows of Richard Rich; we call him the greedy baron. He owns great tracts of land he bagged for himself after the monasteries fell, including Leez Priory, a little north of here. The princess sends back her reply, begging the pleasure of welcoming him and his guests to a drive hunt in her park on the morrow.

I join the grooms and kennel hands in a great surge of activity. Although I hate the thought of a hunt, it is a welcome change from the melancholy that's hung over the palace in the past couple of days. As if in concert with the general change in mood, the rainclouds move off, letting the sun warm the brick floor of Stable Court till it steams.

I help Fitz move the wooden bench out of the tack room so that we can sit against the courtyard wall. We close our eyes and tilt our faces to the sun.

'You'll be brown as a nut by the time summer's done.' He flicks my bare arm. 'The browner you get, the less likely you'll be invited to join the ladies again.'

I give a snort. 'After the last time, that's never going to happen.'

His hand caresses my arm, making light circles on my skin with fingers dark as a tanner's from polishing saddles. I'm aware of nothing else, and the pulse of my wrist flutters under his touch. Here with him, with the sun on my face, I feel perfectly content, as if nothing bad could ever happen.

A moment later our peace is broken by the head groom, who walks briskly through the archway into the stableyard. A small man with brown wrinkled skin like an old apple, he favours me for being a horse-lover, one who understands his animals.

He claps his hands. 'Come on, you two, look sharp! Lady Mary's coming. Wants to see her gelding.' He winks at me. 'She'll be wanting to thank a certain person.'

The princess strokes the velvet nose of her gelding. He nuzzles at her palm, then breaks off to nip and butt at the girdle chain round her waist, lips pulled back from his long yellow teeth.

'Ah, Querido, you know exactly where I keep it, don't you!'

Laughing, she removes a sliver of sugar from the purse that hangs from her girdle chain. Expensive stuff to be feeding a horse – no ordinary servant is permitted near the sugar loaves locked in the confectioner's cupboard. With it, I worry that Querido's colic will return, but in Lady Mary's mind nothing is too good for her beloved gelding, though his stomach may have something to say about that.

As she stands in Stable Court next to the horse, I real-ise she's barely taller than him, so thin and slight that she must feel a feather on his back. Most of her ladies choose sweet-natured palfreys, but I guess such a horse wouldn't suit Mary's spirit. Maybe, when he picked out the geld-ing for her, King Henry recognised something bold and intense in his daughter – uncrushable qualities inherited from Mary's pious and unyielding mother, Catherine, as well as from his own headstrong nature.

Her fifteen-year-old favourite, the laughing-eyed Mistress Dormer, stands next to the princess. I think of the afternoon in the withdrawing chamber when she

witnessed the dogfight. Glancing at Turnspit, I am pleased
to see that he is behaving himself, sitting straight as a pike-
staff at my feet. I wonder if he's trying to prove a point
after their last encounter.

'So the colic has improved?' Lady Mary asks the head
groom. 'Is he quite recovered?'

'Pulse is quieter, my lady. Sweating's gone and his
breathing's not so fast,' he replies. 'You'll remember he was
pawing the ground and trying to roll? He's stopped that,
thanks to Mistress Wisbey.'

'I must say, the horse does seem in better spirits.' She
smiles at me and, abashed, I drop a little curtsey. 'Don't
you think he looks well, Mistress Dormer?'

'I do, my lady. But weren't you saying that you don't
intend to ride tomorrow?'

'I was. And I am not.' The princess rubs her temples,
and her features rearrange themselves into a furrowed expression of pain. 'My head hurts too much.' She resumes
stroking Querido, then adds: 'You can go. It'll give you a
chance to wear that new hat.'

Mistress Dormer's expression brightens. 'My lady, do
you know who the baron's bringing?'

'Oxford, I know that. And the dreaded Tallon will be
with him, no doubt. What a basket of snakes that will be.'
The princess gives a tired smile. 'I warrant they've been
sent by Northumberland to spy on me.'

My head swims. Why hadn't I thought of this before?
I should have known there was a risk Tallon would come.
I sway on my feet, take a breath to steady myself.

'Are you all right, girl?'

'She's pale. Maybe she's sick,' says Mistress Dormer.

The princess's face is a blur. She reaches out to grasp my arm, and my turmoil grows.

'It's talk of Tallon that's done it. She's scared because she set a flock of ravens on him.' The princess raises my chin with her forefinger. 'Am I right? Is this about him? Look at me, girl.'

I meet her eyes and an understanding passes between us. She lets go of my arm.

'Stay inside the palace tomorrow,' she says to me, quietly. 'Don't even think of going with the grooms to the meet, even if they need extra hands for the horses.'

I nod, but she reads the fear in my eyes.

'He won't know you're here. But even if he does, he won't dare touch you. Not under my roof.'

I wish I had her confidence.

I run to find Fitz. He is in the tack room, tidying the bridles and harnesses. He drops what he is doing the moment he reads the distress on my face.

'Have you heard?' I collapse onto the bench.

He sits down beside me. He doesn't touch me but gnaws on a thumbnail, elbows on knees. His hair falls over his eyes, and I wonder, not for the first time, if he uses it as a screen to hide behind.

'Tallon's coming to the hunt.' I press my hands together, holding them between my knees to stop them trembling.

'I heard.' He gets to his feet. 'Dela ... there's something I must tell you ...' He takes my hands.

'What is it?' I knew there's something he was keeping from me. I've tried to pretend everything is all right – that we are sweethearts who trust each other completely – and there's been a part of me that's despised myself for it.

He brings my hands to his face and presses them to his cheek. As he takes a breath to tell me, I glance up and see Lucretia. Breathless with running, she stands in the doorway, her green eyes wide with shock as she takes in the sight of us together. She gasps, and he opens his eyes, quickly dropping my hands. But it is too late for that.

Her face reddens, and at the same time a blush of shame spreads over my cheeks. Fitz and I have been creeping about like thieves. She must have noticed. The tumbler may be a jester, but she's no fool.

'How could you do this to me!' Her eyes spit green fire.

I manage to bleat, 'I'm sorry ...' but Fitz interrupts.

'Lettie, it wasn't her fault.'

This only make things worse.

She looks from him to me, then to him again, holding her red cheeks as if she has a toothache. 'You said we'd never have secrets. I'm family to you, Fitz, remember? Better than family, because it's the one we choose. You said that. Did it mean nothing?'

'We were going to tell you ... we didn't want to hurt you.'

His explanation sounds lame, and he knows it. I wish Fitz hadn't said 'we' – it'll only make Lucretia think we're in league against her. I see in her eyes a desire to hurt, and when she speaks, her voice is rough-edged, its accent more pronounced than usual.

'Why should I be surprised that you're a *farfallone*? A skirt-chaser ... a liar.'

He freezes like a coney caught in the light of a lantern.

At his reaction, Lucretia's pinched face shows a sour victory. 'He's just like his father. Isn't that right, Fitz?'

He holds out a hand to stop her. 'Don't …'

'The *frutta* doesn't fall far from the tree.'

'Lucretia …' His voice is strangled, doesn't sound his own. He grabs her shoulder.

She twists out of his grasp. 'Don't you dare come near me!' Her eyes are hard and sharp as flints. 'Ask him who his father is, Dela. Go on, ask him!'

He won't meet my eyes. Something earth-shattering lies between us, and it will take only one word more for the ground to split open and swallow me whole.

I back out of the tack room, looking from one to the other in dread lest either of them should say that word.

CHAPTER 15

I curl up on my side under my bedsheet, knees to my chest. I want my head to be empty, but thoughts keep knocking, clamouring to get in. I put my hands over my ears as if that might help. Sensing my despair, Turnspit is ill at ease, pacing the flagstone floor, and at some point he takes up position as sentinel at my door.

I don't leave my chamber to go to supper. Lucretia's words have shattered me, and yet she never even finished what she had to say. If Fitz were to touch me now, I'd break into a thousand pieces.

I ignore the quiet knock at my door. Hearing his voice, I remain curled up tight.

'Please, Dela, let me explain ... It's not what you think.' He's quiet, but there's an urgency in his tone.

I walk to the door, place my mouth to it. 'Is it him? Tallon?'

Neither of us breathes. The world has stopped turning, I'm sure it has.

'Please. I need to explain ... Open the door.'

My heart thuds in my chest. I have to answer or he won't go away. 'Leave me. There's nothing you can say.'

If I'd sounded angry he might have tried harder, but he must have read the deadness in my tone. It is this, I'm sure, that persuades him to go.

His footsteps on the brick floor of the courtyard grow faint till I can't hear him any more. Only then do I fold up piece by piece, until I'm curled next to Turnspit.

A banging on the door rouses me from a sleep of troubled dreams. I must have found my way to bed at some point in the night.

'Dela, please! You've got to let me in!'

Turnspit stands my side of the door, wagging his tail.

I let Lucretia in, without knowing if she's looking for a fight or wants to make things right with me. I want to get in first, tell her I'm sorry, but she doesn't give me the chance.

'Don't say anything. Not a word!'

She paces back and forth, refusing to sit down. Her eyes are red; I can tell she hasn't slept.

'It's Fitz! We need to stop him!' She gabbles a broken string of words, half of them Italian. I grab her arm in a bid to get her to speak more slowly, but she wails, 'Oh, what have I done!' and bursts into tears. 'I wanted to hurt you … and him. Oh, Dela, how could I? … I knew what Tallon had done to Fitz's mother, and how horribly he'd bullied him.'

Hastily grabbing my smock and kirtle, I throw them on. 'Where is he? What happened?'

'I couldn't sleep so I went to his chamber,' she says. 'I was scared … didn't want to lose him. I thought, what if he won't speak to me? I wanted to say *mi scuso* – but he wasn't there! … I knew something was wrong.'

Lucretia tells me she ran down to the stables and found him saddling the Barbary mare.

'I grabbed the bridle, but –' her voice cracks '– he raised his whip to hit me.'

'Did he say where he was going?' I pull on my boots, fumble with the strings of my cap. 'Please don't say the hunt.'

'He said it needs to be done.'

'What?' I have her by the shoulder, shake her till her hair loosens from its pins and tumbles down her back. For a moment – just a flash – I see a river of rust-coloured blood. 'Lucretia! *What* needs to be done?'

'He's going to kill his father.'

Turnspit leads the way as Bessie canters out of the stable-yard. In my hurry, I haven't tightened the girth properly and my saddle keeps slipping, though not enough to unseat me. I give no thought to Lady Mary's advice to stay out of sight. How could I? Whatever Fitz has done – whoever his father is – none of it matters now. My lips move with snippets of prayers as Bessie's hooves gallop along the rutted turf. The hunting party must have set out at first light. I can see their hoof-marks on the dusty track.

Turnspit stops and sniffs the breeze. I pull Bessie to a halt behind him. Catching the whiff of something, he growls low in his throat, hunching his shoulders.

I let him take the lead, and he threads his way through the trees, upwind of the hunters and their greyhounds. I realise he aims to come at them from the rear, where they are least likely to spot us. My heart batters at my ribs. I don't even know what I'll do when we come upon them. What if fate is playing me a nasty trick and sends me straight into Tallon's hands?

Turnspit picks up his paws one at a time, putting them

down soundlessly. He freezes like a statue if he hears a noise – Bessie taking her lead from him, not even crunching on her bit – and leads us to a spot behind a thicket of brambles. The hunt party is about fifty yards away. I can hear the tinkle of women's laughter, the strident voices of the men. It is a moment before I pick out the figures – the greens and browns of their riding clothes blend into the colours of the forest so cleverly that it allows them to hide in plain sight.

My eyes scan the group looking for Fitz, but I can't see him. Then my gaze settles on the three men at the edge of the gathering, nearest to me. Each has a muscled leg thrust forward, hand on the heavy crossbow at his belt. Greyhounds stand at their side, eyes fixed on their masters' face.

The stocky one in the centre I guess to be Lord Rich. To his right, the man with grey hair, his greedy eyes fixed on Mistress Dormer, must be the Earl of Oxford. The third is Tallon. Tall and unmistakable, the gleaming waves of black hair, the proud set of his head … then he half turns, and I see the side of his face, disfigured by the pits and scars the birds have gouged in it. Everything else in the forest fades to nothing; all I hear is the blood rushing in my ears.

As if he feels my eyes upon him, his head flicks round, hand tightening on the crossbow hooked to his belt. Has he seen us? Turnspit's hackles rise, but he makes no sound.

Just then I spot Fitz behind a stand of birches. No sign of his mare. He moves stealthily in the direction of the group, sword drawn. Suddenly he breaks cover, and, as he does so, Turnspit dashes to block his way. A gasp from the ladies, then Fitz makes a dart at his father. On seeing his son, Tallon's face freezes in shock.

Turnspit will not let Fitz past. He marks him, blocking his

steps every time the boy moves. I cannot hide in the trees any longer, and with a nudge to Bessie we canter into the open.

'Fitz! Don't!'

He turns in shock just as Tallon pulls the string of his crossbow into lock and raises the bow, aiming the bolt at me.

'Dela! Watch out!' Fitz leaps into the breach just as his father looses the bolt. With a hiss, the missile reaches its target – only it is not the one Tallon aimed at.

'Fitz!' I shriek.

He clamps a hand to his shoulder with a look of surprise, then as the pain hits he crumples to his knees.

Tallon struggles to load another bolt in his crossbow. Fearing he'll lose me, he clicks his fingers at the greyhounds. 'Go! Get her!'

Three dogs dart in my direction, thin legs moving in a blur of speed. Bessie screams and tosses her head, the whites of her eyes rolling in panic. I see bone-white faces, the jags of their teeth. They'll be tearing into her in a moment.

My head spins and I almost fall from the saddle. *Oh God, what have I done?* The forest whispers with a flurry of leaves and the whisper grows into an angry storm, twigs and branches shaking in tune with my fury. At Tallon … at myself.

It is white-hot rage, not fear, that makes me shriek.

The greyhounds stop in their tracks. They cringe, ears flat against the sides of their narrow skulls. Eyes fixed on me, they tilt their heads, cocking their ears as if waiting for some silent command.

Then they're away, racing back to their masters. No longer submissive, they dash at the three men wildly, with a volley of high-pitched barks so deafening that the ladies cover their ears. From all over the clearing the other sighthounds rally to the call of the three dogs.

The pack bunches, then leaps at Tallon and his friends, going for their faces. The men shield their heads with their arms as the force of the dogs topples them.

Amidst the screams and frenzy, in the quiet eye of the storm, Fitz is crumpled, motionless, on the forest floor. He is on his knees, head slumped to his chest, a crimson stain spreading slowly across his fawn-coloured jerkin. I urge Bessie forward, but Turnspit comes hurtling at us, barking loudly with such authority that the mare stops in her tracks and wheels round. I tug her rein to pull her back again, desperate to get to Fitz, but she ignores my command and canters into the trees, following the dog. All I can do is look helplessly over my shoulder as I wail Fitz's name.

It is hours later when we return to the palace. Even in my shocked state I knew it would be too dangerous to go straight back there. We hid deep in the woods, and I prayed to the Holy Mother hour after hour while Turnspit lay across my feet.

'*Sancta Maria*, don't let Fitz die. I'll do anything if you'll only save his life.'

It is late afternoon when we slip into the stableyard. The head groom hurries out at the sound of hooves on the brick floor and takes Bessie by the bridle while I dismount. As we lead her to the water trough, he darts a nervous glance over his shoulder.

'How is Fitz?' I ask. 'Tell me he lives.'

'I haven't heard. He was breathing when they brought him in.' He places a hand on my shoulder. 'The lad's young. Strong.'

'Where is he?'

'Mistress Clarencieux has him in her chamber. Doctor Scurloch is with him.'

'Do you think they'll let me see him?'

Sympathy softens the eyes of the wiry little man, but I don't want any of it. I just want to see Fitz.

He chooses his words carefully. 'They're not of a mind to be kind to you … It's not safe for you here.'

My lip trembles. I've heard those same words from Ned, and only now do I realise the full truth of them. There is nowhere in this world that will ever be safe for me.

'You must go,' he says. 'Lady Mary wants to see you. I'll look after Bessie.'

I find myself in the same quiet writing closet where I had to face the princess before. This time it will not turn out well.

She is seated at her table, but not alone this time: Mistress Clarencieux stands beside her. The lady-in-waiting is diminished somehow, as if her small round figure has been punctured. I expect vindictiveness from her but can read nothing of that sort in her red-rimmed eyes. I recall how she favoured Fitz, her eyes softening whenever she spoke to him.

It is the princess who is livid, barely managing to contain her fury.

'I wish they had hunted you down, put you – and us – out of our misery.'

I flinch but say nothing.

'I gave you succour, girl. A roof over your head … friends, when you had nobody. Is this how you think to repay me? By using witchcraft to get the hounds to attack their masters? These men will use any excuse to have me locked up, and you've just handed it to them.'

My knees, dipped in a curtsey, tremble with the strain. The desire to ask if Fitz lives is so strong that it overrides any other feeling.

'My lady ... the groom, Master Fitzjohn. Does he live?'

At the sound of his name, Mistress Clarencieux hides her face in her hands, attempting to stifle her sobs.

So that's it then. He must be dead.

The princess ignores my question, and in refusing to answer I realise how great she deems my fall from grace. Nothing I say will move her, nothing will she hear.

'Listen, witch, I will spare your life, but that is all. Leave now, with nothing more than the clothes on your back. You will not return to your chamber or take your horse. The dog will stay here at New Hall, work in the kitchens.'

I give a gasp, wring my hands. Turnspit seems to understand, because he gives a little whine and flattens his ears.

'Please don't punish him. He's done no wrong.'

'He can turn the spit, as he was bred to do,' says the princess. 'He has no place being anywhere else, just as your kind have no place among the God-fearing. To think that I gave you a home! ... But now I know that your witchcraft is the devil's own work. It could bring peril on us all.'

She dips her head to study the parchment on the table, making it clear she never wants to look at my face again. I remain in my half-curtsey, trembling.

But she has one last thing to say, and she does it without raising her face:

'If you ever dare come near me or my attendants again, I will have you killed.'

3

A Fight for
the Throne

Chapter 16

Cloak Lane, Walbrook, London, July 1553

It is midnight. St John's has just tolled the hour, and for a moment I think I'm back at Ned's, hearing the bell in St Peter's watchtower calling the men to the jetty. I sit up in bed, thinking there must be a ship foundering on the rocks out at Mersea; I'm in that strange channel between sleeping and waking where dreams swim like fish, too slippery to hold. Then I remember where I am and what I've lost, and a sharp skewer of pain runs through me. Every morning since I got to London two weeks ago I've had to suffer it, and it never gets any easier. Fitz … Turnspit. I've lost them both, and it's my fault, all of it. The bolt from Tallon's crossbow was meant for me; Turnspit is caged in a wheel because of me.

I get out of bed and walk to the window. It still feels strange having floorboards under my bare feet rather than beaten earth. On the other side of Cloak Lane, the dark square bulk of the church's crenellated tower hides the moon. I draw little comfort from its presence, no more than I've been able to find solace in prayer, finding myself entirely numb, except in those moments on waking when the skewer through my chest reminds me I'm alive.

Lucretia's glover uncle, Signore Alfredo Pisanelli, took me in. It was he who told me the streets aren't usually so empty. Even during the day, it is an unwholesome, sullen sort of quiet where folk keep to their houses much of the time. Those who are out on business walk quickly, heads lowered so they do not have to meet each other's eyes. Yesterday, when I returned from my daily walk to the wharf, I said to Alfredo that men seemed to be crossing the street to avoid each other. 'They are fearful,' he explained. 'Northumberland's agents swarm through the city. Cockroaches in the cracks. The duke has told them to arrest anyone who dares speculate that Edward is dead.

'The horse dung the duke shovels at us!' he went on. 'You saw that notice on St John's door, saying the king feels better ... walks in his gardens ... picks a rose ... *mio culo*! What lies! The boy is clearly dying. And that *coglione* wonders why we can't trust each other.'

It is true that the duke has made a grave error in treating Londoners as if they have cloth ears and not a brain in their heads. An anger simmers in the streets, yet Northumberland continues to spin falsehoods that any child can see through. He's buying time, pretending the king is getting better, while he shores up his own position. At all times of day, we hear the marching feet of soldiers and the heavy rumble of gun carriages on Cornhill. Even a fifteen-year-old marsh girl can guess that the duke is readying himself in case Mary should rise up to claim the throne. And still he tries to contain us like flies in a box. The city gates are opened later in the mornings and closed earlier at night, hours before the nine o'clock curfew bell tells folk to put out their fires and get to bed. He has us penned in.

I open my window and inhale the night air, smelling as I do so a slight whiff of rot from the street. It makes me think of the king's bloated body, and a picture comes into my mind – that of a dead seal Rob and I once found floating in a marsh pool, greenish-black and puffed to twice its size.

The glover tells me all kinds of things when I'm bent over my stitching. He said that Cloak Lane would have reeked a whole lot worse in the days before the Wall Brook was paved over, when it used to run like an open sewer past St John's. He told me the lane took its name from the Latin word *cloaca*.

'Romans built this city. Never forget that, *piccolina*. My countrymen … were … here … first.' He leaned over to tap my forehead at each word as if that might help the fact of it sink into my brain. 'Do you know your Latin? Or are you an ignoramus?'

I said I knew a little Latin, but that I was definitely an ignoramus.

'Hah! At least you're clever enough to admit it. *Cloaca* means sewer, *cara*. Ditch of stinking water.'

I poke my head out of the window and listen. I'm sure I can hear the noise of the brook running beneath the lane. Alfredo also told me that there used to be a wooden bridge next to the church, dismantled many years ago – Horseshoe Bridge, it was called. The name hovers in my mind like a ghost, and I take a drop of comfort in that tiny thread that binds me to Ned.

The glover says it was the skinners who made the Wall Brook foul from washing their hides in the stream all those years ago. His daughter Elisa has married a skinner – a rich alderman. The Skinners' Hall is further down the hill, a grand building that I pass on my way to the wharf on those afternoons when I follow the course of the hidden brook until it gushes in a brown torrent into the Thames at Dowgate. The river draws me to it, with its wherries weaving back and forth under London Bridge, while barges move up and down majestically, their rust-coloured sails barely flapping in the hot, still air. Standing at the wharf, I close my eyes and listen to the gulls, trying to pretend I'm at the edge of Goldhanger Creek, looking across to the little island of Osea. Soon my face becomes wet from a slow and steady leak of tears, though I'm unaware I've even been crying.

Signore Pisanelli calls me *faccialunga*: long face. He says it to make me smile, and I do – but only because he reminds me so much of Lucretia with his red hair and green eyes. 'We are as like as a pair of gloves,' he admitted when I commented upon their similarity.

He knows my story, and how his niece saved me when I stood outside New Hall thinking everything was lost. She darted through the gates like a flame-haired sprite and handed me a purse, saying, 'Here's money to get you to London. A ring, too. Give it to my uncle Alfredo. His house is next to the Tallow Chandlers' Hall. You can't miss it – he flies a flag with the red fleur-de-lys of Firenze from the gable. He'll look after you, *mia poveretta*.'

And he has, with a generosity of spirit as abundant as that of his niece.

On the ground floor of Alfredo Pisanelli's big, comfortable house is his shop where he measures and fits gloves for customers. The large window facing onto Cloak Lane has the benefit of catching the eye of churchgoers on their way to the services at St John's. His gloves, made from Witney doe-skin whitened and softened with pot-ash alum, are so fine that only the richest merchants and nobles can afford them.

Signore Pisanelli mostly concerns himself with paying court to important customers, as well as any task that requires special artistry and imagination. He is often to be found dipping into his strongbox of precious gems like a bright-eyed jackdaw or laying spirals of precious metal in flamboyant fern-like curls on the cuff of a hawking glove, after which one of the girls sews them to the leather with couching stitches.

'It will be good for you to learn the glover's trade, *faccialunga*,' he told me on my first day in his workshop. 'I'll teach you all the stitches. And put you in stitches with my jests.'

He is fond of wordplay, taking such delight in it that he often has to stop whatever he is engaged in to mop at his green eyes with a kerchief.

It turns out that the glover is right. Learning my round and prix stitches for the seams has been the best thing for me. With my brain taken up in this way, there is little space to brood over Fitz and Turnspit.

It is thus with some relief that I enter the workshop this morning. The chamber lies at the back of the shop and is almost entirely taken up with a cutting bench down the side wall and a stitchers' table under a back window that looks out onto a small walled garden. The two embroiderers he employs need as much natural light as they can glean, candles being not only expensive but ruinous to the eyes. Sometimes, on a still, bright day the girls take their sewing boxes outside.

Today I can tell that the glover is in an especially talkative mood. As he bends over Colin, the apprentice, the thumb of his left hand is hooked into the pocket of his red silk-damask doublet while the forefinger of the other points to the piece of doe-skin the tow-headed boy has just cut out. Master and apprentice are as different as it is possible to imagine: Alfredo, a sprightly peacock of a man; Colin, solid as a Saxon farmer, with a pink-and-white complexion and a slow, shy smile. At first glance, the boy seems a most unlikely type to be a glover, but his large, meaty hands are surprisingly deft.

'Aha! *Faccialunga* has joined us at last!'

I bid them both good morning and take a seat at the stitchers' table under the window. A few days ago, if I had been the last into the workshop, Alfredo's greeting would have made me colour in shame, but then he had taken me aside – 'No arguments, *ragazza*. Red eyes need sleep, else you will stitch your thumb to the leather' – and ordered me to stay in bed for an extra hour in the mornings.

The two girls seated beside me are twins from Florence, Alfredo's home city. Like Colin, they work quietly, seeming to communicate without the need for words, handing thread or pins without so much as a glance at each other. It makes me wonder if my silent talk with animals is so very strange after all.

The glover comes over to sit at our work table. Bright-eyed, he tilts his head the better to see my stitches. He makes me think of a boisterous robin as he perches on a stool in his red doublet.

He gestures to the pair of gloves to which the twins are putting the finishing touches. 'For the Duke of Northumberland. The great Lord Protector. Pah! The *coglione*!'

'He still hasn't paid, Signore Pisanelli?' I ask.

'No. But if he asks, I make. You don't refuse, even when he says to the merchants, "Put your money in my war chest. Fifty thousand pounds, if you please." That *coglione*!' He thumps a fist to his red breast. 'The *nobili* in my city are not like this! In Firenze they pay artists to paint, *architetti* to build. And you English? Pah! You blow things up! Gunpowder, that's what you like. Poof!'

I know when he says 'you English' he doesn't really mean me. With my dark curls, he forgets I'm not a Florentine like him. I venture to ask him why, if he despises the English so much, he has made his home in London. I regret my question immediately, stammering an apology when his eyes fill with tears.

'Italians are not afraid to cry. Not like you English brickheads. You ask why I stay? Love … *amore*.' He sighs and wipes his eyes. 'I fell in love with an Englishwoman, but she died and broke my heart. Left me a beautiful daughter – my Elisa. So I stayed for her. Now she is married, but it is too late to go home.'

We have a pause, while the glover checks on Colin's progress at the cutting bench, but it isn't long before he's back and engaged upon his favourite subject.

'Your countrymen are good-for-nothings, *faccialunga*. Every one of them. They kill deer, eat too much, get gout. That is all they do. How can you run a country like this?'

He chuckles. 'The de Medicis know how to run things. A *fiorentino* uses his head. *Mio nonno* made the gloves of Niccolo Machiavelli, did I tell you that?'

He has told me on several occasions, and by now I feel I know a few of Machiavelli's ideas. The Florentine statesman had a very low opinion of people, it seems to me. If someone is not a greedy liar, he must be a foolish gull. But where honest God-fearing folk like Ned fit in I don't know.

When I make the point to the *signore*, he narrows his eyes and considers it carefully. 'A man has to be a fox ... to keep out of traps. There is a place for deception, *piccolina*.'

I have watched the glover when he hasn't known I've been looking. That I've done so doesn't make me a spy, merely a sleepless girl standing at her window in the thick of night. More than once, a man wrapped in a cloak with a hat low over his eyes has come to the door and given three quiet knocks. He then exchanges a packet with the *signore*, and something tells me the transaction has nothing to do with gloves.

Colin, the apprentice, and I take a break at midday in the courtyard garden. We perch on a bench under the mulberry tree in the middle, while the twins keep themselves to themselves, huddled together eating their bread at the far end.

Alfredo has left for the afternoon to visit one of his titled customers. 'A man,' he'd said, 'who is too fat and lazy to come to the shop.'

'Do the customers not take offence at his rudeness?' I ask Colin. 'You know, he reminds me so much of Lucretia, his niece.'

At her name the apprentice colours, his feelings making themselves plain on his pink-and-white cheeks. He takes a mouthful of bread and waits for the blush to die down. 'He can afford to say what he likes. If they don't care for it, he refuses to work for them. That soon stops their mouths.'

'Maybe they like his bluntness,' I say, thinking of the favour fools receive. 'A man likes to know where he stands.'

Colin nods, chewing thoughtfully on his bread. 'He likes to play it that way.'

'What do you mean?'

'What they see is but one part of the man. And he's grown rich on it.'

It doesn't surprise me that the glover is a man of parts, a subtle player. I think of the mysterious moonlight visitor, and it stops me from asking more.

CHAPTER 17

The next morning, the glover asks me if I would like to come with him to pay a visit to Sir William Cecil, the secretary of state. The *signore* has been asked to present himself in person to deliver a pair of embroidered gloves for a portrait sitting.

'Let us put a smile on your long chops, *faccialunga*,' he says, grasping my chin between his thumb and forefinger. 'An outing will blow the cobnuts away.'

I always find the glover's mistakes with words more amusing than when he actually tries to make a jest, but today I hardly notice, alert as I am to a change in him. He is wound a little tighter and talking faster than usual. I wonder if the secretary of state's summons doesn't concern something greater than a simple pair of dress gloves.

I change into the best of the clothes Elisa, Signore Pisanelli's daughter, has left folded in the wooden chest in my chamber. While the housemaid helps me to dress, lacing up a crisp white chemise and slipping a dark-green damask gown over my kirtle, my mind wonders what use I will be to Alfredo. I'm not so soft as to imagine that his only reason for taking me is to put roses in my cheeks. It feels like New Hall all over again: the pinch of grand clothes and mixing with high-born folk who are far from being my kind.

The glover tells me about Sir William as we walk to the wooden landing stage where the wherries pick up foot passengers. The secretary of state, he explains, likes to think he is a person important enough not to care two figs that the glover is below him in station. 'He tells me to come through the front door, bring my daughter, make myself at home while I fit him for his gloves.

'Pigwash, of course. The man says one thing, believes another. He is obsessed by rank.' He chuckles, nudging my arm with his elbow. 'But I will outfox him. I know he is up to something. I can smell it!'

So I am not the only one thinking that there is more to this outing than a pair of doe-skin gloves.

'He watches for a change in the wind.'

'How so, *signore*?'

'If a man knows his Machiavelli, he can read Cecil.'

Just then we have to step aside for a stable lad with a handcart of horse dung. I am watchful of my fine skirts and hold them out of harm's way, and only once we are again walking down the hill do I ask the glover if he means that Sir William is a slippery man.

'A clever one. He will use a person if he can.'

'How would he use you?'

'He knows I hear things. Courtiers spill secrets in my ears.' He lowers his voice as we reach the landing stage. 'Knowledge is power, *faccialunga*. Never forget it.'

I nearly ask the glover how he intends to use me, but find another way to put it: '*Signore*, how will I be of help to you?'

He smiles, and I notice one front tooth crosses over the other just like Lucretia's. 'I want you to play the fox. We will be foxes together. You will play the simple girl – the country girl who does not know Cecil is a wolf. *Comprendi?* Charm him with your sweetness, *piccola*, while I keep on the right side of him.'

All this talk of foxes and wolves exhausts me. I *am* a simple country girl, so why I should play at anything is beyond me.

Once we are out on the water, I raise my face to the sun and close my eyes, listening to the splosh of the oars and the creak they make in the rowlocks. Every so often, one of the watermen shouts as he steers his way through the river traffic. I let these sounds wash over my senses, thankful that the glover keeps silent until the wherry bumps the side of the landing stage at Whitehall. His excited state makes me nervous.

We make our way into New Palace Yard, skirting the Grand Conduit, a fountain topped by a gilded dome. Signore Pisanelli tells me it runs with wine whenever there's a coronation. 'We will get drunk, *cara*. Very, very soon.' He taps his nose. 'Say no more, eh? Or the *coglione* will have us arrested.'

Even at this early hour, New Palace Yard is bustling with statesmen who push past us in mantles that make their shoulders unnaturally broad. There are churchmen too, hands clasped at their waist, making their way to the north-west side of the court where the great stone abbey stands, its delicate finials needling the pale blue sky.

We head for an arched opening in the north wall. From here a passage leads us to Cannon Row, where we find Cecil's grand townhouse.

'Sir William likes it here with all the dukes and earls,' the *signore* tells me, leading the way up a flight of stone steps to the door. 'His *nonno* kept an inn at Stamford, did I tell you that? His enemies never let him forget it.'

We are shown into a wainscoted chamber by a page. Cool and dim, it affords immediate relief from the swelter outside – its dark corners lit by candles, and the casement window half-shuttered against the July heat. Two men are seated opposite each other at an oak table, an ivory chessboard between them. One of them, a strikingly handsome man with widely spaced intelligent eyes, gets to his feet and greets Signore Pisanelli warmly. The other, a small man with a lustrous copper-coloured beard, finishes his move, taking the queen with a flourish.

'Damn you, Throckmorton,' laughs the standing man, who I guess is Sir William. 'You wait till my back is turned, then rob me of my queen.'

'Your king is done for, my friend. You are finished.'

'You'll be finished if you don't watch what you say.'

I sense their teasing is part of a show put on for us, encouraging us to relax, lower our guard. Beside me, Alfredo gives a smart bow, bringing his gleaming boots together with a click. I give a passable curtsey, having had enough practice at New Hall not to make a mess of it.

Sir William looks me up and down. 'And who is this fair mistress? Your daughter, *signore*?'

The glover gives my name and explains that I am his daughter Elisa's friend from Essex who has come to assist him now that Elisa is not free do so.

The other man, Throckmorton, asks me which town in the county I'm from.

'Maldon, sir.' I keep my eyes lowered.

'Wasn't Maldon your seat a few years back?' Sir William asks his friend.

'It was.' Throckmorton's expression takes on a morbid cast. 'I didn't care for the damp air. Glad to be out of it.'

Sir William's cool grey eyes settle on me again. 'Though it doesn't seem as if the marshes have done you any harm, mistress.'

I do my best to play the simple country girl, giving the nearest to a dimpling smile I can manage. It seems to work, and the two statesmen look at me approvingly.

'So what is the news from Walbrook, glover?' asks Sir William. 'What are the good aldermen saying?'

'They are minding their words ... and minding their money, sir.'

Sir William taps the side of his nose. 'I understand you, *signore*. Say no more.'

Alfredo proceeds to take a silk-wrapped package from his bag, and the two men exclaim over its perfumed contents.

Sir William holds the heavily embroidered cuff of one of the white gloves close, the better to see the detail. 'There's fine work here. I'll pay you the honour of holding them when I sit for my portrait, good *signore*, as promised.'

'Pay me that honour by all means, sir, though pay me in coin if you will.'

'Ah, ever the wit, glover!'

Sir William clears his throat and fiddles with one of the ivory pawns. 'The thing is, Pisanelli, I need to know if we count on your loyalty. We'd like to speak freely.'

'I am a loyal man, sir. And I can speak for Mistress Wisbey. The girl can hold her tongue.'

'Good ... that's good.' Sir William glances at Throckmorton, who gives the barest tilt of his head. 'I wonder ...
did you hear what happened on Sunday, *signore?*'

'I saw the notice go up on the church door. Pray for
the king, it said.'

'That's right, and so we should.' Another pause. 'I suppose you've heard the rumours.'

'*Tsk*. There's a saying in Firenze – gossips need gloves,
to stop their wagging tongues.'

'That would soon fill your coffers, sirrah! I bet you
glovers put that one about. Anyway, these rumours of
which I was speaking – that the king is dead – they're false.
He lives. Sir Nicholas has just come from Greenwich, so
you have it from the horse's mouth.'

'We heard the king was seen at his window,' the glover
says, addressing himself to the red-bearded Throckmorton.

'You heard right. There was a great crowd outside the
palace to see him. A gentleman of the king's bedchamber
bade them go home, saying the air outside was too damp
for the king. But they didn't believe a word of it, wouldn't
leave till they'd seen Edward with their own eyes. In the
end, the gentleman had the king wave from the window.'

'*Bene, molto bene.*' Alfredo is all smiles.

'*Bene*, my foot. It's anything but *bene*,' exclaims Sir William irritably, tapping the tip of the queen's ivory crown
with his forefinger. 'The boy is little more than a cadaver.
They had to hold him up or he'd have fallen ... Anyway,
more importantly, none of this helped quell the rumours
... of poison and whatnot.'

There is another pause, during which Alfredo waits
patiently for one of the others to speak. Most folk I

know would prattle to fill the silence, but he seems quite at ease.

'Northumberland is giving out that Lady Mary's to blame for the king's illness,' says Sir William. 'Countering the whispers that he himself is poisoning Edward with that ridiculous rumour of his own.'

'How does he say she's to blame, sir?'

'Swears she cast her evil eye on her brother when she last came to visit. Of course, no educated man would believe it, not of the pious Lady Mary. It's unimaginable … laughable.'

In the cool brown shadows of the room, Sir William strokes his beard. 'I make the presumption – correct me if I'm wrong – that as an Italian you are perhaps closer to the spiritual governance of Rome than we Englishmen.' He holds up a hand to stay the glover's protestations. 'Not that I accuse you of papist sympathies – of course not. Nonetheless, I am guessing you will support Mary when the time comes … in the event there might be another … contender.'

The glover blinks, then swiftly recovers himself. 'The princess favours my gloves, that's all.' He gives a flourish of his hand. 'What can I say? I am an artist, a *fiorentino*.'

Sir William returns a tight smile. 'We didn't bring you here for a pair of gloves, *signore*, exquisite though they are.'

The blankness has returned to Alfredo's face. He feels the veiled threat underlying the mention of Rome.

'All I require of you is to listen, nothing more. Say naught to anyone. And if they ask, this conversation never happened. Our business concerned only gloves.'

The glover inclines his head.

'You will have noticed the king had lines of text removed from the church service. Those where the congregation gives their blessing to Mary and Elizabeth …'

I think back to the Sunday before last, when the priest paused for the briefest moment before closing the gap in the words and making as if the blessing had never been there. I know the words by heart – we all do. But none of us dared catch one another's eye, knowing it was safer to look down at our laps.

'Neither lady,' Cecil explains, 'was born of a marriage that was legitimate, so the king has decreed they have no place being named in the service.'

Sir William says 'the king', but we know he means the duke. It suits Northumberland to have the princesses branded bastards so the throne can be his for the grabbing.

'Now this next part concerns you more closely. It hasn't escaped our notice that your niece has found favour with Lady Mary. You must be wondering what will happen to the girl should the princess be imprisoned. Could the fair Lucretia tumble her way out of trouble, eh?'

There is no sign of emotion on Signore Pisanelli's face, not so much as a flicker. He merely tilts his head in acknowledgement. Sir William's widely spaced eyes are fixed on him with such a stare, I am surprised the glover doesn't babble with nerves.

'Yes, well. Now we come to the important matter, so listen hard. Yesterday, Northumberland wrote letters to Mary and Elizabeth, requesting their presence at the king's bedside. The net is closing around them. It is a trap. The duke wants to lure them to London so he can lock them in the Tower. Throckmorton has already sent a message to Lady Elizabeth, warning her to stay at Hatfield, pretend she's sick.'

Throckmorton nods. 'She readily takes counsel from us.'

'But not so Lady Mary, and that's the point.' Cecil strokes the fringe of his new glove with a thumbnail while he waits for his words to sink in. 'She wouldn't trust anything that came from us. And anyway, I doubt she can resist coming to Greenwich. The lady is nothing if not dutiful.'

Throckmorton gives a little snort. 'She'll be keen to get to Edward's ear – whisper a Hail Mary in it while he's too weak to stop her.'

Sir William gives a sharp glance at his friend, then his eyes settle once more on Alfredo. 'We think Lady Mary will have left Hunsdon by now, her manor in Hertfordshire. So this is what we'd have you do. Take a message to her. Catch her on the road if she's already set out.' He smiles, as if he's describing the rules of a new game for our entertainment. 'Just think, glover. You will have the double satisfaction of saving a princess *and* a tumbler.'

Sir William Cecil has a position of power in the king's government, and I'm sure neither Cecil nor Throckmorton is a Catholic. So while I see that they would want to help the Lady Elizabeth, a dutiful Protestant, I cannot understand why they should do the same for Mary. I think of Machiavelli saying that a man has to change with the times if he wants to rise to power and stay there. It makes me think of a hermit crab moving from shell to shell, each one bigger than the last. Maybe Cecil and Throckmorton think to say 'aye' to the duke, seeming to side with him, while secretly seeking to gain favour with the princess in the event she ends up on the throne.

There is a moment of silence, then Alfredo inclines his head to say he has understood. Not for the first time, I marvel that for a talkative man he has shown such restraint with the two statesmen, never once letting his tongue run away with him. I sense he is mixed up, as Ned once was, with a group of Catholic sympathisers loyal to Mary. Ned's lot were only ever local Blackwater folk, I'm sure, but Alfredo seems to be an altogether bigger player.

The secretary of state rises from his seat. The talk as the glover and I prepare to leave takes on a looser tone now that the important business has been dealt with.

Sir Nicholas asks me how I like Maldon.

I murmur that it suits me well and show my dimples.

Sir William, having signalled to his page that his guests are leaving, spreads his smile among us, generous as thick butter on a knife. 'A fine town Maldon, full of salt and good herring. Isn't that where Sir John Tallon is from?'

He addresses his question to Throckmorton so never sees me flinch, the blood draining from my face at Tallon's name.

'Haven't you heard? His greyhounds attacked him. Some local girl made them do it. A witch, by all accounts.' Throckmorton holds out a hand to stay Sir William's laughter. 'I know, I know. But I heard it from Rich who was there. He received a few bites himself.'

Sir William turns to me. 'Now that *is* a story. Did you hear of it in Maldon?'

I shake my head, unable to speak.

Throckmorton, keen to get on with his story, doesn't wait for my answer. 'Tallon has turned into a raging mad-man. Thinks the girl is lying low somewhere.'

'Has he done anything about it?'

'Only burned her village to the ground.'

A small sound escapes me – a tiny yelp – and Alfredo reaches for my arm to steady me.

Sir William, engaged in fetching a purse to give the glover, notices nothing of my upset. 'Burning a village? That's a bit excessive, isn't it?'

'He thinks one of the locals has been harbouring the girl. An old fishwife. He set light to her house first.'

'And the fishwife?'

'Inside it, apparently.'

Sir William raises his brows. 'That's one way to flush the girl out, though not a method I'd choose.' He gives a wry chuckle. 'Burning a haystack to catch yourself a mouse? I cannot think that has made him too popular.'

Throckmorton shrugs. 'He doesn't care to be popular. He's a strange, cold-blooded fish. That's why Northumberland gives him the vilest jobs no one else will touch.'

'Someone has to pick up the dirt, I suppose,' says Sir William, picking a speck off his new gloves. '… As long as we both keep our hands clean, my friend …'

Goldhanger! Burned to the ground.

I must go at once, see with my own eyes. Sal … is she alive? And Rob?

Every trace of the numbness that has kept me cloaked in a state of half-living these past weeks vanishes. Against the sharp urge to be there, every other consideration pales into nothing – even the stark fact that the inhabitants of Goldhanger will be sure to turn me in.

Back at the house, Signore Pisanelli darts about with brisk efficiency. He says he will lend me one of the two horses he keeps at a stables a short walk from Cloak Lane; the other he will ride to Hunsdon. I didn't have to raise with him my need to get to Goldhanger – he was already making plans for the journey before I had a chance to open my mouth.

'I'll take Leonardo to warn Lady Mary. You can have Angelo. Fifty miles will be nothing to him,' he boasts, giving a sharp click of his fingers. 'Not like your fat English horses.'

When I become tearful at his generosity, he brushes away my thanks. 'Make sure you rest him every two hours and let him drink. And remember to throw a pail of water over his back to cool him down.'

While Colin is sent to instruct the groom to ready the horses, I fill a pannier with everything I'll need for the journey and go upstairs to change into my old clothes. My hands are trembling as I put on my smock and kirtle, but shock is only part of it. A steely hatred has me in a grip so strong, it leaves little room for other feelings. I want to rip Tallon to pieces, tear out his heart and eat it. I will do anything, go anywhere, suffer whatever the fates hurl at me. There will be no need of ravens or dogs this time. I will use the strength of my own bare hands.

Chapter 18

An invisible grey pall hangs in the evening air over Goldhanger. I can taste the bitterness on my tongue long before I turn off the Maldon road into Head Street. If I didn't know better, I'd think the farmers had been burning their wheat fields after bringing the grain into the barns, but the smell is too acrid for that.

Barely able to breathe from anxiety, I ride along the deserted street in the failing light. At first, I am relieved that what I see doesn't nearly match Throckmorton's description. I remind myself that a tale grows bigger with the telling, each new storyteller emboldened to add a bit more colour.

Goldhanger survives. Head Street is untouched, as are the church and tithe barn at the far side of the square. The Bell stands, though the whitewash between its timbers is greyed with smoke.

So far, so good.

At the end of the road, I give a small tug to Angelo's rein. He bears right into Fish Street and, as he does, all at once the breath is knocked from my chest and I have to clutch the pommel of my saddle to prevent myself from sliding to the ground. The flames must have swept through every one of the thatched cottages on either side of the lane, helped in their passage by breezes from the sea. There would have been little the villagers could do. I imagine them now, dashing around in panic, before scrambling to organise themselves into a chain, passing pails hand to hand from the pump. And all too late.

Nothing remains of Sal's row of cottages but a few blackened ridges where the walls stood. I dismount and step carefully over ashes and charred timbers, hardly knowing what I'm looking for but hoping to find some clue that Sal lives. I see the dark shape of the hearth, blacker than the rest. Her iron cooking pot still stands in its place, but other than that there is no trace of Sal's belongings – the wooden stools and trestle, spoons and bowls. All gone.

I take Angelo down to the jetty where Sniggler Nick, an old eel-catcher, stands stoop-backed over the blackened hull of his boat. He stares at it in surprise, as if the truth of what has happened is only just dawning in his head. I lead the horse over, and he fixes a pair of muddled eyes on me.

'Master Nick, I am so sorry.' I gesture to his boat, then behind me to Fish Street. My mouth opens and closes, unable to shape itself round whatever has happened here at Goldhanger. Eventually, I have the courage to ask, 'Sal – does she live?'

The sniggler scratches his head, muzzy-eyed, trying to catch hold of my question. 'It were Sal they came for. Torched her cottage first, then the flames got to the rest.'

'Does she live?' I repeat helplessly.

'Nay, lass … Rob was out at sea, or he'd have been murdered too.'

'Where is he now?'

The eel–catcher points a shaking finger. 'He's moved into the farrier's house. Taken Bridey with 'im. There's a few folk there.'

Before I turn and walk back up Fish Street, I take a last look at the burned boats. None of this damage at the jetty has been caused by that first torch to Sal's thatch. Tallon's men must have come down here and set light to each of the fishing boats in turn. They must have wanted to be sure that the villagers of Goldhanger didn't have the means to put food on their table.

And all because of me.

Smoke coils up from Ned's chimney in the dusk. They will have banked down the fire by now, ready to turn in for the night. Gentle clucks come from a wooden coop in the yard, while in the stable the pigs grunt along to Bridey's snorts.

I wonder how many have moved to Ned's. There were a few families in Fish Street, but they can't all have taken shelter here, surely. My stomach coils itself slowly into a knot. I'm the cause of their misfortune. What will they say? What will they do to me?

Luckily, Rob finds me before I have to face them. As Angelo and I stand at the gate, plucking up the courage to enter the yard, he comes out of the stables, rubbing the dirt from his hands. When he sees me, he stops and stares.

'Rob?' I take a few steps towards him, leading Angelo by his rein.

'Dela.' He doesn't move. Then it's as if he wakes up suddenly. 'Come. You'd best come.'

He takes the reins from my hand and hurries us towards the stables. I can feel the urgent pressure of his palm pushing against my shoulder.

Once we're inside, he gives me a wooden ladle of water, and I gulp from it. Angelo is no less thirsty, and while he drinks from his pail Rob rubs him down.

'Is she really gone?' I have to ask it. Nothing has sunk in yet.

He nods, dry-eyed. 'She didn't give you up. Would never. Even if she'd known where you was.'

'I know.' I don't need to tell him I'm sorry. He knows I am. And what use is sorry anyway? It won't bring Sal back. 'I'm going to kill him,' I say.

'You won't get to him. I went up to the Hall to do the same. But he'd gone. Gatherin' soldiers. Davy the groom told me.'

His broad shoulders slump; I can see how weary he is. The pair of us sit on a hay bale, and I can hardly keep my eyes open myself.

'Ma told me about your dog. The spit turner.' Rob gives a little snort. 'I've never heard her so keen on a hound. She don't like 'em as a rule.'

It feels better talking of Sal as if she's still with us.

'Turnspit's at New Hall with Bessie. I miss them so!'

He reaches out and places one hand to my heart – palm against my chest – the other to his own. 'I'm glad you came. I dunno what the others'll say. But I'm right glad.'

'Who's here?'

'The Dickenses. John Wright. Tom Sherrin.'

'Oh. Tom will want to turn me in.'

He nods. 'Though it's Fowler you'd best watch out for. Since Tallon left, he's been lordin' it, getting up folk's noses.'

'He's only a gamekeeper. He can't do much, can he?'

'I wouldn't be so sure about that. Thou should see 'im – makes us all sick. After the fire an' all.'

I rise to my feet slowly, stiff as an old woman.

'Not goin', are ye?'

I make a strange sound – something between a sob and a laugh. 'No, I'm not. I was going to make myself something to sleep on.'

'You can kip in the hayloft. Folk don't need to know you've come.'

'That's where I've always slept, above the horses. After Ma died it was the only place I could sleep. I think it was the sound of Bessie's huffing that helped. When the silence got in my head, it used to scare me.'

'It's them pictures I can't stand. It's like I saw it. Ma tryin' to get out. Burnin' up. Hair, apron, cap, all of it.' He sees my expression and presses his big fists to his eyes. 'I always end up frightenin' you.'

'Best to speak of it, else those pictures in your head only make you mad.' I sit back down and take his hand. 'We won't breathe again unless Tallon's destroyed. If he's out there – even if he hasn't caught me – those pictures in our heads will never go away.'

'An' Ma will have died for naught.'

We hunker together, hand in hand, feeling the gaping hole Sal's left behind.

'She always said ye was special,' Rob says quietly. 'I used to get torn up with it. Had it in my head she cared more for ye.'

'I didn't know ... I'm sorry.'

He holds up a hand, brushing my words aside. 'That was when we was littluns. Then you grew ... straight as a withy ... honest with it. Tellin' folks exactly what you thought. I could see Sal were right. She told me, if the day comes and she's pushin' up daisies, I must look out for you ... I reckon that's now.'

I hug him, and it feels good to feel his broad shoulders, the comforting smell of salt and sweat.

Climbing the ladder into the loft feels strange to me. I did it all those nights when this was home, but now I have none of the comfort it used to afford me. It's as if the world is spinning away into the night, and I can't get my footing.

'*Faccialunga*! I've got a hungry horse down here!'

I sit up and rub my eyes, thinking at first that I must be at the house in Cloak Lane. *What on earth?*

Then there's the creak of feet on the ladder. A head emerges, on which sits a jaunty black hat with a dyed green plume. Two bright emerald eyes, surrounded by laughter lines, and a small neatly cropped red beard. Alfredo!

'Get up, sleepybones. I've got two starving horses, one strange little dog, and a lovesick *ragazzo* down here.'

'Wh ... what?'

Alfredo's head disappears again. I jump up, pull on my kirtle, and am making my way to the ladder when Fitz emerges through the open trapdoor. I stare, unable to believe it is really him. I thought he was dead, and yet here he is, though I notice he seems a thinner, paler shadow of himself. Below his hazel eyes, his hollow cheeks are flushed, though beneath the spots of colour there's a sick pallor to his face. He moves stiffly, without his usual cat-like ease.

We stare at each other awkwardly for a moment but are saved by a cross bark from the stable below.

Fitz turns back to the ladder. 'I'd better help him up.'

The barking gets crosser. 'I'm coming. I'll lift you up, don't worry.'

Moments later, a tufty hairball launches itself across the hay bales, and a long pink tongue swipes at my face. Laughing, I try to duck out of range, but there's no getting away. I wrap my arms around Turnspit's warm, wriggling body, and he gives a great wheezing sigh.

Fitz perches on a bale and waits while I pull myself upright. I put my bare feet on the boards so that Turnspit can sit on them. It's his favourite place, back resting against my shins. I know he won't let me out of his sight in case we lose each other again.

'How is your shoulder? Does it hurt?' I ask Fitz.

'Not so much.' He shrugs lopsidedly. 'I just wish I didn't get so tired.'

'Why are you here? How did you know? ... Sal ...' My words falter.

'Alfredo met us on the road from Hunsdon. He told Mary she was heading for a trap. Lucretia wanted to come when she heard that you were here, but he told her to go with Mary. Said it was her duty to protect the princess.' He looks down at his hands, unwilling to meet my eyes. 'When he told us about Sal ...'

I know what he's thinking – that it's his father who did it, the man he should have killed, and that if he'd only managed to do it Sal would still be alive.

'I thought you were dead!' I blurt, wiping my eyes furiously with the back of my hand.

He stares at me helplessly, then puts his good arm around my shoulder. 'I wanted to come to you.' His voice is a croak. 'I wasn't fit. Lucretia said she'd sent you word.'

'I never got it.'

'We knew you'd be worrying about us.'

I think of the numbness, the nights spent gazing onto the dark street, wondering, fearing. 'You have no idea ...'

'Turnspit was allowed to sit with me. Mistress Clar-encieux let him.'

'I thought of him. All the time ...'

'I wish you'd known we were all right.'

A moment's silence, then he comes to sit beside me. 'You've got hay in your hair. Sticking out all over the place. You look like a scarecrow.' He starts to remove it, stalk by stalk. A moment later, there's a creak on the ladder and Alfredo appears, hopping nimbly into the hayloft.

'Turtle doves, we have things to do – *cose importanti*!'

He is followed by Rob, who stoops almost double to avoid the rafters before sitting down on a bale next to the glover, looking bemusedly at the jauntily dressed Italian and Fitz picking hay out of my hair.

'I brought ye summat to eat.' He hands us each a mus-lin parcel. 'You'd best get it down. They'll be seeing to the animals any time now.' He doesn't need to tell me that I mustn't be seen; fear for my safety is writ large on his broad, weatherbeaten face.

Alfredo gets straight to business. 'You two need to get to Mary and my niece, *pronto*. This charming *pescatore*,' he gestures at Rob, 'informs me that Tallon rides north. Doing the *coglione*'s dirty work, no doubt.'

The glover's eyes meet mine, serious in a way I've rarely seen them, though I've had hints of this side of him before. I think of Sir William saying that Tallon is always given the vilest tasks no one else wants to do, and my heart gives a squeeze. I'm certain Tallon has been sent to finish Mary off. Northumberland will want it done before her followers have a chance of gathering in any great number. And one thing's for sure: Tallon won't stop at the princess. Not one of her party will be left alive to tell of the slaughter.

Fitz breaks into my thoughts. 'The princess and her party are heading to Kenninghall, her palace in Norfolk. I've been there a few times. They'll be taking the road to Thetford from Bury. The princess always stays the night with Lady Burgh, her friend at Euston Hall. Kenninghall's a few miles east of that.'

I can almost hear the glover's mind whirring. 'You'll be on your own, you two. Lady Mary's told me to get to London, keep an eye on what is going on there for her.'

'The roads will be full of watchers. Soldiers too.' I hate how my voice comes out in a bleat.

'Only one thing for it!' he says, with a snap of his fingers. 'You must sail. Why else has Sant'Andrea sent us a *pescatore*?'

Rob scratches his thick tufts of hair – so like Sal's. 'I don't know what's what with all that pesky talk, but I do know that ye can't grow a pair of wings. And my boat, she flies like a witch.'

'You'll do it?' I say.

'The wind and tides will favour us. I know the shoals and sandbanks better than the lines on my hand,' he says comfortably. 'We'll sail twice as fast as ride. But you'll need horses once we get to Lowestoft.'

'I have gold enough,' says Fitz, patting the purse at his girdle. He gets up unsteadily, wincing at the pain in his shoulder.

As he does, we are aware suddenly of a loud cluck-ing and squawking coming from the hen-coop outside. Turnspit gives a low growl.

Fitz moves to the open gable end of the hayloft, from where he has a view of the yard. 'A fox nosing round the chickens.'

Rob joins him and his face freezes. 'That ain't no fox.' He and I glance at each other. ''Tis Red, Fowler's dog. Best keep out of sight, Dela.'

'Who is this Fowler?' asks Alfredo, as we hurry to join Fitz and Rob at the gable.

'Tallon's man. A gamekeeper,' I tell him miserably. 'He's come for me … must have heard I'm here. He's the one who stuck Turnspit in the wheel. He invents ways to torture animals.'

Alfredo peers down at the scene in the yard, eyes fixed on the figure crossing it. '*Beh!* I thought more of you, *faccialunga.* That freckled grease-clout?'

We watch as Fowler sidles in the direction of the stable, pointy face squirrelling from left to right, keeping an eye out for any movement. His feet make no sound; he stalks like a cat. I reflect how he always manages to pop up without warning, giving folk a fright.

'Well,' Alfredo says, pulling on his gloves, 'I will have

to deal with this pale and spotted weasel. And you two lovebirds and the *pescatore* will escape while I do. *Capite?*'

Fitz cannot peel his eyes away from Alfredo. I can tell what he is thinking: the glover and his niece are uncannily alike. Not only in the vivid colour of their hair and eyes, but in the way they talk rapidly, giving sweeping gestures with their hands.

With a flourish, Alfredo puts his plumed hat on his head, skips down the ladder, barely seeming to touch the rungs, and is out in the yard before we know it.

He flicks his white-gloved hands at Fowler, his feet dancing nimbly towards his opponent. 'Hen thief. Out of our yard. Out! You miserable English worm.'

Fowler's eyes are like two round pennies in his freckled face. Speechless, he takes three steps backwards.

'Go back to your *nonna*. We – don't – want – you – here. *Capisci?*'

After his initial surprise, Fowler recovers himself and approaches the glover. 'I'm the man who decides who is and isn't wanted. I'll tell you plain, froggie. We – don't – want – no – foreigners – 'ere. So beat it, before I set my dog on you.'

A change comes over the glover's expression, a blade-like sharpness.

Unaware of it, Fowler reaches out a grubby hand and shoves his arm. 'We've got no time for your sort. Pah! Look at you in your fancy velvet. Get back on your ship, Frenchie.'

Alfredo's eyes narrow. His gaze never leaves Fowler's face, not even when he reaches down with lightning speed and takes a dagger from his boot – a thin stiletto knife, rubies flashing on its hilt.

Fowler edges back, his eyes fixed on the blade. He doesn't give a thought to where the glover is pushing him. It is only when the backs of his thighs meet the lip of the water trough that his stare breaks. Too late! A grunting cry, a splash – and he's over.

He raises his dripping face to find Alfredo nose to nose with him.

'Be careful who you call a Frenchman, freckled milk-sop. You've got off lightly this time. You're lucky I don't press my fist down on your head. Drown you like a *ratto* in a bucket.'

I wish the mallards could see Fowler now. The thought barely has time to form in my mind before I am tugged away by Fitz. Rob is already halfway down the ladder, and I scamper after him, Turnspit under my arm.

CHAPTER 19

It is a relief when Rob tells us he won't need our help to sail. 'You three get down there in the bows,' he says as we climb aboard. 'Else you'll only get under foot.'

Hunkered down in front of the mainmast in the space usually reserved for Rob's catch, we watch as he moves about the boat, surprisingly nimble for a man as big as a barn door. The wind changes as the estuary widens out, and he stoops forward, one hand on the tiller, to help the great red foresail across. The squarish mizzen at the stern, fixed to its own tiny mast, looks after itself, flipping back and forth to catch the breeze. It's fortunate it does — Rob may be the best sailor in Goldhanger, but he only has two hands, and there is already plenty for them to do.

A flock of ravens fly out of the thorn trees at the tip of Osea as we sail by. They croak and swoop in the wake of our boat. I look in vain for the grey head and stippled wings of my friend, and my heart sinks a little when I don't see him among them.

Turnspit is perched at the bow, a squat figurehead. Squint-eyed, ears driven back by the wind, he twitches his pale brown nose from side to side to catch the scent of fish. It's no wonder he hated the kitchen so much — he's a born sea dog, at home on the waves. Unlike his mistress.

Fitz is surprised to find that I am a nervous sailor. Noticing my knuckles whiten when Rob's boat heels over in a sudden gust, he puts his good arm about my shoulder and hugs me to him. I like saltwater between my toes, but only when my feet are firmly planted on the mud of the marsh – not soaked in the freezing bilgewater of this tipping, creaking tub. I've never learned to swim, and the thought of Rob's boat being the only thing between me and fathoms of grey water is terrifying.

Our skipper is hunched at the stern, elbow crooked round the tiller. For a moment I have the feeling that he is a part of his boat, carved from the same beechwood he used to make it. I take comfort in his quiet confidence and lose a little of my tension. With him at one end and Turnspit the other, I tell myself I'm in good hands ... and paws.

The boat heels, and as it does so I catch sight of the wooded high ground of Mersea island, the square tower of its church rising above the trees. We will soon be over the sandbar.

'She won't want to hug the coast for long,' Rob tells us.

He always speaks of his fishing boat as if she were an actual person, in this case a wayward mistress who wants to kick up her skirts and take us right out to sea. He says the *Sally Forth* – named after Sal – will capture more wind the further out we are. And there's less chance of our running onto sandbanks or rocks lurking beneath the surface.

'We'll pass through the Wallet, but after that we'll keep out beyond Knock Deep. If I were to take her twixt Bawdsey Bank and Shipwash Sands she'd break up like an apple box. She don't take kindly to the Aldeburgh Knapes neither.'

I clench my jaw grimly and clutch Fitz's arm with white fingers.

'Hush, Dela. He knows what he's doing.'

I rest my head against his shoulder, and Turnspit comes down from the prow to give my face a lick, nestling into my other side. Even he isn't a match for the great grey waves that are starting to slap at the hull.

'You're wet,' I say to him, rubbing his tufty fur with my cloak.

We're heading north now, a brisk sou'wester behind us. The boat has levelled out, running with the wind up the Wallet. It doesn't feel as if we're moving nearly as fast as we are, but then I look at the shore and see we're already passing the mouth of the Colne. There's the low hill topped with the beacon, below which Horsewash Spit protrudes like a pointing finger. The other side of the spit lies St Osyth's Creek and the tide mill. I can just make out the stretch of greensward that belongs to the priory – one of the many estates given to Lady Mary in her father's dower. I point it out to Fitz.

'It's no longer hers. Northumberland grabbed it off her. Thought she might escape the country from there.'

In my mind's eye, I can see her running down to the creek, cloak flying behind her, a foreign ship waiting at anchor ready to take her away. I wish she had gone – I'm not ready to forgive her. But if she had, I suppose England would never get rid of the evil Northumberland. My feelings are in a knot – pulled tight and difficult to unpick.

I don't share my thoughts with Fitz, saying only, 'I wonder if she wishes she'd done it … fled the country when she had the chance.'

He shrugs, forgetting his shoulder, and winces. 'Maybe. Who knows? She'll either be running scared or be raring for a fight. Maybe a bit of both.'

This makes me feel even more frightened for Lucretia, but I keep it to myself. It is so easy to spread fear, and things are hard enough for Fitz without my infecting him with it. I glance at his pale face. The frown of pain is still there. If anything, he looks worse. It's clear he isn't well enough for a journey like this, but if I'd told him to stay with the glover he'd never have agreed.

Now we're on an even keel and no longer throwing up spray, Turnspit is back at the prow. He leans forward, neck stretched out, and for a moment – dazzled by the sunlight bouncing on the water – my eyes see a wolf standing there. I cannot imagine why my mind plays this trick on me: Turnspit, with his short legs and sparse, wiry hair – not to mention the cross little cobnut eyes – looks more like a boar than like a wolf.

Watching the dog gives me courage. Fitz needs me to be strong, and I have to be so for Lucretia. We must help her, and if we assist the princess in doing so, perhaps that is no bad thing. Although I know Lady Mary hates me – and I cannot find it in myself to like her any better – there are important matters at stake. I think of the old Blackwater song that my mother used to sing to me, the one Ned remembered. The words of its last verse seem to work on me like a spell, binding me tighter to my course. Ned was right – the song does speak to you.

'There's a girl with the wolf on the marsh beside the sea,
Hey, ho, the grey waves a-rolling.

Salve Regina, *we follow Mary,*
Hey, ho, the east wind's a-blowing.'

We sleep soundly for a while, wrapped in my cloak, Fitz's
cape a bolster for our heads. Tired after his night's journey, Turnspit comes down from the prow and curls in the
crook of my knees, where he snores noisily.

I wake hungry, and Rob hands us salt herring and ale
– all he managed to grab this morning in our rush to be
gone. Fitz picks at his food, which worries me: he must
be running a fever. He ends up giving most of it to Turnspit, and a little later, thirsty from the salt fish, the dog finds
himself a small puddle of rainwater to lap in a crease in
one of Rob's oilskins.

'We're making good time. Got her on a tidy reach,'
Rob says between mouthfuls. 'Comin' to Sizewell Bank
now. There, see? Broken water.' He points, and over the
port bow I can just make out stripes of colour in the middle distance – moss-green and grey – and the tell-tale
ruffles of white.

'How long till we reach Lowestoft?' Fitz asks.

'Couple of hours at most. A channel takes you twixt
two shoals – Newcombe an' Holm. Known round here
for being widow-makers.' Seeing my alarm, his face falls.
'Oh dear, done it again. Scared thee.'

'No … don't worry. You didn't.'

'Anyways, don't fret. Them banks and rocks ain't never
got me yet. I'm more likely to drown in a pottage bowl
than out here.'

I think of Rob's shaking fits, and how he's never had
one in his boat. Now that Sal's gone, he'll spend even

more time at sea with nothing but the birds for company. It will be lonely for him.

Fitz and I tuck ourselves against the curving side of the hull under the lip of the gunwale, safe from the sea spray. I know he needs to sleep; I can see the faint sheen of fever on his brow. He has his eyes closed, head resting on my shoulder, and I think he has drifted off, but then he starts to speak. And it's as if his strongbox of childhood secrets is finally beginning to open.

'My father preferred women who didn't stand up to him. Ones like my mother … and I hated her for it …'

I think of Fitz's outburst at New Hall after Rosie the kitchen maid had let herself be bullied by the scullions.

'I kept thinking, why doesn't Mother just take me and leave?'

'Tallon broke her spirit, that's why. That's what he does.'

I think of the dogs and pups I've tended to, the ones with whip sores and broken bones. More times than I care to remember, I've seen them go back to licking the hand of the master who's hurt them.

'Are you his only child?' I ask.

'As far as I know. He named me Fitzjohn. Reckoned that if King Henry could parade his bastard Fitzroy around, my father could do it with me.

'He gave me a dog – I refused to beat it. He gave me a horse – I wouldn't hobble it. Finally, he shouted at me for being a weakling like my mother.'

'I can imagine.'

'I spent hours at the butts till I could shoot an arrow straight. I hoped that would be enough for him, but he couldn't leave it at that.'

'Let me guess. He took you hunting.'

'When I was ten. It took two days and nights. When the mastiffs grew tired, he had others replace them. I begged to go home, but he wouldn't let me.'

Fear and sadness flit across Fitz's pale face as he speaks. I recall how arrogant and uncaring I'd thought him at the beginning. Now I realise how exhausting it must have been to try to maintain that front, all the while struggling to keep these memories locked away.

'The hart was massive ... majestic. We exhausted him finally, and he turned, ready to fight us off. Only there were four fresh mastiffs and the two of us against him. He was so close, I could see the white scars in the fur of his face ... the pupils of his eyes big with fear. But even though he was done for – and he knew he was – he was still so ... fierce.'

'What did you do?'

'Nothing. I turned away, refused to take my father's sword when he offered it.'

Turnspit gets up and stretches. Muzzy with sleep, he takes a moment to find his sea legs, skittering on the boards as he makes his way to Fitz's side. He sits down and leans into him, while Fitz – hardly aware of the dog – relives that day in the forest.

'After that, my father wanted nothing more to do with me.'

'Must have been a blessing, wasn't it?'

He shrugs. 'Once he'd given me to Oxford – who let me join his players – he had no reason to help my mother.'

A pause as he clears his throat. 'I think that the disgust he felt for me, he took out on her.'

'She died?'

Fitz nods. 'The worst thing is I don't think anybody even noticed she'd gone.'

'You noticed.'

He rubs his forehead with the back of his hand. 'Yes … I suppose so.' He moves his body, trying for a more comfortable position, and winces with pain.

But this isn't the only thing bothering him; I can tell there's more.

'Dela … I worry that I'll grow to be like him.'

'Of course you won't. You're completely different.'

'It was strange, you know … at the hunt, when he saw me.'

'Why? What did he do?'

'It was the way he looked at me. He seemed pleased. And there I was, about to kill him.'

'He must have thought you'd come to your senses, grown into a bloodthirsty killer like him. No matter that you were bent on murdering him.'

'Exactly. Though he didn't look so pleased when you cantered out of the trees shouting my name.'

'He must have hated that. His son friends with his sworn enemy.'

'Only friends?'

His tawny eyes meet mine and a current, warm and strong, flows between us.

Soon after, the weather changes. Rob turns into the wind and reefs his foresail. Now a westerly squall is in our teeth, slapping at the sails so that they shriek. Standing in a half-crouch at the stern, he braces himself against the force of the waves that slam into the rudder. I marvel that he still manages to wear an expression of quiet confidence, able to move nimbly about the boat without once losing his footing. I look down at my fingers, white from the chill of the sea and from gripping the gunwale.

Then we see gunships off our starboard bow, six or seven of them strung out to the south of us. We're close enough to the lead ship to see the seamen scampering up the ratlines between the shrouds.

'Look at them!' shouts Rob above the wind, pointing to the galleons.

I don't know what scares me more: the ten-foot waves battering against the *Sally Forth* or Northumberland's great warships bearing down on us.

Fitz tightens his arm about my shoulders. 'Must be heading for Yarmouth. They'll have been sent to block the harbours north of Ipswich. Mary won't manage to get away now, and her cousin Charles can't send ships to help her even if he wants to.'

The lead gunship is almost level now. It's like some great floating castle, its poop deck high as battlements at the stern. My eyes are drawn by the black mouths of the cannons ranged at intervals along the gun deck, and I give a shiver. Next to the warship, the *Sally Forth* is but a tiny minnow.

A moment later, Rob gives a yell. 'Lowestoft!'

My eye is caught by the white walls and weatherboards of a huddle of cottages along the straight pale edge of the coast, tucked under a cliff on top of which loom the larger merchant houses and the spire of a church breaking the skyline.

'We'll be goin' about soon,' he shouts through the noise of the squall. 'See the gap in the broken water? That's where the shoal ends. She'll start tippin' when we turn into the channel.'

'We'd best stay low,' says Fitz, helping me tuck into our space in the bows. 'You too, Turnspit.'

'Ready about!' shouts Rob, with a sharp tug at the tiller. As the bow comes round, the foresail whips over, and with a moan and a creak the *Sally Forth* dashes into the spume, tipping so sharply that we have to brace with our feet to stop ourselves from tumbling forward. Rob tacks down the channel between Newcombe and Holm – the submerged rock shoals he'd told us about – clawing his way against the tide. The water rushes under the hull, faster and noisier than before, and, every time a massive wave hits, he disappears from sight in the white of the spray.

By the time we reach Lowestoft, we are soaked through. Rob brings the *Sally Forth* into the wind, lowering her foresail as late as he can and leaving the mizzen flapping. The town has no harbour or quay, so we have to sail through the wavelets to the beach, where I jump ashore with the mooring rope into the shallows.

It is only once the *Sally Forth* is safely pulled up on the shingle that Turnspit emerges, quite dry, having had the sense to worm his way under a large oilskin for the duration of the squall.

Rob gives a snort. 'Thou kept nice and snug, dog. Fair-weather little feller, ain't ye? Straddlin' the bowsprit like a lion – duckin' under when it's blowy. I knows your sort!'

Turnspit turns his back, and I explain to Rob that he doesn't like being teased. Seeing the fisherman's broad face fall, I quickly reassure him that it isn't his fault – how was he to know the dog has such a thin skin? I move closer to give Rob a hug, my arms only just reaching around the barrel of his chest.

'Keep safe, littlun,' he whispers into my hair. 'And look after the boy. He don't look too well.'

'I don't know if I can do it,' I murmur. 'I couldn't bear to let Sal down again.'

'You can do it.' He draws back, grasping me by the shoulders. 'It's just … you need to take your strength and own it.'

Moist-eyed, I give a nod, despising myself for whinging.

Rob takes the mooring rope and coils it round his arm. 'Right, tide's a callin', wind's at my back. You two give the bows a push. Make it quick, I don't want them gunships spottin' me.'

Chapter 20

A farmer sells us a pair of horses, promising they will be good-tempered and sturdy. He takes one look at Fitz's pale face and careful movements and suggests we stop for the night with his friend the miller, whose mill house is a little way up the Waveney River in the direction we're headed. When we get there, the miller and his wife are friendly enough and ask no questions, providing us with clean beds and a meal, for which we gladly pay them. Fitz sleeps a little, but it is an uneasy doze, full of dreams and fever.

The next morning, we leave the mill at first light and follow the river, hearing only the peep-peep of the moorhens and the occasional plop of a trout surfacing. Turnspit trots ahead, and we follow him unquestioningly, no longer wondering how he always seems to know the way. Lulled by the quiet, we progress with little sense of urgency.

This soon changes when we meet a man with a cart full of turnips. He tips his hat and brings his horse to a stop. 'Where's ye headed?' he asks.

'The Thetford road,' answers Fitz. 'Are we far?'

'Nay, young master. A mile, no more. The ways meet at Scole.' His two round eyes stare at us with unbridled curiosity from a head shaped like one of his turnips. 'Came that way myself, matter of fact. Though ye'd best take another.'

Fitz is immediately alert. 'Why is that?'

'Soldiers. Came up the Ipswich road last night. Camped at Scole.'

Startled, I'm aware that my first instinct is to flee as quickly as possible, back in the direction we've come.

Fitz shows more presence of mind. 'Are they on the move yet?'

'Only round the honeypot. There won't be a crumb left once they've done wi' Scole. Provisioning, that's what they calls it.' The man leans over the side of his cart to spit on the ground. 'There's an odd-looking feller runnin' the show. Pockmarked face. Has a look of the grim reaper about him. Quiet voice … yet all them soldiers doin' his bidding in a snap. They're squeezin' the villagers dry.' He gives a wry laugh. 'Lucky for me, the devil-man turned his nose up at my turnips.'

Fitz meets my eyes and a silent call of alarm passes between us. Sir John Tallon. Must be. My insides are taut as a rope tugged two ways, the whining coward getting the upper hand. Then I think of Lucretia, and how we need to warn Mary. I have to be cool-headed, strong.

The man is staring at us strangely, and I realise that shock must be written all over our faces. Fitz collects himself enough to ask him which route we should take to avoid the village, and the man directs us to a bridleway that loops below it, meeting up with the Thetford road further along.

Before we part, I think to ask one last thing. 'If you please, master, have you seen or heard anything of other riders? A small party of nobles coming from Thetford?'

'Nay, mistress, nothin' like that.' He gives a chuckle and points at Turnspit. 'You'll be passin' through huntin' country, sure enough. Make sure them nobles don't chase the little feller, mistake him for a sow.'

Fortunately, I don't think Turnspit, who always seems to sense an insult, hears the turnip man. He is already running in the direction of the bridleway. Bad enough to be told you look like a boar – but a sow?

I'd like to say that our horses fly with the wind at their hooves, but they don't. That being said, they do their best to put as much distance between us and Tallon as possible with a willing temperament and stolid gait that remind me of Bessie's.

We loop close to the village on a narrow track, a hedge of whitethorn shielding us from sight. I follow the bumbling, freckled backside of Fitz's grey, willing her to go faster. We can hear the soldiers breaking camp – the noise of it fills the clear morning air, punctuated by sharp bugle calls bidding them rouse themselves. The shrill sound drills into my skull. We must hurry.

The going is easier once we join the Thetford road. We have a clear view behind us, and I cannot help looking back, watching for a tell-tale dust cloud on the horizon. When Fitz glances over his shoulder, he flinches as if someone has whipped him. His wound must be paining him worse than ever.

He catches my worried expression and tries for a confident smile. 'We've got ahead of them. It'll turn out well, you'll see.' He points to a church tower peeping through the trees ahead of us, a jaunty red-and-white pennant flying from its battlemented grey stone roof. 'Lopham Parva – I recognise the tower. Not far now. A lane runs north to Kenninghall from there. We'll stop at the village, water the horses, see if anyone has news of Lady Mary.'

It is then that I spot the dust cloud behind us. 'Fitz …' He follows my eyes. 'We must hurry.'

The pump in the village square is busy. How can we afford to wait our turn? The line is bunched into little knots of gossiping women who seem in no hurry to do anything but wag their heads. I cast a nervous glance at the road behind us; the dust cloud is bigger, I'm sure of it.

Fitz leaves me with the horses and walks over to three women at the head of the line. Busy lifting pails with arms fat as hams, they shake their heads in answer to his question, then flirt with him, sending peals of full-throated laughter across the square. One of them pinches his upper arm as if she's sizing up a flitch of bacon. I don't know how he can bear to let the seconds trickle through his fingers like this.

But it is worth it in the end. He comes back with a full pail, and the mares dip their heads to suck up the water. Once Turnspit has had his fill, Fitz hurries back to the pump. And it is then that it happens.

I sense something at my back and twist round, but it is too late. A hand grasps my arm, pinning it behind me. The shout dies in my throat; a cold steel blade nicks my skin.

'Animal witch.'

I know that nasal drawl. It belongs to Sir Godfrey Knowles, Mary's hunt master, a man who never liked me.

'You and your groom friend are coming with me. You'd better not try anything.'

My immediate terror of having my throat cut abates, but my heart sinks. This is not how Fitz and I planned to take our intelligence to Mary. Being dragged like a convict on a rope is unlikely to impress her. I'm sure she will make good her promise from the last time we met and have me killed.

Two miles along the Thetford road, we meet up with Mary's party who rein in their horses and watch the three of us dismount. Knowles gives me a shove, knocking me to my knees. The time for curtseys is long gone.

Lady Mary keeps a careful distance, mounted on a chestnut gelding so tall for her that she appears marooned on its back. I immediately pick out Lucretia in the small group of riders. She stares at me with green eyes vivid against the pale skin of her face. I sense her willing me to save myself.

The princess fixes a pair of stony eyes on our captor who shifts uneasily on his great black hunter, his face reddening under her stare. Having thought he was bringing Lady Mary a prize – like a cat setting down a live mouse at its mistress's feet – he is bemused that she doesn't give him praise. At New Hall, I always recognised Knowles for the weak-chinned nobleman he is, desperate to win her favour.

'The girl is a succubus sent by the devil. I will not look at her.'

The princess is scared of me. I am a plague that will devour her soul should her eyes meet mine. Reduced, travel-stained, exhausted, she has no resistance – so she keeps her face averted.

Fitz, standing beside me, tries to speak. 'My lady, if you please…'

'No. Hold your tongue. I do not … will not trust you. Any more than I will her.' Again, the fear in her voice. Does she think Fitz has been seduced by me, the succubus, to do the devil's bidding?

'You brought them in, Sir Godfrey. Now you have the task of getting rid of them,' she says coldly. 'You have a perfectly good sword. You were given one simple task, to find out if the way is clear …'

'M-my lady,' he stutters, 'Master Fitzjohn was bringing word of Sir John Tallon's company, approaching from the east.'

I see what the weak-chinned huntsman is doing. He thinks to try a different tack, hoping to get back in his mistress's good graces. Having blocked his ears to our arguments on the road, all of a sudden he remembers his original errand as scout.

Lady Mary's gaze hardens. 'You saw these troops with your own eyes?'

Unable to stand the force of her glare, Sir Godfrey fixes his gaze on the pommel of his saddle.

'Did you seek any further intelligence? Did you?'

'N-no, my lady … The groom, he –'

She raises her whip hand, and he flinches.

All this while, Lucretia's eyes have never once left us, but now she leans towards the gentlewoman mounted on a dainty grey next to her and whispers in her ear. It takes me a moment to recognise Mistress Dormer, the princess's young favourite. Her countenance, robbed of its usual monkey-like playfulness, is quite stern. She nibbles on the thumb of her glove for a moment, then brings her mare close to Lady Mary's side to confer with her.

The princess passes a tired hand over her brow. 'Mistress Dormer has counselled me to let you speak, Master Fitzjohn.'

He steps forward. 'My lady, we have travelled from Essex to find you. Sir John Tallon and his men were camped at Scole last night. A hundred horse, maybe more, headed this way. They will have reached Lopham Parva by now.'

She stares at him for a moment, and I wonder if she is too exhausted for the words to sink in. Then, all of a sudden, her features twist in distrust. 'Hold your tongue, boy! All I hear is the devil talking. You feed me intelligence and expect me to swallow it? You and this witch. Well, I won't!'

Fitz sways, losing his footing. I think he is going to fall.

Mary turns to Mistress Dormer. 'How could I possibly believe the boy when his very bones have been infected by the witch? The girl follows me like a curse!'

But her companion's attention has been caught by something on the horizon. 'My lady, forget the witch. Master Fitzjohn has it right. Look!' Her gloved hand points back along the way we've come.

Dust from hundreds of hooves, kicked up from the dry road, is whirling our way.

Desperate, Fitz cries out, 'They have come to kill you, my lady. You have no time! We're here to help. Please!'

The princess's hand is pressed to her chest as if to still her racing heart. Instead of answering him, she turns to the horseman on her right, a man in a faded pigskin hat who looks more drover than courtier. 'Master Kepple, you know the tracks through these forests. Is there another way to Kenninghall?'

'Only a much longer road, my lady. You'd be doubling back on yourself,' he answers. 'By which time, if they've taken the short route, they'll cut you off at the top.'

She stretches her stiff neck and squares her shoulders. 'What can we do?'

The man scratches the bristles on his jaw. 'Split up, I'd say. The only thing for it. Confuse them enough, maybe they'll follow the wrong tracks.'

Mistress Dormer raises a gloved hand. 'If I may suggest something, my lady?'

The princess inclines her head.

'You want to be rid of the witch, I see that. But the girl hates Tallon – why else set her ravens and the hounds on him? Should you not use her first? Why not change places with her? Exchange your hat with her cap, her cloak with yours, and maybe they'll mistake her for you. Tallon will chase her whilst you slip by unnoticed.'

The princess frowns, perplexed. 'And you'd do that, witch?'

I nod my head. 'Yes, my lady.'

Her eyes are narrowed, distrustful of me as ever. 'All right. Let us try this plan.'

CHAPTER 21

To anybody's ears, it would sound like madness. Our task is to ride east, leading our enemy on a wild goose chase into the royal forest. Criss-crossed with paths and rides, hopefully it will prove a maze in which we can lose them. Fitz remembers enough of the terrain to know that is cut through by a river, and beyond that a heath to the north-east. All this we will have to traverse if we are to reach the fortified palace of Kenninghall whose walls, we hope, will defend us against Tallon and his soldiers. Ordinarily, I would be far too scared to set foot in a royal forest, knowing that, if I did, I would likely be arrested for trespass and have my thumbs nailed to the pillory.

As Mistress Dormer ties the strings of my travel-stained cap under Lady Mary's chin, the princess seems beaten down with exhaustion. She droops, very like the feather on the French riding hat that Lucretia is presently engaged in pinning to my curls. Once this exchange of clothing is done, the four of us in the decoy party – Fitz, Lucretia, Turnspit and I – watch in silence as the princess and her seven attendants turn their horses around and canter away, back in the direction of Thetford.

Fitz gives a brave attempt at a smile. 'We'll be able to buy them some time at least.'

'I hope we can do more than that.' Lucretia tries to sound bold, but all I hear is uncertainty in her voice. 'You and I can juggle eight balls, swallow a fire blade, perform all those tricks … remember?'

If she thinks Sir John Tallon is a man easily gulled, she has much to learn. We have an unwinnable fight ahead. The four of us must pit ourselves against a hundred horsemen, not to mention a hunter who will never give up. Lucretia casts me a sidelong glance, and I know she is wondering if I can exercise my gift to get the cavalry horses to buck their riders off. But she knows it doesn't work like that. I might as well ask for the moon.

The morning sun grows stronger with every second that passes. A heat haze shimmers above the dusty yellow road. Beyond it, a mud-coloured smear bleeds into the sky, caused by the relentless hooves of Tallon's cavalry soldiers. Riding towards the threat feels like lunacy, but I trust Turnspit will show us the way.

Half a mile along the road to Lopham Parva, the two farm horses break into a heavy trot, encouraged by Lucretia's light-footed mare. I exchange an uneasy glance with her and we slow them to a walk. Both of us can tell Fitz is struggling. The jolting gait of his horse is rough on his shoulder – we can see it in the tense line of his jaw and the stiff way he holds himself. How will he bear up if we are forced into a chase? Turnspit seems to understand our concern, so he sets the pace carefully, every so often darting a watchful glance at him.

Riding down this same stretch earlier, as Sir Godfrey Knowles's captives, Fitz and I spotted a deer running onto a track, off to our left, that led into the woods. I wish I could remember exactly where. It might be our best hope.

As if reading my mind, Fitz asks, 'Dela, remember that path we saw before? I'm sure it was about here.'

'It can't be far.' My voice sounds more confident than I feel.

The dust cloud ahead is starting to take on a more defined outline. Through its whorls and eddies, I can make out the spiked mass of a troop of soldiers, their pikes and pennants pointing skywards. The hoof-beats are still a distant rumble, like the grumbles of thunder before a storm, but the sound is getting louder with every second.

And then I see it: a break in the trees. Turnspit has it in his sights already; he gives a sharp bark, and, in that split second, I hear a bugle call, harsh and insistent.

'They've seen us! Quick!'

Our sweating mares need no encouragement. In a moment, we have left the hot dusty road and dived into the cool dappled green of the forest. Turnspit takes us on a winding route, avoiding the broader rides. He gives tiny yaps that our horses seem to understand.

Lucretia takes the lead, her red hair rippling like wildfire down her back. Behind her, Fitz looks like a ghost boy. I can tell from his rigid white face that he is desperately holding onto what little is left of his strength. His hair is stuck to his forehead with sweat, his eyes shining with the brightness of fever.

Another bugle call. With a quick glance behind him, Turnspit takes us deeper into the thicket, following the half-paths made by deer and foxes. Lucretia is first to follow, her grey mare weaving through the undergrowth without trouble. Fitz is hunched over in his saddle, holding the reins loosely with one hand. His freckled farm horse stumbles her way over tree roots, the woolly hair of her fetlocks catching in the brambles. A moment later, she trips heavily, and Fitz tumbles headfirst from the saddle, his foot catching in the stirrup. The horse recovers herself and lumbers on, dragging him behind like a rag doll.

'Lucretia! Grab the reins!' I shriek at her.

Luckily for us, all three horses come to a sudden halt. We've come to the edge of a high bank topped with beech trees whose exposed roots dangle like woody tentacles over the mouth of a cobwebby hollow. We free Fitz's foot from the stirrup and sit him up against the trunk of a beech. His eyes are closed, lashes dark against bloodless cheeks. He cannot go on.

'You stay here with him,' I tell Lucretia. 'Hide down there.' I point to the cave behind the tree roots. 'I'll draw the men away.'

Her eyes flick to Fitz. 'It won't work. Their hounds will find us anyway.'

'Not if I take the horses. The scent will confuse them. Just keep out of sight.'

She nods, grabbing my hand. 'Take my mare, she's faster. You mustn't worry about us. I'll look after him.'

Once I'm in the saddle, she brings the two farm horses and hands me their reins. I try to paste on a brave smile, telling her I hope to see her at Kenninghall later, though I don't think either of us believes it. The last I see of her, she's crouched over Fitz, then the noise of the hunt rips through the forest, and I'm away.

I release the two mares and manage to dissuade them from following. My hope is that they might draw off some of Tallon's men. I can hear them now: the crashing of

branches, soldiers shouting, their mastiffs' barks. I tell myself that at least we are still ahead of them. If we can keep
up a good pace, we have a chance.

Then I come down to earth with a crash. Our way is
blocked by a river. Turnspit pauses, sniffing the air. Before
he can choose a new path, something rushes out of the
trees. A flash of white and russet. And then it is upon us.

A muscular scent hound makes a dart at my horse, who
rears in alarm. Turnspit throws himself at the dog, going
for the back of the neck. His teeth grip, but the other
is too strong for him and wrenches himself free. Turnspit
dances round his opponent like a boxer, next going for the
throat, using the force of his powerful front legs to help
him ram the other dog head-on. They roll in a snarling
mass of teeth and fur.

I scream Turnspit's name, but it is too late. He falls —
they both fall — into the river, still at each other's throats.
I dismount quickly and, ripping off my hat, throw myself
onto the bank. Thinking to catch Turnspit by the scruff,
I stretch out an arm, but just when I get the chance the
other dog is uppermost, holding Turnspit under. In a panic I grab at him, but he wriggles from my grasp, and the
current takes them both.

'Turnspit!'

At my cry the little dog breaks free, and I see his pale
nose raise itself bravely. He is in the middle of the river,
paddling for all he is worth. I scramble to my feet and sprint
along the bank. His strength is starting to give out. Desperate, he scrabbles for a floating branch and hooks his forepaws over it, but, just as I think he's safe, it rolls over. Losing
his balance and the last of his strength, he is swallowed up.

'Turnspit!'

I plunge in.

The storm of yesterday has swelled the river, littering it with branches and leaves. There is no sign of either dog. I clamber along the riverbed, weed dragging at my legs. Under my feet, the stones are slippery; it is almost impossible to keep my footing. I am terrified I will fall and get sucked under. I peer through the brown murk desperately.

Just then the mastiffs pour out of the undergrowth, six of them circling, noses to the ground. Butcher dogs, trained to rip the face off a man – their skulls one big jaw filled with knives. I stumble and fall. The floodwater closes over my head, rushes into my mouth. I'm drowning, fighting to get upright, but it tugs me downstream.

The current tumbles me over, then suddenly I am the right way up, on my feet again. I move through the water at a crouch, trying to calm myself, keeping only my eyes above the surface. I can see a bend ahead. If I can get past it without the mastiffs or soldiers seeing me, maybe I can scramble onto the opposite bank. If I'm lucky, the northerly breeze will keep my scent from the dogs. Maybe Lucretia's mare will help by drawing them away. My mind scrabbles while my eyes scan the muddy water. I fear Turnspit may have drowned, but a part of me clings to the hope that he has escaped and is waiting for me further downriver.

Shouts now, coming from the other side of the bend. They have found Lady Mary's hat and will guess that its wearer has jumped into the river. I struggle onto the bank and stagger along the edge of the reeds, looking for Turnspit. He is not there. And, with that, the tiny flicker of hope I've been nursing is snuffed out.

I have no time for grief or despair. The men's voices are close – horsemen are rounding the bend on the other bank – and terror has me in its grip. My skirts cling to my legs. How can I run in these wet clothes? I pull my kirtle over my head quickly, then I take to my heels, wearing nothing but a knee-length linen smock and my boots.

The mastiffs cross the river. They are gaining on me fast – I can hear it from their barks. The breath tears in my chest, roaring raggedly in my ears. I run blind, with no idea where I'm going. I need a plan: they'll be upon me in a moment, and then it will be too late. Stopping, I cast about wildly. I need to find a tree to climb. That way I might save myself ... for a while at least.

I spy a spreading chestnut and run to it. The lowest branch is just out of reach. I jump, and my fingers just touch it, grazing the bark. I can't get a grip. A quick look over my shoulder. A white blur, pounding feet ... and the mastiffs tear into the glade.

Raw fear drives me to leap higher than before, enough to grasp the branch and swing my legs over it just as the jaw of the first mastiff snaps shut, inches from my foot.

The branch is too low; I need to get to the next. Tallon has bred these butcher dogs for war, trained them to tear a horse down. They have the power in their hind legs to jump higher than a man. I stand, my back to the trunk, eyes wide in terror as one by one they spring, swiping at my legs with hooked claws. I have to climb, but how can I? My body is rigid with fear.

When the first dog's teeth graze my boot, slashing through the leather, I have no choice. Desperate, I reach upwards, and my hands catch hold of a branch three feet above my head. Gripping hard, so that the bark cuts my fingers, I manage to swing my legs and lock them around it. Another scrabble, and I'm astride. I lean back against the trunk, wipe the sweat from my eyes.

How long do I have? *Think, Dela!* Tallon will take a few minutes finding the best crossing place for the horses, but does that even matter? It's not as if I can get away.

Snarling, the mastiffs circle the tree, black eyes in their flat white heads fixed on me.

Just then, a magpie flies onto the end of my branch and gives a loud screech. Another joins it. *Two for joy.* I almost laugh at that, but then I think … maybe, just maybe … *Use your gift, Dela. Own it.*

I make a picture in my mind's eye: magpies diving down to jab at the eyes of the mastiffs. *Come, birds! Do my bidding, I beg of you.*

But they don't swoop down on the dogs. Instead, they fly straight at me, flapping and screeching. They have nestlings, I realise, and must think I'm a danger to their young. Gripping the branch between my knees, I cling on desperately, but with all the batting of wings and scratching claws I find myself slipping. I can't hold on.

As I fall I make a grab for the branch and manage to catch it with my fingers so that I dangle, my feet almost on a level with the mastiffs' heads. They lunge and snap, and I kick at them.

I close my eyes and the sky turns black. A rush of air, the beating of wings. For a moment, I think the magpie pair have somehow summoned a flock to help them. I open my eyes a crack.

Ravens. A black, flapping mass that descends upon the dogs with guttural cries. Hanging from the branch, I move my lips in a whisper.

You came!

Beneath me, the dogs haven't given up snapping and clawing at my legs, and I can't hold out much longer. Numb from gripping the bark, my fingers are slipping.

The ravens fly in battalions, five at each mastiff, each bird as swift and deadly as a cormorant diving for a fish. From high up, they tuck in their wings and plummet, arrow-like, to pierce the flesh of the snarling butcher dogs. I cannot look down, but I hear the battle, feel the storm of their wings.

The mastiffs snap and twist as the ravens' beaks do their work, the birds timing their dives perfectly. Then at last I hear it – the tide of the battle turning. Growls of aggression become yelps of pain as one by one the dogs give up and run away.

I drop to the ground, rolling to absorb the shock of my fall. Lying curled on the forest floor, I keep my arms about my face, though my attackers have gone. All is quiet, save for the distant whining of the fleeing mastiffs. I open my eyes. The battlefield is littered with feathers, but no dead ravens, thank goodness. One of the mastiffs lies on its side, stabbed through the eye to its brain, still twitching, as if chasing a coney in its sleep.

The forest feels different to me now, more threatening. The trees whisper like spies; I could swear that eyes, hidden in patches of dappled shade, watch my movements. A distant bugle call sets the mastiffs barking, some way off now. The soldiers have crossed the river, and once they're reunited with the dogs the hunt will resume in earnest. There is no time to lose. I think back to Fitz's description of the terrain, and where I will need to head to get to Kenninghall. North-east, he said. Across the heath. The problem is that the sun is high in the sky; I cannot hope to work out my direction from it. I pray that some inner sense will take me roughly the right way. If only I had Turnspit, my navigator-in-chief, to help me.

Pushing aside bracken and branches, I stagger through the undergrowth, taking the fox paths I guess he would have chosen. After what seems like an age, I emerge, scratched and bleeding, onto a broad ride. Ahead of me, I glimpse brightness through the beech leaves and my heart lifts. An open stretch – one that might signal the start of the heath.

When I break through, my eyes cannot believe what I see. Sun sparkling on water ... a river. And there, on the opposite bank, the plume from my hat.

I sink to my knees and bury my face in my hands, feeling the heavy weight of defeat crushing my shoulders. I am useless, hopeless, not worthy of this fight. How could I have ever thought I was?

Heaving sobs next, my frame quaking as they come. My ears are so taken up with the noisy sounds of self-pity that it is a while before I am conscious of anything else.

A splash ... a scuffling. I raise my head and listen, push away the hair from my eyes.

At first I think the wet, dark-brown shape emerging from the rushes is an otter ... but it isn't.

In a moment, I have my arms around Turnspit, lips pressed to the bedraggled nest on top of his head. He sets about licking the scratches on my face and arms, then stops

and cocks his head, ears pricked. He sniffs the air, pale nose
twitching from side to side. Soldiers, coming this way.

Time to run.

The trees thin out the further we head from the river, a
scattering of birches and pines, under which the bleached
grass and the odd patch of furze are the only ground cover.
We must be nearing the heath, but this terrain makes me
nervous. Fewer places to hide.

Turnspit pauses, forepaw raised. His nose has picked up
the scent of something … smoke. Probably wildfire: the
whole forest is dry as tinder. I take a moment to catch my
breath, bend over to ease the stitch in my side.

Then I see them. Four soldiers on horseback, coming
this way. No sign of dogs. A pause while they scan the trees
for movement. Heart pounding, I duck down behind a
gorse bush. One of the men is Tallon, I'm sure of it. Seated
on a great black charger, the figure has that particular alert
quality, the hawk-like set of his head.

Turnspit's gaze turns from me to the open ground
before us. His eyes fix on a group of pine trees on the far
side, from which a spiral of smoke rises. Surely, he can't
want us to break cover? They'd see us in an instant. A girl
on foot in a white smock … I wouldn't stand a chance.

He gives a yap; I remain in a crouch. Growling, he fixes
me with insistent brown eyes. *All right, Turnspit. You win.*

We race across the open ground. Behind us, a man
shouts, 'That's her!'

A moment later, a bolt hisses past my head. I run harder,
weaving wildly to dodge another missile, then another.

Galloping hooves pound the ground behind me, then I'm under the cover of pines.

Turnspit leads me to a clearing, ringed by trees, where the last embers of a fire are smouldering. A woodsman's hut stands at one end, a track beyond it. My mind skitters over my choices. Hide in the hut? Keep running? The track must surely lead to a lane. Desperate, I turn to Turnspit for an answer. He gazes at me with unwavering cobnut eyes. He has a plan, I know he does. But what?

I dive behind a pile of logs neatly stacked beside the woodsman's hut. I'm only just in time: a crack of brush-wood, and the four horsemen enter the clearing.

They spread out quickly, Tallon making sure to block the track behind the hut. 'She's got to be here. Just look!'

Motionless beside me, Turnspit growls low in his throat. For a moment all is still, as if the air has been sucked out of the clearing, then Tallon dismounts. I hold my breath, waiting for his next move. He leaves his horse, walks towards the hut.

Turnspit makes a dash for the smouldering bonfire, a twiggy branch of dead brushwood in his jaws which he drags along behind him. Dropping it next to the fire, he leaps into the embers and kicks hard, throwing up a cloud of ash and sparks. The pads of his paws must be scorched to blisters.

Tallon pauses, stares at Turnspit, and motions to one of his men to see to him. Then he heads towards the hut, intent on finding me.

It all happens in a moment. Sparks from the embers catch the dry brushwood. It takes only a second for the fire to flare and spread, and very soon it lights the stack of logs behind which I am hiding. Sleeve over my mouth and nose, I run for it, catching Tallon off guard. Deciding not to pursue me on foot, instead he grabs the reins of his horse and leaps on its back. He'll ride me down in a heartbeat!

The flames lick quickly at the dry bracken and pine needles; very soon, they leap from tree to tree. Three of the horses panic, screaming as they take off through the pines, tails alight like tapers. I make for the track out of the copse, Turnspit at my heels, barely able to see anything through the smoke. Before we get there, Tallon's stallion suddenly looms in front of us, pawing the ground, blocking our way out of the inferno.

'Give up, Dela. You can't get away,' he shouts. 'Come. I'll lead you out.'

The smoke tears at my lungs, making my eyes stream. I dither, while Turnspit barks, then we back up, making for the middle of the clearing. The heat fries my hair, my arms. Dimly through the smoke I see that Tallon, instead of taking the safe route out of the blaze, is coming back for us. The flames are all around him now, and his stallion wheels, eyes rolling wildly, trying to turn. But Tallon will not give up: he is determined to get to me, even though I'm finished anyway. He tugs at the rein, and his horse rears up, shrieking in terror. When his cape catches fire, I don't think he is aware of it, and as his stallion bolts through the blaze it streams out behind him like a flaming standard.

I am curled in a crouch, arms over my face, but Turnspit won't let me rest. Dragging at my torn smock, he gives a low growl. How can I possibly walk? I can't even breathe. But, somehow, I stagger to my feet, and through half-shuttered eyes I take a few stumbling steps in the wake of the little dog while smoke rakes its path to my lungs. I bend over and cough, try to take a breath, then cough again. Turnspit tugs at my smock and the linen rips; he will not give up.

Finally, without any breath left in my body, I manage to stagger along the path he's found for us through the blaze, praying that Tallon isn't already positioned at the end to block us.

Instead, though, I hear a delighted shout ahead: 'Dela! Turnspit!'

Where the track meets the lane, Lucretia waits for us astride her mare. Beside her stands my sturdy farm horse. At first, I think she must be a ghost of my imagination, but there is something so robust about her — cross-toothed grin splitting her face — that I cannot doubt that she is here in front of us.

She dismounts and pulls me into a hug. 'The mares came back, all three of them. We couldn't believe it!' She draws back and holds my shoulders, the better to study me. 'My goodness, *ragazza*, you are a sight. What did they do to you?'

'Where's Fitz? Is he all right?'

'Two of the stablehands at Kenninghall were sent to find us. They brought a bloodhound with them — had given it my scent,' she explains. 'They took Fitz back with them. I refused to go.'

'Lucretia, how can I ever thank you!'

'By not thanking me,' she says gruffly. 'A Pisanelli would never leave one of their kin in trouble. *Certo che no!*'

I swallow the lump in my throat at her words; my eyes are streaming enough as it is. 'Did Lady Mary's party reach Kenninghall safely?'

'Yes, thanks to us.' She taps my arm briskly. 'Now let us not stand around making sheep's eyes. Tallon's men have backed off for the moment, but we must hurry.'

CHAPTER 22

When the Duke of Norfolk built Kenninghall Place he spared no expense in making a fortress of his fine new redbrick palace. But neither the moat and drawbridge, the gatehouse with its sharp-toothed portcullis, nor even its well-stocked armoury could save him – the most powerful noble in the land – from being locked in the Tower once King Henry had had enough of him. After her father's death, Lady Mary had been given the palace in her dower. I pray she hasn't inherited Norfolk's bad luck with it. Kenninghall's walls will have to prove strong in her defence.

It is late afternoon when we ride up to the mighty gatehouse, a tired Turnspit tucked at my side against the lip of my saddle. We find the place humming. Hundreds of country folk – yeoman farmers, smallholders, farm workers – have taken over the outer court. After the horrifying day we've had, it seems strange to witness such high spirits: comrades helping each other to pitch tents, tether cows and horses, shoulder sacks of grain. The scene reminds me of the fair when it comes to Maldon; I half-expect to see children bobbing for apples.

On seeing us, Mistress Dormer hurries out of the porter's lodge. 'Thank heavens you're safe!'

I hand a wilting Turnspit to the porter, who quickly drops him on the cobbles and wipes his hands on his doublet. Feeling the pain of my bruises, I dismount gingerly, while Mistress Dormer instructs a groom to take our horses to the stables.

After clasping Lucretia's hands in welcome, she turns to me. 'Goodness! Where is your kirtle? You look as though a hound from hell has torn you to ribbons. Didn't your animals help this time?'

I'm about to reply crossly, but Lucretia interrupts with 'How is Fitz?'

'Mending well. But you mustn't mind that now – I have something far more important to tell you. The king is dead. The Spanish ambassador sent his courier with the news.'

I've been expecting King Edward's death – we all have – but I feel the shock of it anyway. Beside me, Lucretia is wide-eyed, and I realise I'm not alone in feeling the ground shift violently beneath my feet.

'What is to happen now?' she asks.

'He changed the succession before he died. It's what we feared. Lady Jane Grey is to have the crown.'

'And what of Lady Mary?'

'Having none of it. She's sent her man Hungate to London with a letter telling the Council they must proclaim her right and true title to the throne.' This new shock silences us. 'There is no going back from it. Mary has thrown down her gauntlet.'

After a pause, Lucretia says, 'I feel almost sorry for the Grey moppet. Never a day when she wasn't bullied. I never cared for the sour little milksop, but I wouldn't wish this on her. The duke has her by the throat.'

'And he will bring the full weight of his fist down on Mary's head if she tries to get in his way.'

Mistress Dormer's eyes are fearful. I remind myself that she is not that much older than me. Until the rest of Mary's company arrives at Kenninghall, she carries the burden of being the queen's only lady companion.

'Robert Dudley, Northumberland's son, is on his way to arrest Mary. Four hundred mounted troops. And when the duke gets her letter, he'll send more — thousands more.'

'What of Emperor Charles?' asks Lucretia. 'Has he said he will back her claim?'

The lady-in-waiting shakes her head, eyes darkening. 'His letter advised her to go quietly. Make her peace with Northumberland. Get to a priory, save herself from the Tower. He says she hasn't a hope of defending her title. Not when the duke holds the mint and the armouries. And with his warships blocking the eastern ports …'

'So she's bent on ignoring her cousin's advice.'

'You know what she's like. Never one to be told what she shouldn't do.'

I picture the princess as I saw her this morning — braving it out, but grey-faced with tiredness. As soon as she got here, she must have faced this new situation, straightened her narrow shoulders. It's true what Mistress Dormer says. She is a fighter — you can see it in her eyes.

'She called everyone into the great chamber — even the sweaty scullions — and announced herself queen. You should have been there. We were in tears … hugging one another.'

'So what now?' asks Lucretia.

Mistress Dormer's eyes lose their sparkle, elation leaking from her as she regards the milling throng in the outer court.

'We have to pray that some of the richer landowners turn up tomorrow. Ones with troops and arms. I doubt if any of these men know how to handle a proper weapon. Catapults for stoning crows, if we're lucky.'

I think of the rumbling gun carriages making their way out of London and gaze at the honest, weatherbeaten faces of the men. Tears prick my eyes. 'But they're here to defend the queen! That must count for something. Look at them – they've come to fight. *Want* to fight for her!'

These men are my people, familiar to me as home. It could have been my father here. He'd have been the first to sling a rope around his cow and make his way to Kenninghall. I'll warrant they have come for one thing – Northumberland's head, safely on a spike where they can see it. They've never forgotten that he was the one who slaughtered Kett's rebels on Mousehold Heath, only a few miles from here. Three thousand men of the soil. A crime that not one of these good comrades will ever forgive. If protecting Mary is what it will take to bring the duke down, they'll happily give their lives to do it.

Mistress Dormer looks on me kindly. 'You are right. These men are lions. But we need more help, proper weapons. Pitchforks and pruning hooks will be of little use against the might of the duke's army. Even now, Mary has everyone who can hold a quill seated in the great chamber, making copies of the letter she sent to London. They're going out tonight to some of the richest landowners in the country. Let's hope her couriers have wings on their feet, or we're doomed.'

We walk past the washhouse where the launderers are busily sorting out linen. Mary has arrived without warning, and it has thrown the household into frantic activity. From this outer courtyard, we pass through an arch into a smaller one.

'Ewery Court. It will be quiet till the rest of the company arrives. You'll want to be together, I imagine. I'll tell them to bring linen and a ewer, have some clothes sent down.'

She shows us to our chamber and hesitates a moment in the doorway. 'You've done well, Mistress Wisbey. The queen will give her thanks in time ... But, for now, it's best you keep scarce.'

I am not given the chance. We have just finished washing our faces and hands and helping each other into our gowns when we hear a knock at the door. Lucretia opens it to find a maid, breathless with running, her face blotched red beneath her cap.

'If you please, mistress, her majesty commands the witch girl's presence in the great chamber.'

Lucretia darts a glance at me, then back at the girl. 'Calm yourself, girl. Did she say why she wants to see Mistress Wisbey?'

'All I know is there's a great speckledy raven standin' on the table. Starin' and squawkin' at the queen.'

We hurry to the east wing. My mind is in a turmoil. The grey raven – it has to be. If he's come to help Mary, he won't get any thanks for it. She'll be the first to call him the devil's bird.

When we enter the great tapestry-lined chamber, my eyes are drawn immediately to my old friend, halfway down the long oak table, standing taller than the top of the queen's head. Faced with the bird's fluffed-up majesty, Mary has shrunk a little into herself, as if it is the bird, not she, who is the royal one.

As I look from one to the other, two things are clear to me. The queen is obstinately set on her opinion that the raven is an instrument of the devil, and the bird is trying, yet failing, to perform an elaborate courtship of her. He has raised the feathers above his eyes so that they appear to be two fluffy ears sticking out at the sides. The ones on his breast and throat are exaggerated into shaggy hackles; those on his flanks are puffed out like a Spaniard's doublet. His wings are spread a little at the shoulders, further creating the look of inflated pride. He takes strutting steps towards the queen, backs off, then comes at her again. Making cooing, impassioned calls to woo her, he gives a little bow every time he approaches.

Wide-eyed with fear, she seems both horrified and relieved to see me. 'What is the bird doing? He's yours, is he not? Call him away! His eyes …'

This part of his courtship, in particular, unnerves her. The raven thinks that the blinks of his second eyelid – flashing white – are alluring. It works on the females of his flock, so why not on the queen? But when the white skin lowers over his beady eyes, I can see that the contrast against the black of his feathers might appear to be sinister to one who does not know better.

I hurry to explain the misunderstanding. 'Your grace, it is his courtship ritual. Nothing more.'

Rochester, her beanpole of a comptroller, gives a discreet cough. 'Your grace, she speaks the truth. My father explained the white-eyed trick to me when I was a boy.'

'You say "trick", sir. The devil is keen on tricks. This bird is a lure set to trap me. I won't hear otherwise.'

'He's no lure!' I burst out. 'The raven's come to pay his respects.' The injustice of it hurts. The bird is doing his best, but she refuses to see it.

'Quiet! You've done quite enough. Just get rid of him. After that, I'll decide what to do with you.'

At my feet, Turnspit gives a growl. The raven, still intent on his courtship, makes an elaborate bow, skipping from foot to foot. Then, like a foreigner who has failed to make himself understood, he finally gives up and struts towards the pile of parchment scrolls.

It is only now that I see what the men are doing at the other end of the long table. Quills in hand, a handful of scribes write furiously, pausing only to dip their nibs into the ink. They are preparing parchment letters, pleas for help, ready for Mary's couriers.

Lucretia ventures to speak. 'Your grace, I think it has something to do with those scrolls. The bird thinks to tell you something.'

The queen's lips tighten. She hasn't yet forgiven the tumbler for her outburst this morning. 'Methinks the devil seeks to distract us from our course. Those scrolls are all that stand between our victory and utter devastation.'

She cradles her forehead in her hand. 'Though I hardly think the couriers will get there in time. We'll need Cheshire, Devon … not just the eastern counties.'

Then her head snaps back and she fixes a pair of cool grey eyes on me. 'It's bad enough I have to contend with the devil-girl and her mangy dog. This horrid bird is all I need.'

As she says it, the raven grabs a scroll in its beak, fastening on the red ribbon. He flies to the open window and stands on the stone sill.

'I think he wants to deliver it!' Lucretia blurts out. 'You could try telling him who to take it to. One of those rich landowners we need so badly.'

In response, the bird dips his speckled head.

'I will hear no more of this. The devil clearly has your tongue,' Mary snaps.

Rochester clears his throat. 'Your grace, the girl's magic has helped you before …'

'So you admit she's a witch and yet think to use her?'

Rochester flushes and sits back in his seat. Meanwhile, the raven gives a gurgling croak from the back of his throat. It rises in pitch, filling the huge chamber with sound. The queen stares at the bird, transfixed, hand to her chest. He takes a few sideways hops and waits. His call is answered by a harsh, rattling cry from the trees outside.

Another raven swoops down to the sill, cocks its head, and dives to snatch one of the scrolls. Out it goes, and another takes its place – swoop, snatch, and it's gone.

Mary starts up from her chair, eyes popping from her head. 'Make them stop! Do something! Stop them!'

Rochester stumbles to his feet, knocking over his chair. He and Mary flap their hands, shouting at the birds, but they continue to come – one after the other – till all the scrolls have been taken. It only takes seconds, then the table is empty.

After the ravens have gone, a hollowness grips the room. Pointing a trembling finger at me, the queen explodes, purple with rage.

'All I asked … *all* I wanted was that bird off the table. But you couldn't do it, could you? Satan has you by the throat, so you do his bidding, not mine. And now the best chance I had of being queen has flown out of the window. I should have you dragged back to the forest, let the creatures eat your innards – the ones you call friend. Then you'll know what treachery feels like.'

I draw myself up, lock eyes with her. I can't hold my tongue. 'You don't know what a friend is. And if you go on ignoring the good folk trying to help, you will lose.' My voice is clear as a bell in the still room. 'I've fought for you – got clawed and cut to pieces. I saved your life, though you'd have had me killed. And now the ravens try to help, yet you're too stubborn to see it. You should be thanking them. Thanking me.'

Mary stares, her eyes black in her chalk-white face. Beside me, Lucretia brings her hands up to cover her cheeks. Turnspit sidles into my skirts. Even he can see that I've gone too far.

CHAPTER 23

I kneel in the chapel on cold, hard tiles, hands tied behind my back. The lower part of my face has been fitted with an iron muzzle, its bars covered with wire mesh. That way I cannot bite anyone or vomit toads from my mouth. My knees hurt; the rope cuts into my wrists; metal digs into my sore face.

It is morning. A cool, clear light plays on the tapestries that line the walls. The scenes of Christ's Passion fit my mood perfectly. *Despised and rejected … a Man of sorrows, acquainted with grief.* My eyes are fixed on the foot of a Roman soldier, stitched so lovingly that I can see where his boot has become worn at the toe. My gaze travels from the scuffed leather to the sinewy flesh of Christ's thigh as He tries to climb Golgotha, bent double under the weight of the great wooden cross. Here, on my knees, I know exactly how that feels.

Not far away, seated in a pew, Mary consults with her chaplain, a mild-faced, blinking man whose small body is drowned by his cassock.

'I woke this morning, chaplain, and it was clear in my head. I knew I must bring her to you.'

'H-how can I help your grace?' stammers the man, running a finger between his collar and neck.

'I have been thinking of my Spanish grandmother, Isabella, and the work she did to rid her country of infidels. She had her Grand Inquisitor – a man of the cloth – preside over her tribunals. And although I cannot expect you to fill such a role ...'

The man swallows nervously. 'R-role?'

'To help me clean my country of heresy. It is a contagion – one that easily spreads. We have seen it, have we not?' Her gaze is bright, penetrating.

'I-indeed we have,' The man's tiny head wags nervously under his square hat with rounded earflaps.

'We must begin now. Do you see?'

'You mean with this g-girl.'

'I do. It is my duty to protect my people. I have an authority, divinely ordained. I confess all this new responsibility feels strange ... heavy on my shoulders ... but I will start as I mean to go on. Innocent Christians must not be led astray by heretics like this witch. I cannot let it happen.'

'N-no, indeed.'

'The question is, how shall we sweep the devil from our house? She must be dealt with, or she will drag us under.' She takes a breath, waits for his contribution.

'I've heard that sorcerers cannot speak the scriptures aloud,' the chaplain offers hopefully. 'If we have her recite the P-Paternoster maybe the d-devil will leap out ... show himself.'

'She is too clever for that. The devil is a trickster, after all.'

'He is indeed, your grace.'

She smiles, warming to her theme. 'I've come to you as my teacher, a learned man who must help me decide. I warrant you know every word of the Bible, as well as our Lord's doctrine concerning witchcraft. I myself made it my study this morning after Mass.' She reaches into the purse suspended from her girdle and draws out a sheet of parchment, which she brings near to her face and consults with a squint of her near-sighted brown eyes.

'Deuteronomy has it clear: "*aut qui ariolos sciscitetur, et observet somnia atque auguria, nec sit maleficus, nec incantator, nec qui pythones consulat, nec divinos, aut quærat a mortuis veritatem*".'

The chaplain, certain of his text, translates without stammering. 'Let no one be found among you who practises divination or sorcery, interprets omens, casts spells, consults with familiars, talks to the dead.'

She nods vigorously. 'And here in the Apocalypse: *Ego sum Alpha et Omega* – you know the verse, don't you. "Those who practise magic arts, the idolaters and liars, shall be consigned to the fiery lake of burning sulphur".'

She turns her bright gaze up to his face. 'You see it, don't you? My grandmother Isabella had it right. Burn them at the stake. Give the heretic a foretaste of hellfire and she will recant.'

'Though she'll die whilst she does it,' the chaplain ventures to remark.

'That's as may be. But I have to cleanse my company of this witch! *Maleficos non patieris vivere*. Suffer not a sorcerer to live … You know it, I know it.'

The chaplain's square hat with earflaps bobs as he nods his head.

Two of Mary's guards take me down the stone steps to the cellar. They make a show of dragging me, though I am perfectly able to walk. Like everyone else at Kenninghall, the men are keen to put their back into any task they're given, such is their eagerness to serve the queen.

We pass through the wine cellar, and as we make our subterranean progress under the great hall the air grows mustier by the second.

I spent last night here, deep in the bowels of the earth. The guards call my cell 'the oubliette', after the French word for 'forget'. Though, in truth, it isn't one of those – neither do I have to be dropped through a trapdoor, nor will I be forgotten. The queen will make quite sure of that.

I have to feel my way to the bucket they've placed for my needs. Little else in this dark cell: just a pitcher of water beside a pile of old straw that crumbles into dust under the weight of my body. At least the guards have unstrapped my iron muzzle so I can drink.

I am glad Turnspit isn't with me. Lucretia hid him in her skirts last night as they came to drag me off. I am too hollow – too low – to support him. I've moved beyond fear to a strange place where I feel no interest in anything at all. Build the bonfire, set up the stake – it's all the same to me.

The girl I was, before my gift was thrust upon me, is a stranger to me now. I've forgotten who I am. On re-flection, maybe the oubliette isn't such a bad name for this place.

It is strange not knowing if it is day or night. After a while, I lose all sense of time. I'm topsy-turvy, as I was the day Rob and I took turns in a cider barrel while the other rolled it down Fish Street. I am equally confused when it comes to sleep and wakefulness. Which is which? Am I asleep or awake? It's hard to tell.

As the hours pass, snippets of my life spool through my mind like coloured threads. Years ago, I saw a man being dragged out of the water after falling into the mill race. After coughing up the muck from his lungs, he told us how his whole life had passed before his eyes. Later, I watched him walking off – thoughtful, as if wondering at the choices he'd made and whether it wasn't too late to repair them. Is my mind playing a similar trick now that I am close to death?

The years have brought a string of lost causes. My father's fight against the land enclosures. My mother's bid to get him released. Ned helping a worthless spy. Mary trying to get the better of Northumberland. Sal believing me to be special, worth protecting. What a load of hogwash. Special? That is the biggest joke of all. The ground is littered with my mistakes, the people I've hurt. And the thing they call my gift? Nothing but a sick joke with ugly consequences.

Mary is right: it is better that I die.

Fitz sneaks in. I don't know how he got past the guards – they're not in the mood to be bribed. At first, I think he is part of my dream. It is only the smell of him – hay and saddle leather – that persuades me he is real.

He sets down his lantern, puts his hands through the bars to touch my face.

I shrink away. 'What are you doing here? You must go!'

'I had to see you.' His expression is earnest, open.

There's still a part of me that wants to reach out to him, but I couldn't bear to be responsible for the death of another person. I know what will happen if he's caught with me. 'It's not worth it. *I'm* not worth it. Just go.'

'Don't say that. We aren't giving up. You mustn't either. Jane's here. She arrived with the others this afternoon. We're hoping she'll have better luck with the queen.'

'Tell her not to bother.'

'Don't be like that. There's still hope. We'll get you out somehow.'

I flare at him. 'You just don't understand, do you?'

He recoils a little. 'What? Why are you being like this? This isn't you.'

'And just what is *me*? You think you know, do you?'

'I think you're the bravest person I've ever met.'

'Well that just shows how stupid you are.'

He doesn't say anything but stoops to slide something under the bars of my cell.

In the glow of his lantern I can see it is one of his drawings. I move a little closer, pick it up. The sketch is of Turnspit – lying on his back, begging to have his stomach tickled.

'I drew it that night I brought Bessie to New Hall. You told me not to tease him. Do you remember?'

I pick it up and inspect it in the light, committing it to memory before darkness once more makes it impossible to see. 'I remember,' I whisper.

He stoops to pick up the lantern.

I have one thing to ask before he goes. 'Fitz … can you do something for me?'

He comes close to the bars, presses his face to them. 'Anything.'

'When it comes to the time … you know … when they do it … I don't want Turnspit to see … None of you should be there. Those pictures stay in your head. I don't want that.'

He nods, and I can see the tears glitter in his eyes.

They come for me the next morning, strap on my muzzle. The same two guards do the dragging, one each side, gripping me under the arms. This time they need to half-carry me. Faint with lack of food, I stumble along, feet bumping the stone steps as we come up from the cellar. Terror grips my throat – a raw fear that takes me by surprise. All this time I've been waiting numbly, wanting to get it over with – so why am I shuddering, clawing to get back to my cell? I had no idea that my instinct to survive would be so strong.

When we emerge into the bright light of morning, the shock of it makes me close my eyes.

'Come on, we haven't got all day.'

Gingerly, I open them a crack.

Mary's loyal farmers have built a great bonfire in the courtyard outside the chapel. They are standing next to it, rows of good-natured fellows, proud of their handiwork. The logs are arranged neatly to form a pyramid, at the centre of which is a tall, straight stake. Waiting for me.

I hear no shouting or jeering. This is no ordinary execution. Mary has had the fire built outside the chapel for a reason; she wants them to know this is a solemn event, held in God's name. My eyes sweep the rows of tight faces. They look away quickly when they catch my stare.

I am the devil. They want me dead. It is all there, written on their weatherbeaten faces.

Mary's chaplain stands with her on a raised platform. Behind them, the stained-glass windows of the chapel flash red and gold in the sun. Both figures look tiny next to the towering pyramid of logs. Swallowed up by his embroidered surplice, the chaplain looks almost as terrified as me. Beside him, Mary stands severe and straight, England's devout queen in waiting.

I told Fitz not to be here, to keep the others away. But now my eyes search desperately for a friendly face. I didn't realise how much I would need someone familiar – loving – to whom I could anchor my gaze once the flames lick my body. *I don't want to be alone. Not here, not now.*

Then I see them. A row of white, pained faces. Lucretia the tumbler, Jane Foole, and Fitz. My friends. I am relieved to see they haven't got Turnspit with them. I couldn't have borne that. He wouldn't have stood it.

The tears come, coursing down my cheeks. Fitz knew I wouldn't want to face this alone. They are here for me. The fear that has me gripped – tight bands round my ribcage – loosens a little. *I can do this.*

The two guards help me to the stake and tie my arms tightly around it. They pause and look at the queen, wondering if they should remove my iron muzzle. Mary shakes her head. *She's still afraid of me. Even now.*

The chaplain begins to intone the words of the Creed. The crowd joins in, and a low Latin hum reverberates around the redbrick walls of the courtyard. '*Credo in Deum Patrem omnipotentem, Creatorem caeli et terrae …*'

One of my guards appears with a flaming torch. He glances at Mary. This time she gives a nod. He touches it to the base of the bonfire. A small bluey-green flame flickers, not yet hungry, content to consume the kindling before it spreads. Behind my muzzle, my nose picks up the smell of smoke. It reminds me of the quiet warmth of Ned's hearth on a winter's evening. I picture him on his knees, teasing a flame with the leather bellows. Strange comfort now. I close my eyes, pick up the words of the Creed, hinge my thoughts to God, ask his forgiveness.

'… *crucifixus, mortuus, et sepultus, descendit ad infernos* …'

A bark, a shout. I open my eyes to see a small brown shape storming into the courtyard. Turnspit, dragging with him a plump nobleman whose standard he has by the teeth.

'Blasted cur! Give that back!'

The nobleman looks up to see Mary watching him from her platform, hands clutching her white leather prayer book.

'Your grace …' He gets creakily to his knees, hand across his chest. Behind him, a mounted battalion of blue-coated soldiers file into the courtyard, two by two.

She steps down from her platform and approaches him. 'Sir Henry Bedingfeld. You are welcome, sir. So welcome.'

The knight speaks loudly, as one who is hard of hearing. 'I came from Oxburgh as soon as I heard.'

'Who brought you word?'

'Not *who*, but *what*. I'd just sat down to supper when a great speckled raven swooped in. Your scroll in its beak. Nearly fell off my chair. Said to the wife, "Grace, dear, 'tis a sign from the heavens."'

Mary darts a look in my direction. 'The raven belongs to the witch. It may be a sign, but it is riddled through with the devil's trickery.'

At this, Fitz breaks from the row of onlookers and dashes forward. 'She is innocent! On your side. The raven proves it. Stop the fire!'

'I will not listen to you, boy. The witch has reeled you in, made you her creature.'

The flames lick their way over the sticks. Turnspit, having rushed to the bonfire, now scrabbles at it, desperately trying to stamp out the flames with his four small feet. I shriek, but that only makes him try harder to scramble up to me.

Lucretia breaks from the ranks and throws herself in front of the queen. 'If Fitz is her creature, then I am too! She has done everything to protect your majesty. Please … *per favore,* save her!'

Sir Henry's bulging eyes stare at me, then back at Mary in bewilderment. 'The raven was hers?'

'One of her familiars. The dog is another.'

'Ah, I see how it is … though it's hard to see the little slip managing all that.'

'All what?' asks the queen.

'I haven't told you the half of it, your grace. I'm not the only one, you see. Southwell had a bird too. Said it wouldn't stop squawking till he'd mustered his troops. He's right behind us now – with cavalry stretching halfway to Norwich.'

Mary stares at him, at a loss for words.

Fitz, who is being held back by a guard, struggles in the man's grip, shouting, 'You *have* to let her go! You have it now. The proof!'

'I have no such thing! Quiet the boy's mouth.'

Through the haze of smoke, I spot Lucretia. She dashes to the fire, holding her cap over her nose, and grabs

Turnspit with a swift scoop. His fur has begun to frazzle; I can smell it. Soon it will be me. The flames are close to my feet, the blaze roasting hot. I begin to whimper, between the scattered words of the Creed.

A muttering swells in the men who throng the courtyard. Their mood has turned to unease. But still Mary stands firm; the queen is not for turning.

Until now, the chaplain has stood at Mary's side, eyes closed, intoning his prayers, but now he summons the pluck to stammer, 'Your grace, you have your mind set on this being the devil's work. But consider this. The Lord works in mysterious ways.' He gazes at her from under his square hat, then plucks up his courage. 'I think Bedingfeld had it right when he took the bird to be a sign.'

'A bloody great sign, if you ask me,' Sir Henry bellows. 'Forgot to tell your grace that the Earl of Bath is a few leagues south. I'll warrant he had one of her ravens too.'

Mary takes a breath. Her voice when it comes is carried in wild shouts from one person to the next.

'Stop the fire!'

Chapter 24

Framlingham Castle, 17th July, 1553

I walk with Turnspit on top of the high curtain wall that encircles Framlingham Castle. Gazing across the flat Suffolk plain, I see men with pennants far below us, small and spiky as stag beetles as they stream along the road leading to the postern gate.

I turn to look at the redbrick buildings inside the enclosure, huddling into the comforting skirts of the great flint wall. *My friends are safely tucked inside*, I reassure myself. Fitz, Lucretia, Jane – even Alfredo, who arrived last night from London.

He came with the latest news. 'The duke's councillors slunk away when the *coglione* left with his army. They'll want to cling to Mary's skirts now.' He lifted his voice in a mocking falsetto. '"We didn't mean it, the duke made us do it!" English scumbags, the lot of them!'

'And Lady Jane?' Fitz asked.

'Alone in the Tower. She'll be for the chop-chop-chop.'

I imagine her, crowned just yesterday, all alone in her great canopied chair of state, crying her eyes out.

'I feel sorry for the Grey moppet,' said Lucretia. 'None of it's her fault, *la povera*.'

I am so engrossed in my thoughts as I make my way along the wall walk that I never notice Mary – not until Turnspit and I are almost upon her. She stands alone, a small, solitary figure scanning the road to the far horizon – reassuring herself, perhaps, that every inch of it is covered with Englishmen ready to fight for her to be queen.

I hesitate, thinking to turn quickly and retreat, but I am too late. She beckons me to her. We stand side by side, and I am reminded of the early days with Fitz when we found it easier talking without having to look into each other's eyes. How different that is now.

Eventually, she breaks the silence. 'We have thirty thousand troops at the last count and still they continue to come. I've made Radclyffe my commander-in-chief – you'll remember him from Woodham Walter. A good man. It's a shame he had to choose such an objectionable wife.'

I don't answer. What am I meant to say? Are we to ignore the fact Mary had me tied to a stake? Anyway, it is not for me to comment on Lady Radclyffe's nature, objectionable or otherwise.

'It's over, you know. We've won. A bloodless victory, thank heavens. Robert Dudley has given up and declared for me. And the duke's retreated to Ware with what little army he has left.' She gives a little snort of disgust. 'We've heard that his soldiers are leaving him. Even when he tries to bribe them, they won't stay.'

'And here they keep on coming,' I murmur.

'Thanks in part to you.'

Startled, I turn, meet her eyes.

'You said that I do not know what a friend is. Or rather, you shouted it.' The corners of her mouth twitch. 'You were wrong, though. I value my friends. Very much.'

I don't know what answer to give, but she seems to want one. 'I think, your grace, you have a hard time trusting folk.'

She gives a sigh, rubs her temples. 'That may be true.'

And it's no wonder. Neither of us says it, but it hangs in the air. Mary had a father who cared little, and the wicked stepmother Anne who wanted her dead. And even now, the one man she had come to rely on – her Spanish cousin, the Emperor Charles – has ignored their ties of blood and faith and let her down.

I know the story, but can I really feel what it must have been like for her?

'You remind me of myself when I was fifteen, Dela. The moment I met you at Woodham Walter I saw it. The scowls, the bursts of temper … saying exactly what you think. And the love of animals, of course. Even the bad-tempered Turnspit.' She bends down to scratch his head.

I expect him to turn his back on her, but he doesn't.

He licks her – just once.

CHAPTER 25

Goldhanger, two months later

'You should have been there.' Fitz sits next to me on a moss-covered log. Turnspit lies on his back at his feet, mouth agape, while he scratches his belly. The September sun is gentle; a breeze teases the silvery leaves of the willows that border the creek.

'Well I wasn't there,' I say flatly, picking moodily at the moss. As soon as the words have left my mouth I regret saying them. Fitz has ridden all the way from London to surprise me, and I *am* happy to see him, of course I am. But I can tell he finds it hard to understand why I would choose to come back to Goldhanger rather than share in the triumph of Mary's ride into London. Can't he understand that I cannot bear to be anywhere near her? That I wanted nothing more than to scurry home and creep into my hayloft.

He wants to tell me all about it, though. His hands move like birds, swooping in excited gestures as he helps me picture what it was like in London: the bonfires and street parties; men throwing coins in the air for urchins to scuttle after like crabs.

'And the noise, Dela. I had to cover my ears. Bells rang from every steeple in the city. And when the guns fired from Tower Wharf you couldn't hear yourself speak.'

'I'll wager Mary liked that.' I cannot help the sourness seeping into my voice. 'Sorry, Fitz. I don't know what's got into me. Alfredo was right, I *am faccialunga*. I can't seem to shake it off.'

I don't share with him how I wake in the night grinding my teeth. I lie on the straw, muttering bilious words to Turnspit, saying that if the queen wants to think herself a saint with a great halo glowing around her stunted sparrow's body that's her business. Was it God's miracle that she succeeded, that all those English lords and farmers came in their thousands to help her? I'm not so sure. All I do know is that I'm not inclined to trail behind her. If she likes to think that she's God's chosen maid sent to bring the country back to the old faith, let her. But I still have the image burnt into my mind of the stubborn little woman forcing the iron muzzle on me and glaring while I nearly roasted. Turnspit may have deigned to give her hand a lick, but I'm keeping my distance.

Fitz puts his arm around my shoulders, but I cannot nestle into him. My shoulders and elbows are sharp-edged, resisting his efforts to pull me close.

He isn't put off, though, and reaches to tuck a tendril of hair behind my ear so he can read my expression. 'When I said you should have been there, I really meant I *wish* you'd been there.' He watches my face closely, determined to make his feelings plain so there can be no misunderstandings between us. 'I've missed you and Turnspit. Alfredo's started calling *me* long-face now.'

A smile tugs at my lips; I snuggle in closer. 'How is he? And Lucretia. I wish I could see her.'

'They're both well. She keeps slipping out of the palace

and off to Cloak Lane. I fancy the moonstruck calf has something to do with it.'

'Colin? The apprentice?' I ask delightedly. 'I remember how he blushed whenever her name was mentioned, but I never for one moment thought ...'

'I know what you mean, they do make an odd pair. Lettie won't admit to liking him, of course. But he gave her some gloves, and Jane caught her holding them to her cheek.'

'Dreamy-eyed.'

'Exactly. Just like you now,' he adds roguishly, stroking my neck with his thumb. 'Jane may be dull-witted, but she's always quick to notice when someone's in love.'

'I suppose it's not all that strange, Lucretia and Colin. Maybe it's the perfect match. After all, she loves gloves almost as much as tumbling.'

Talking of gloves makes me a tiny bit homesick for Alfredo's workshop and the quiet *whish* of thread as the stitchers pull it through the soft doe-skin. Another world.

I look down at my roughened hands, the tough hide of my boots. 'I'd never make a courtier. It's better I'm here. The villagers were good to me once Rob told them I helped in sending Tallon to the Tower.'

'You're not missing anything in London, anyway,' he says. 'We hoped Mary would ask for a masque — a proper celebration — but all she wants is religious plays. It's tiresome.'

I feel sorry for Fitz. I remember the way his body moved on stage, speaking in its wordless, magical way to the audience, the expressions on his face making them laugh till they clutched their sides.

'Maybe Mary thinks she has to be serious now she's queen.'

'Well it is a serious business, I'll give her that. She sits half the day at her prayers, the other half biting her nails, wondering whether she should take Lady Jane Grey's head off. She's always been indecisive. The Privy Councillors run rings round her already.'

'Why did she keep them on? She'll never be able to trust them.'

'She's enjoying being bountiful. Making a point of it.'

'Well at least she beheaded Northumberland. Folk here were so happy when they heard. Danced outside the Bell as if it was May Day.'

'Same in London. The duke was led through the streets to the Tower, hugging his hat to his chest. It didn't fool anyone. They could see it in his eyes – he wasn't sorry, he was furious. By the time he reached the gate, they'd tipped their pisspots on him and pelted him with rotten eggs.'

'I wish I had seen that!'

'It was weird. I think he thought right to the end he'd bring Mary round. He converted, you know. Got himself some rosary beads. But she didn't believe it. Nor his whinging that none of this was his fault – that he'd only ever been doing the King's bidding.'

'Well, it's good news he's gone.'

Fitz smiles and takes my hand, lacing his fingers through mine. 'That's not the only good news. You know how I said Mary's enjoying being bountiful?'

'Yes.'

'She's grateful to you. I know she isn't one to say sorry – doesn't ever like to admit she's wrong. But she means to do well by you.'

'How do you know? What did she say?'

'She asked me to tell you she's giving you Barrow Farm.'

My eyes widen; I can't take the words in. 'The farm?' I stutter. 'My father's farm?'

'It's yours, and a goodly sum of money to help you buy livestock, seed, tools, that sort of thing.' He jumps to his feet, pulls me up and spins me round, though he has to watch out for his toes. He knows I am the world's worst dancer.

We sit down, his arm around my waist. 'There's more. I hope you'll be pleased.'

I nestle into the hollow of his shoulder, feeling the comfort of it.

'Mary's given me my father's estates. I've asked that they be made over to the folk of Blackwater as common land.'

'Didn't you want the Hall? You'd be set up for life.'

'You know me better than that. I'm going to have the place torn down.'

'So you don't want to live here?' I ask quietly, feeling my back stiffening against him. I know I should be rejoicing wholeheartedly at his news, but I can't help thinking that if he wants no part of Goldhanger, maybe that means he doesn't care for me either, or not enough to stay.

'I never said I didn't want to live here.' He chews the side of his cheek and his hair flops conveniently over his eyes so that I cannot read his expression.

'So?' I prompt.

'So … it may be a bit soon to say it. I don't want you to run away in fright.'

'Do I look as if I'm running away?'

He pushes the hair out of his eyes and comes out with it straight. 'I thought you might want a helping hand with the farm.'

I can't speak, but I don't need to: I'm grinning from ear to ear. He speaks fast, so that it's clear to me that he's had all this worked out in his mind, gone through again and again, and it's no spur-of-the moment idea.

'I need to finish up in London first, get Mary's permission to leave court. After that I can stay at Ned's with Rob if you don't want to wed yet. I don't want you to be alone, and I don't care to be apart from you. Not ever.'

I raise my head to his, and he takes my face between his cupped hands. He searches it with his eyes, his thumbs stroking my two cheekbones, and again I have the feeling that he's committing my features to memory, the better to sketch them later. He kisses me then, and our longing is like a thirst, and he draws me tightly to him as if he never wants to let me go.

At our feet Turnspit gives a moaning whine. Fitz pulls away and we sit up, bleary with passion.

He leans forward to scratch the dog's ears. 'I think he's feeling left out.'

Only now, as I straighten my kirtle and cap and the thrum of hot blood in my veins begins to quiet, does a thought strike me. 'What about Tallon? Mary's stripped him of his land, but will she have him beheaded?'

His fingers stop their scratching. 'She's let him go.'

He's known this all the time, yet he hasn't told me.

'Why?' My voice is a strangled yelp. 'I thought she'd keep him locked in the Tower at the very least. He deserves to die, like the duke!'

'Mary thinks she can afford to let my father go,' Fitz says helplessly. 'The duke was too dangerous. He'd only have plotted against her.'

Heart battering, I can't take in any of it. 'But Tallon's hated too! He should lose his head!'

'Of course. I only wish I could do it myself, hold the axe.'

'He'll come back here.' I wrap my arms about my chest, cold in spite of the sun. 'I can't stay now!'

'Mary told him he can't set foot in Essex. He's banished from the county.'

Fitz's tries to sound confident, but he knows I'm right. Tallon has every reason to come back: he has unfinished business.

'Look, you're not alone this time. We'll see this through together.' He squeezes my hand. 'You too, Turnspit. You're our secret weapon.'

The dog raises his head from his paws and huffs through his nose, outraged at being woken, then goes back to sleep.

I cannot help a snort of laughter. 'He'll need to do better than that.'

'He will. He's just keeping his powder dry.'

A few days later, the sun ups and leaves and the air takes on a dank fogginess. Autumn is on its way. It has been such a long, dry summer that the farm women have already finished gleaning; the fields are bare and tidy, and folk are getting ready to hunker down beside their hearths.

This morning, on waking, I had the strange feeling that something was missing. It is only now as I'm standing in Bessie's stall that I realise the house martins are no longer twittering in their nest under the eaves. They must have left yesterday, heading south before the cold weather sets in. I give a shiver, unable to stem the low tide of loss their desertion brings with it. I tell myself they'll be back in April to line their mud nest with new feathers, raise another brood – but the bleak feeling persists.

In the late afternoon, Rob senses my mood the moment he enters the stables.

'Feelin' the turn in the weather?' he asks, watching me brush Bessie's mane miserably.

'The house martins have gone.'

He reads my meaning at once. 'They'll be back ... Fitz too. He's a good'un. Don't ye fret.'

Yesterday Fitz left for London. I told him to go, knowing that he can't rest till he's told Mary he won't be her courtier. I blink back my tears, wipe my face on my apron. I am so used to losing folk; maybe that's why I find it hard to believe he will return.

'Come now. This ain't like thee.' Rob scratches his tufty black hair thoughtfully. 'D'ye think just when your bucket's full o' sprats some wight'll come tip it o'er?'

I nod.

'He'll be back. I never saw a lad so keen on a lass. Just set your mind on the harvest supper. He'll be here by then. Mind, he'd best stuff the toes of his boots wi' straw if he means to dance wi' thee.'

I give a *humph* of a laugh and rest my forehead on his shoulder. He's right. It won't be long now.

As he leaves the stables, he glances up at the hayloft. 'Summat up with Turnspit? He's been sat up there lookin' out all day.'

It's true. For hours, he's been staring out at the yard and the lane beyond, head thrust forward, ears pricked.

'Maybe he's sickenin',' Rob adds.

We both know perfectly well that the dog isn't sick.

He's on his guard.

'Where's Turnspit?'

I glance down at my feet. Earlier, the dog left his perch up in the hayloft gable and followed me to St Peter's. For the past hour I've been plaiting straw for harvest crosses with Sal's neighbour, Annie, while she rattled on about her daughter's handfasting.

'He's probably down at the jetty nosing after fish guts. Shall I come look wi' thee?'

'It's getting late. I'll go. You stay here.'

At the jetty, the Bedwell brothers are hard at it, despite the lateness of the hour, caulking their fishing boat. I ask the older of the two if he's seen Turnspit.

He carefully straightens, one hand on the small of his back. 'Scraggy little dog? I know the one.'

Anxious, I shift from foot to foot.

He turns to his brother. 'Luke, didn't ye say ye saw Fowler with a dog?'

The other gives a nod. 'Yep. Where the track meets the causeway.'

'That can't be Turnspit. He wouldn't wander that far.' My tone is harsh with frustration and worry.

Luke recoils. 'No need to bite my head off. Never said it were your dog.' He goes back to his work, then, relenting, raises his head. 'Tell ye what I saw. I thought he were Red at first. But this one had stubby legs. Bit like a sow.'

My heart sinks. 'Where were they heading?'

'Onto the causeway. Fowler was shoutin' fit to burst and that dog weren't takin' no heed. Stickin' his legs in the dirt, though the rope was chokin' him like this.' He raises a stalk-like neck and bugs his eyes, his tongue lolling from the side of his mouth.

His brother gives him a look and pats my arm. 'One day we'll get a rope round Fowler's scrawny neck. And a good long drop wi' it.'

Gathering up my skirts, I tear up Fish Street and don't stop until I reach the water's edge facing Osea. Brushing the sweaty hair out of my eyes, I scan the mile-long, winding tidal track to the island. I can barely make out the snub-nosed western tip of it where it meets the causeway, just a spiky black line of wind-twisted thorn trees. Then, even as I watch, the line blurs as a sea mist drifts its way up the estuary.

The tide is on the rise, but it'll be a while yet until the causeway is covered. When the water comes, it moves much faster than a man can run. If I'm quick, I should have time to scour Osea for Turnspit and make it off the island before it's cut off from the mainland. The sea is not the only danger. The shingle-covered mud either side of the marker stones looks firm enough to the eye, but much of it is treacherous.

I haven't been to Osea in a long time. My mother used to bring me in the days before Tallon got so tough on poachers. I used to boast that I was so sure of my footing that I could make my way over the causeway blindfold.

One time she tested me, and I closed my eyes, counting the steps, following the bends and curves by instinct. She said it must be another gift I have — an inward eye — though it didn't help me one bit when I had to navigate Thetford Forest without Turnspit.

At the thought of Turnspit, any misgivings I have about quicksand or the tide vanish. I step onto the causeway and walk quickly, watching the island keenly for signs of life. I make sure to keep a close eye on the track beneath my feet as well, and it is lucky that I do, for on the first bend I spot paw prints in the wet mud.

Hold on, Turnspit, I'm coming for you. Maybe he senses my words, because as soon as they form in my head a barking starts up, coming from the island. My relief at discovering he's alive is short-lived. In the next moment, his voice is cut off abruptly, mid-bark. In my panic, I tear across the causeway, leaping over the ruts and puddles wildly, desperate to get to Turnspit before Fowler does him any more harm.

All is quiet as I reach Osea. I am sharply aware of the crunch my running feet make on the narrow strip of shingle. Once I'm on the rough marsh grass, I pause for a moment to peer through the wisps of mist. At first, I think the flat land is strewn with large, pale rocks, then my heart gives a violent thump when one of them moves. The hump raises its head. A grazing sheep.

I remember the island well enough to know that the south-eastern end, where the Blackwater channel is deepest, has a rough beach at low tide. Here is to be found the island's only safe anchorage, and above it a rough stone hut. I reckon I stand the best chance of finding Fowler and Turnspit there.

I follow the curve of the southern shoreline, picking my way around the watery bogs that pepper the marshy ground. At one point, a flock of dark-bellied geese fly overhead. I turn my head sharply at their cries, which sound uncannily like a pack of dogs barking. The geese have journeyed south early this year, come from the northlands to feed on eel grass in the Blackwater.

The sea mist thins out as I round the bend, and for the first time I have a view to the mouth of the estuary. The light has started to dim with the approach of dusk, but I can just make out the hut and, below it, a fishing boat resting on the shingle above the tideline. As I continue to hurry along the shore, I spy a movement near the boat, then a figure sets off along the stony beach, heading in my direction. My eyes squint in an attempt to pick out the detail. I don't think the figure has a dog with him. A tall man, by the looks of it. On his own. And the way he moves is nothing like Fowler's rat-like scurry. I know that confident stride, the raptor's set of the head.

Tallon.

Heart in my mouth, poised to make a retreat, I cast about for an alternative way to the hut. Then I think of Turnspit, and my desperation to save the dog keeps me walking up the beach towards Tallon. As we get closer, I feel the tension vibrate between us. He is in no hurry, moving with the ease of a man used to holding the strings of power.

We are ten feet from each other, staring in silence. Now that we are close, I can see that in his looks, if not his spirit, he is diminished. His hair is dull and sweated to his scalp, an untidy beard covering the lower part of his face. Above it, the pitted surface of his cheeks is an angry red, shiny with the scars from his burns. His boots and breeches are grey with dried mud.

I wonder how long he has been hiding out here on Osea. He has taken a risk coming back to the Blackwater.

If for a moment I'd felt emboldened by his reduced state, once I meet Tallon's eyes the shock of his grey stare kicks the breath out of me.

'Good of you to pay me a visit.' Smooth, polite, unhurried.

I cannot play his games. I have too little time if I am to find Turnspit and get off Osea before the tide cuts us off. I tear my gaze away, and my blurted question sounds loud to my ears. 'Where's my dog?'

He is startled at my bluntness. 'I have him,' is all he says, giving me a look of such hatred that I find it hard not to recoil.

I sense that if I curl into myself, giving the upper hand to him, all will be lost. 'Fowler had no right to take him.'

Tallon's eyes snap. 'You need to learn your place, witch. You seem to forget that my man raised him. He has every right to take him.'

I push past him, setting out for the stone hut. Instead of grabbing my arm, as I'd half expected, he falls into step with me.

'Where's my dog?' I repeat, as if I haven't listened to a word he's said.

Now he reaches out to yank my arm, stopping me in my tracks, pinching hard. 'You and the dog are *nothing*. Vermin.' He smiles, almost his old self.

What I say next wipes the smile from his face. 'Why are you here? Osea isn't yours any more. And you're no longer a 'sir' either. Just plain John.'

I can hardly believe the words that have come from my mouth. The pinch of his fingers tightens on my arm.

'*You?* Telling me what is and isn't mine? A freak who should have been drowned at birth!' He snorts. 'Did you think I'd let you and my bastard son enjoy everything I've worked for? I saw you both at the creek. He looked so pleased with himself, thinking he'd got it all. The land, the title, the girl. Dropped like a plum into his lap, without his having to do a stroke of work for it.'

He pauses to wipe the spittle from his beard. I can see the rise and fall of his chest under the dirty cloth of his doublet. I have a sense, an instinct, that I must keep stabbing at the gaps in his armour as they reveal themselves, seeking out the tender spots. If I can make him lose his cool, perhaps he will slip up.

I choose my words carefully. 'Fitz is kind … noble … honourable. His mother must have been a wonderful woman.'

With each of my words, the pinch on my arm grows tighter.

Trying not to wince, I plough on: 'He's nothing like you. Doesn't even want your horrid Hall. He's going to tear it down. *And* he's giving your precious land away as commons.'

Tallon absorbs this latest shock in silence. It is bad enough that Fitz should have his possessions – but to give them away?

Finally, he erupts. 'The boy revolts me. Weak and useless like his mother. No wonder the pair of you cling to each other. You're all of a kind, every one of you. Marian was no better.' He pauses in his rant, settling on something he knows will hurt me the most. 'Your mother should never have chosen that idiot Wisbey. She could have had wealth, status, servants. But would she listen? Too headstrong, too *stupid*. Did you know, I watched her while she saw Wisbey hang. Her face screwed up like a bawling child's. It was quite entertaining. What a fool she was. You're all fools.'

I will not listen to him. I must close my ears to his poison. Tugging my arm from his grip, I take off again up the stony beach. We are nearer to the hut now. I can see Fowler leaning on a spade, watching our approach. No sign of Turnspit.

Tallon doesn't stop me. I'm sure he means to kill me once he has Fowler on hand to help in the deed. Now, as we get close, I can see why the gamekeeper is holding a spade. Next to him is a freshly dug hole in the ground and, beside that, a strongbox. So this is what Tallon came back for. Treasure. It occurs to me now that maybe he would have let me and Fitz be, never sought to take his revenge, if he hadn't seen us together by the creek. It was our happiness he couldn't bear.

I search for something to say that will unnerve him. His rage might make him clumsy. If I can get him to lose his cool, maybe he'll find himself laid open, like a clam before it is torn from its shell. He'll make mistakes. Or at least I hope he will.

'I can imagine what's in that box,' I say scornfully. 'All that treasure you stole from the abbeys and churches. You're a dirty thief. They should nail your thumbs to the pillory, just like you did to lads who dared poach on your land. The land you stole … which isn't *yours* any more.'

He takes a breath, struggles to control his temper. 'You are scum. And like scum you will be washed out with the tide.' He gives the ghost of a smile. 'Did you know that crabs always eat the eyes first?'

'They know I'm here. They'll come to find me.'

'I'll be long gone if they do. And they won't find you ... mistress crabmeat.'

Leaning on his spade, Fowler stares at us open-mouthed. Bemused at my daring to jeer, he fixes his squirrelly eyes on his master's tight face. In one brisk movement, Tallon reaches for the dagger at his belt. Taking my chance, I tear myself from his grip. He swings round to block my way, but he expects me to run back to the causeway. Instead, I dash towards the hut and the gaping Fowler.

'Turnspit!' I shriek.

Fowler's eyes give him away as they dart to the hole in the ground. He raises his spade but hasn't the chance to brain me with it, for I hurtle straight at his slight body, the force of my shoulders bringing him down.

As he falls, I grab the spade with one hand and pull a heavy, wriggling sack out of the pit with the other. I am only just in time. Tallon leaps forward, his dagger aimed at my chest. He thrusts, and I swing the wooden shaft of the spade to block it. I don't dare step back, knowing he'll only take another lunge, so I push forwards, my torso hugging his.

Tallon's dagger hand is pressed against his chest. He retreats a step, and again I shove him with all my might, my face against the cloth of his doublet. I feel him recoil – his disgust at my closeness – and instead of grappling me to the ground he takes two more steps backwards to free his arm so that he can take a lunge with his knife. But, with that, he's over, sprawling face down in the claggy soil, half in, half out of the hole.

Instead of tackling me, Fowler runs to help his master. Tallon shouts at him – 'Catch her, you fool!' – and the other turns, dithering. In that moment, I swing the spade which smashes into the side of Fowler's head. He drops to his knees, round eyes popping, and slowly keels onto his side.

Quickly, I swoop to pick up the sack. Tallon struggles to his feet, wiping earth from his eyes. Dropping the spade, I turn and run wildly down to the shore.

I have a head start, but I can hear him closing in. I don't dare to look behind – with Turnspit weighing me down, it's hard enough to run without tripping. I concentrate on my feet, careful to avoid the bogs lurking between the tussocks of marsh grass. But before I know it I stumble right into one of them, sinking halfway to my knee. Frantic, I tug at my leg, but I lose a boot, and, with no time to retrieve it, I stagger on. The thrum of blood in my ears deafens me. I cannot tell how close Tallon is. I venture a quick look over my shoulder. Ten paces away. Another moment and he'll be upon me.

I almost throw myself round the sharp bend where the shoreline turns briefly northwards, only to come up against a thick bank of sea fog. I plunge into its wet saltiness gratefully. Behind me, I hear Tallon curse. This is my chance. I need to weave, lose him in a maze of my making. I veer sharply north at once, counting to ten before heading westward again. I know the island, I tell myself. I'm used to sea mists. I can do this. But it's growing dark, and I'm not yet on the causeway.

Soon I am hopelessly muddled. Is that the way, or this? I freeze. Tallon is so close that I can hear his ragged breaths;

he must be a few feet from me. I stagger backwards, stumbling in my panic. I sense him swiping his arms to get at me, but I duck my head and shoulders and run wildly on.

By now I've lost all sense of direction. For all I know, I could be heading eastwards again, and if I am I'll have no chance. I set down the sack, take a sobbing breath.

A brush on my shoulder, soft and fleeting. I give a bleat, thinking it's Tallon. But then see the dark shape of a great bird in the foggy dusk, wings outspread. He is perched on a tussock of grass a little way ahead, his poll paler than the rest of him. *Grey raven!* He gives a low croak, then flies a few feet further off.

I follow the bird as he flits from tussock to tussock, feeling braver now that I have his help. In my head, I hear Sal's voice: *I think he's come to look out for ye. He knows ye need a friend.* A warmth steals over my body, reviving my shaking limbs. *I can do this*, I tell myself.

By now, I cannot feel my arm. It is entirely numb from carrying the dead weight of Turnspit, but somehow I manage to keep a tight hold of the sack. *Sweet Jesus, let him be alive.*

Then the crunch of broken shells, their sharp edges grazing my bare foot, and I'm on the causeway. I can hear a whisper of water; the tide will be upon us very soon. With another croak, the raven flies onto a branch of a thorn tree. He folds his wings, and his head gleams palely in the misty twilight. His task is done; it is up to me now to finish mine.

I stumble westward along the rutted causeway. A mile to go. I fear the tide will outstrip me; it was already on the rise when I set out. I am blind, hopelessly so. I clear my mind, concentrate on the bends and curves of the path. The way is slippery; slimy seaweed obscures the stones that mark the verges of the track. Lugging the heavy weight of Turnspit, I try not to slip as I stagger along in the fog. Inside the sackcloth, he doesn't move, but I can feel a faint warmth coming from his body. I only wish that I could stop to free him, check that he is alive. But I have to keep on running.

Then I hear the thump of booted feet behind me. Tallon has found the causeway. He is faster than me, his legs longer, stronger. What hope do I have now?

But then he utters a curse. A pause in the thud and splash of his boots on the track. I'll warrant he's stepped into the mire. Another curse. I picture him struggling to free his boot from the mud. If I'm lucky, his mistake will have bought me enough time. The gap widens between us.

Then I hear the oddest thing.

'Marian! Help me. I beg of you. *Marian!*'

My mother's name … how strange. Then it dawns on me. In his terrified mind, as the quicksand sucks at his limbs, he is confusing me with her.

I take few paces more, then stop. In Goldhanger we've learned from the cradle never to leave another soul in peril on the Blackwater, not if there's any chance we can save them. It's our code, without which we are nothing.

Turning, I start to stumble back towards the island, barely able to believe what I am doing.

'Where are you? Don't fight the quicksand, it makes it worse. Hold on, I'm coming!'

I listen for Tallon, but his plaintive calls have stopped. Surely, I must have run past him by now. It feels as though I've covered too much ground.

With that strange habit it has, the fog lifts quite suddenly. My eyes scan the causeway. Nothing. No sign at all that Tallon has been here, not so much as a dimple in the mud at the side of the track to indicate where the quicksand has claimed its victim.

I set the sack down, squat on my heels and gently remove Turnspit, untying the rope around his muzzle and legs. Staggering to his feet, he sprawls, jerky as a puppet. He stretches his back legs warily, as if testing for broken bones.

'Come on, boy. The tide will be upon us in a moment.'

He gives a weak wag of his tail.

'We are a fine pair, aren't we?'

It seems to take me an age to push myself up, and all the while I am aware of the water rushing, sweeping up the estuary, filling the creeks, washing over the mudflats – a tide that feeds the creatures of the sea and covers the bones of the dead.

Turnspit cocks his head. He gives a whining bark and staggers, limping, down the track.

I raise my eyes.

A winding string of lanterns lights the way to the causeway, as many as there are villagers. It wends its way towards us, the bob and flicker of the candles sending a glimmer across the dusky wet mudflats. The sight is as merry as any I have seen, as if a hundred marsh fairies have descended upon the Blackwater to dance by the light of the golden harvest moon. My eyes pick out Rob among the villagers, a head taller than the rest. In front of him, leading the line, is Fitz, his wheaten hair bright in the glow of his lantern. Even from this distance I can tell it is him from the agile, loping stride he has, and the way he drops into a squat as soon as he sees Turnspit.

THE END

A Note from the Author

The turnspit dog was a breed that became extinct in the mid-nineteenth century. Originally bred as a kitchen slave, it was doomed to walk a wheel-like cage mounted high on the wall, attached to the roasting spit by a chain.

Characteristics of the breed were short, bowed, and highly muscular front legs, as well as a notoriously bad temper caused by hellishly hot work and the harshest of training, including having burning coals thrown at its feet to make it walk faster.

By the time every inn and manor kitchen had its own mechanised spit the breed died out – no one fancied having such an ugly and grumpy dog as a pet. What they didn't know is that the turnspit dog, if only it had been given its freedom, would have made the most loyal and noble friend.

Nay, there is no turnspit dog bound to his wheel more servilely than you shall be.

> Chapman, Jonson, and Marston's
> *Eastward Ho!*, 1605

* * *

I first read about Lady Mary's botched flight from Wood-ham Walter Hall in Alison Weir's *Children of England*. The account has all the elements of a thrilling adventure: watchers and beacons; a foreigner hiding in a churchyard pretending to be an Ostend corn trader; Lady Mary and Susan Clarencieux desperately filling hessian sacks with things for the voyage, while a nervous Rochester warns the princess that the roads are crawling with watchers and she is in danger of being caught. Her nerve failed her that time – the summer of 1551 – and the emperor's frustrated man had to rush back to his ship to catch the tide. Before he left, Mary asked if he might come back two weeks later and pick her up from St Osyth's at the mouth of the Colne River, but she never got another chance to make her escape.

I took the liberty of inventing a second, imagined visit to Woodham Walter two years later. The real-life Lady Mary was nowhere near the Essex coast by that stage but was staying at Hunsdon House, her manor in Hertfordshire. She had been told to keep at least fifty miles from the coast, and she had last stayed at New Hall some four months earlier in January.

My inspiration for Tallon came from a real-life nasty piece of work: Sir Thomas d'Arcy, a baron who lies buried at St Osyth's Priory. Married to the daughter of Sir John de Vere, Earl of Oxford (whose Maldon townhouse is now the Blue Boar Inn), d'Arcy took over from de Vere as keeper of Colchester jail at the time of the Kett Rebellion. Together with the earl, he signed the death warrant of three local men who had joined the Norfolk rebels. The Earl of Oxford was a notorious womaniser, and it is recorded that d'Arcy and a few cronies took it upon themselves to cut off the nose of the earl's mistress (a punishment in those days for prostitution). After d'Arcy backed Lady Jane Grey as Edward's successor, Mary put him under house arrest, though she later pardoned him.

When Mary was intercepted on the road from Hunsdon and told she was heading into a trap, there is no sure record of who rode out to warn her. Some say it was a goldsmith, Richard Raynes, and that Sir William Cecil and Sir Nicholas Throckmorton were behind it. This left me free to let my fictional glover, Alfredo Pisanelli, take that vital role. Then, when Mary leaves Euston Hall the morning of 9th July, she changes into a serving woman's clothes and rides pillion to Kenninghall Place. Again, I took the liberty of having my fictional Dela exchange cloak and hat with Mary. Later that day, messengers were indeed sent out with letters from the self-proclaimed queen in a bid to bring powerful noblemen to support her, but there were certainly no ravens helping to deliver the scrolls!

In the mid-sixteenth century, Goldhanger Creek would have had barges bringing produce up to a jetty at the bottom of Fish Street. Later, the creek became silted up, and today the village is not connected in any navigable way to the estuary. Back in Tudor times, boats would wait at Goldhanger before the incoming tide provided the necessary depth to take them up the Blackwater to the hythe, Maldon's port. While waiting, sailors would slake their thirst at the alehouses in Fish Street, which was also home to a number of willing doxies (prostitutes).

Back then, the Essex marshes had a high mortality rate due to marsh fever, or ague. We know now that it was caused by a type of indigenous malaria carried by the anopheles mosquito. Dumont's horror of the place and Throckmorton's distaste mightn't have been very far from the truth.

But do go visit – it's a lovely little place, and the mosquitos have gone!

One wing of New Hall still exists, now a school. Woodham Walter Hall has long gone, as has Kenninghall Place. Colchester Castle jail makes a fun visit, and the wall walk around Framlingham Castle is lovely to stroll along.

A Note on the Author

Wanda Whiteley founded manuscriptdoctor.co.uk after a career spent commissioning titles for HarperCollins Publishers. Her first published work was co-authored (as Wanda Carter) with Judy Westwater, a memoir entitled *Streetkid*, which spent three months in the top 10 of the *Sunday Times* non-fiction bestsellers list. After subsequent ghosted collaborations, Wanda decided that if she was to continue script doctoring she should do her authors a favour and have a go at a work of fiction herself. *The Goldhanger Dog* is the result. Now she understands how much pain they go through.

wandawhiteley.com
manuscriptdoctor.co.uk

ACKNOWLEDGEMENTS

Having spent the last decade providing a critiquing service for first-time authors, I knew, when I started to write my own first novel, that early-draft readers would unlock new ideas, new ways through. Even then I hadn't fully comprehended how valuable this would be until vital comments began to trickle in. My heartfelt thanks go to John Carter, who worked at the text tirelessly. Also to Katy Carrington for her formidable editing and Penny Phillips for her excellent proofread. Thanks also to Matilda Melvin, Hattie Earle, Josephine Carter, Megan Frances, Chiara Pinaud-Rebuffo, Daisy Smart, Jasmin Siavoshy, Tracey Sugden, Miranda Burrow, Judith Elliott, Gabriel Burrow, Belinda Budge, Katherine Sharp, Shamim Sarif, Fiona McCarthy, Karen Ferris, Kathryn Gilfoy, Katharine Battle, Janette Ames (who also drew the wonderful Blackwater map), Ayesha Braganza, John Whiteley and Ann Carter. Thanks also to book designer Jacqui Caulton. Also deserving a mention: Apryl and David from New Hall School, Olivia at Maldon Books, and Sue from Gardeners Farm Shop, Goldhanger. And last, but not least, to agent Lisa Gallagher for her wonderful support and enthusiasm.